MY FATHER'S WAR

ALSO BY BARTON SUTTER

Pine Creek Parish Hall and Other Poems
Cedarhome

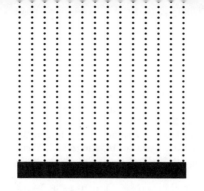

MY
FATHER'S
WAR

AND OTHER STORIES

BARTON SUTTER

VIKING

VIKING
Published by the Penguin Group
Viking Penguin, a division of Penguin Books USA Inc.,
375 Hudson Street, New York, New York 10014, U.S.A.
Penguin Books Ltd, 27 Wrights Lane, London W8 5TZ, England
Penguin Books Australia Ltd, Ringwood, Victoria, Australia
Penguin Books Canada Ltd, 2801 John Street,
Markham, Ontario, Canada L3R 1B4
Penguin Books (N.Z.) Ltd, 182–190 Wairau Road,
Auckland 10, New Zealand

Penguin Books Ltd, Registered Offices:
Harmondsworth, Middlesex, England

First published in 1991 by Viking Penguin,
a division of Penguin Books USA Inc.

1 3 5 7 9 10 8 6 4 2

PUBLISHER'S NOTE
These stories are works of fiction. Names, characters, places, and
incidents either are the product of the author's imagination or are
used fictitiously, and any resemblance to actual persons, living or
dead, events, or locales is entirely coincidental.

"You Ain't Dead Yet" first appeared in *The Iowa Review*; "Happiness" and "My Father's War" in *Crazyhorse*.

LIBRARY OF CONGRESS CATALOGING IN PUBLICATION DATA
Sutter, Barton, 1949–
My father's war and other stories / Barton Sutter.
p. cm.
ISBN 0-670-83777-6
I. Title.
PS3569.U87M9 1991   90-50748
813'.54—dc20

Printed in the United States of America
Set in Bembo
Designed by Debbie Glasserman

To
Annette
and for
Ross and Mary

My heartfelt thanks to Annette Atkins, John Engman, David Jauss, Robert Lacy, and John Mitchell for their generous criticism and encouragement.

Thanks to Rhoda Weyr, my agent, and to my editor, Mindy Werner, for their enthusiasm and support.

I am also grateful for a Loft-McKnight Award, which allowed me to complete some of these stories.

—BARTON SUTTER

CONTENTS

MY FATHER'S WAR

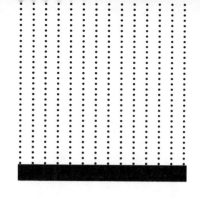

YOU AIN'T
DEAD
YET

Mark flung a final shovelful of cement into the mixer and stuck the spade in a pile of sand. "She'll be done soon!" he hollered at Elmer, who was knocking the forms off a fresh burial vault. Elmer nodded and coughed. Like Mark, he wore a red bandanna across his face. The air inside the Sunwall Brothers' Vault Company was heavy with fine gray dust. By the end of the day his lungs felt so thick that more than once as he sank into sleep Mark had imagined his lungs were hardening, slowly turning to concrete. Still, it was the best summer job he'd ever had. The pay was decent, Elmer was good if quiet company, and the nearness of death made him feel serious, adult, and curiously alive.

Elmer helped him maneuver the mixer over a new set of forms, and they worked hard and fast to fill them before the cement could stiffen. Then they cleared their throats with a shot of cold water from the hose and stepped out into the bright sunlight. They sat with their backs to the wall of the cinder-block building, and the breeze cooled their skin and dried their damp clothes. Elmer's gray shirt was stained with white patches of salt. The man smelled, Mark thought, like somebody's basement. Elmer was a bachelor and so taciturn that, though they had worked side by side all summer long, he still seldom spoke unless Mark put a question to him directly. At first Mark had thought it was the melancholy nature of his work that made Elmer so quiet, but Eddie disproved that idea. Elmer's partner and older brother, Eddie was a glad-hander who spent half his time driving around the county, drinking coffee, smoothtalking the undertakers. Mark preferred the honesty of Elmer's silence. Elmer had gotten his breath back now and broke out his pipe. His tobacco smelled like apples and smoldering leaves. Because there was so much time to pass on the job—waiting for cement to dry, driving to and from the cemeteries, waiting for funerals to finish—Mark had taken up smoking, too. He lit a Lucky Strike. Elmer called them coffin nails.

"Well, that's done," Mark said. "How else you plan to entertain me today?"

"Delivery up to Deep River. We got twins this time. Old man whose wife passed on three, four years back. He buried her in a wooden vault, and I guess the family decided as long as we were going in there anyway we might as well put her in concrete, too. Eddie hauled her vault up there this morning."

"Wait a minute. You mean we're going into the grave, take her casket out of the vault, and transfer it to a new one?"

"That's it. Sort of a transplant. We'll do that every once in a while. Not much to it, really. The Crusher will have her all dug out by the time we get there."

This was a new one, and Mark wasn't sure he liked the idea. He had taken a lot of kidding about this job, but, aside from a few bad dreams, it hadn't troubled him much. Building vaults was just construction work, and setting one in a grave was hardly any different from installing a septic tank. The only funny part was lowering the coffin and placing the lid on the vault. Otherwise the job was surprisingly ordinary. This transplant business sounded spooky, though. Too much like one of his father's jokes.

"Time we got going," said Elmer. "Funeral's at four."

Mark was hoping that Elmer would offer him the wheel, but once he had checked to make sure that the vault was locked in place on the truck bed Elmer got in on the driver's side. Sometimes Mark wondered if the man even knew he was there.

They headed north out of town. Although it had been a warm September, the leaves had already begun to yellow and brown, and the power lines were strung with migrating swallows. Mark mopped his face with the red handkerchief. His father had razzed him about that bandanna all summer. He said Mark looked like an outlaw. He told the neighbors that his son was riding with the Sunwall Boys. Mark would drag in from work, and his father, fixing supper, would turn from the stove and say, "Well, how did the grave robbers do today? Come on, I won't squeal. What did you find? Jewelry? Some nice gold fillings?" Mark was pleased and surprised to hear his father talk like that. They had buried his mother the year he entered high school, and his father had grieved for two years. Mostly at the sink, for some reason. How many times had he wandered into the kitchen to find his father up to his elbows in soapsuds, weeping over a stack of dirty plates? Either the old man had cried himself out, or the teasing was a way to ease the pain. In any case the bandanna had become a standing joke, and Mark had worn it around the house all summer long, pulling it over his face whenever he had a favor to ask. "All right, old man," he would threaten, aiming a finger at his father's belly, "your car keys or your life."

They were on gravel now and dropping into the Deep River valley, raising a wake of dust. Elmer stopped on the bridge and turned off the motor. He was an odd man, Mark thought. He always took time to appreciate things.

The river was slowed here by a series of small dams and backed into marshes and mudflats to form the Deep River Wildlife Refuge. The water was low this time of year, and the breeze blew the rank stink of the exposed bottom through the cab of the truck. Mark noticed a raft of big white birds floating far out. Shorebirds skittered over the sandspits, crying. Near the bridge a great blue heron stood like a prehistoric relic, a patient fisherman with all the time in the world. A flock of blue-winged teal dropped over the ridge, their wing-patches flashing in the sun, and skimmed the water below the bridge, peeling the surface as they landed.

"Pretty," said Elmer.

"I'll say," said Mark. "You do much hunting, Elmer?"

"Not anymore. Used to. When I was a kid. Not for a long time now. Sold my guns here a few years back. Fun went out of it somehow. I still like to look, though."

Elmer turned the key, and the teal, startled, took off. The truck ground uphill, and the steeple of Deep River Lutheran rose like the mast of a schooner against the sky.

Elmer pulled in past the parsonage, around behind the church, and eased the truck down the grassy lane between graves. He parked beside the vault that Eddie had delivered, and they got out, the cab doors slamming like gunshots in the quiet countryside.

The Crusher grinned at them from the grave and wiped the sweat from his face. "About time you boys got here," he said. "And here I was thinking you might like a little extra exercise. Too late now. I'm damn near done."

"Sorry," said Elmer. "We had some forms to fill."

"Yeah, sure. Shame on you both. Leaving a poor old man to break his back in this heat. Could of died of the sunstroke today. Hi, kid. Hand me that water jug, would you?"

"Well," Elmer said, "you couldn't pick a more convenient spot to keel over."

"Ain't that the truth? This wouldn't be such a bad place to be planted, either. It's a nice view. I seen ducks flying up and down the valley all day."

"Prettiest graveyard in the county, I'd say."

"Except for the slant of the hill here gives me a hell of a time. Reach me that level, Elmer. Close enough. You boys relax, now. I won't be a minute."

Mark and Elmer squatted beside the grave and watched the old man work. Of all the people he'd met on the job, Karl "The Crusher" Lundquist was Mark's favorite by far. Built like a bear, The Crusher had wrestled all over the Upper Midwest in his younger days. He said he had beaten Bronko Nagurski in his prime, and Mark believed him. Eddie said The Crusher had retired from the ring after he broke an opponent's neck, but Mark hadn't been brave enough to ask the old man if the story were true. Way up in his sixties now, The Crusher had his Social Security and only dug graves in the summer. The hard labor, he argued, preserved his health. Mark loved to watch him work. His tools were always sharp and bright, and he moved with casual efficiency. He was down to the bottom of the grave now, shaving and slicing, scraping and squaring off. As he worked, he talked.

"Can't bury this one deep enough, if you ask me. Milowski," he spat. "I ought to go down an extra three feet for that bastard. I knew the bum. You seen his place? Silos all over, tractor as big as a house. Made out of money, they say, but the bugger couldn't buy his way into heaven if I was in charge. I never seen the like for luck. If it hails, it hails on his neighbor's place. Milowski picks up the pieces. Born with a horseshoe up his ass. Took every farm on that section. Him and the bank. I seen what he done to his woman, too. They got married, she was the prettiest piece you hope to see. Stop your heart just to look at that woman. High-toned, too, but nice, you know? I can't understand it. Here she is, the prettiest thing in the county, and she marries the most mean-hearted son of a bitch I ever met. And he busted her, too. Just broke that woman down. Worked her like a horse, and she was nothing but a nag by the time she kicked off. They say it was natural, but to my way of thinking it was murder pure and simple, murder over the years. The day she died I told Vera, 'Vera, that man should get the chair.' She knew what I meant. I hear he died of a heart attack, but you could have fooled me. I don't believe the bastard had one. I'd like to see them cut him up. I'd like to see an autopsy. Know what I think they'd find? Liver. A big, fat, black liver right where the heart should be. Wasn't nothing but bile in that man's veins. I swear. The stingy bastard buried his woman in a wooden vault, and, from what I hear, the family felt so bad about it, they figured they put a puke like him in concrete, it's the least they can do for her. They knew. They knew what he done to that woman. Anna Marie, that was her name. Anna Marie, and she was a lady, too.''

Mark looked over at Anna Marie. The Crusher had lifted the heavy load of earth off her vault, and the wooden box, reddish and stained at the corners by some sort of rot, lay exposed. The Crusher had scarred the lid with his shovel.

"That does it," The Crusher said. "How you want to go about this, Elmer? You think we need the belts?''

"Naw, let's try it by hand."

"Okay by me. You boys think you can hold up your end against an old man?''

"Hope your Medicare covers rupture," said Elmer, and he and Mark jumped into the grave. Mark stumbled over a spade and brushed against the wall, creating a small landslide.

"Careful," The Crusher said, "or you'll bury us all."

They forced a pick and shovel underneath the vault, pried it loose, and dragged the wooden box to the middle of the double grave. Then they knelt beside the vault and clawed at the earth until they could work their hands beneath it. "Lift with your legs now," The Crusher said, "not with your backs. Ready? Heave!"

Mark pressed his face against the damp wood and strained. Groaning as if in pain, they hoisted the vault waist-high, paused for breath and a better grip, then lifted on up, slipping and swearing, and then they had her over their heads. Mark looked up at the moldy bottom. He and Elmer lunged and propped their end on the edge of the grave. They hustled back to help the old man. The Crusher counted to three, and they slid the vault like a heavy toboggan out of the grave and onto the grass.

They hauled themselves out of the hole. Mark was trembling.

"Heavier than I expected," Elmer said.

"Yeah, I guess she's a little waterlogged."

Mark looked at the wooden box with dread. "What now?" he said.

"Better sink those vaults," Elmer said. "They'll be here in under an hour."

They put their shoulders to the carriage, in which the heavy concrete vault hung suspended from pulleys and lightweight cable, and rolled it into position over Anna Marie's empty grave. Mark and The Crusher steadied the vault, Elmer turned the crank, and they slowly lowered the concrete box into the hole. Mark jumped down and unsnapped the cables. Sweating in the sun, they wheeled the second vault off the truck and sank it beside its mate. Then they hooked the heavy lids to the carriages and hid one behind the church. Elmer called for a break.

They sat beside The Crusher's pickup and drank from his thermos of ice water. "Hot," the old man said. He poured some water over his head. "One thing about my job, at least you get cooler the further down you dig."

"This heat won't last," Elmer said.

"Nope. Nights are cool already. We'll get the deep frost before you know it, and I can retire again. Used to be, I'd dig right through the winter. Had to burn tires to thaw the ground. What a mess. Cemetery looked like a junkyard. And cold? Christ. Work up a sweat with the shovel, freeze your ass if you stopped to rest. I'm glad them days are over. Summers I don't mind, but come December I'll take the TV and a hot buttered rum. What about you, kid? You must be just about done with this monkey business."

"I leave for the U on Monday. I guess I won't see you again."

"Well, that won't kill you. What you plan to take up up there? The teacher's time?"

"That's it," Mark smiled. "No, I thought I'd try pre-med. I thought I might like to be a doctor."

"Oh, sure, and put me and Elmer right out of work. What do you want to do that for? Christ, there's already too many old buzzards hanging around. Just this morning Eddie was telling me if we don't get a flu epidemic pretty soon we'll all be on welfare. That's the trouble with people today. They all want to live forever. Not me. I was up to the nursing home last Sunday, to see my old pal Swenson? Had himself a stroke last year, and the poor son of a bitch can't hardly talk. About all he can do is sit there and moo like a goddamn cow. And he was the strongest son of a buck! I could of almost cried. So I'm sitting there with Swenson drooling all over this nightie they've got him in, when who comes rolling by but Alma Berg? Hell, I went to school to that old heifer! She's about four hundred years old, and there she is, still hanging around. And for what? She's flat on her back, and they roll her up to the window, and I can hear her mumbling around. Crazy as a goose. 'Sky,' she says. 'Blue sky.' Way to go, Alma. She's about four years old. And then you know what she says? This really got me. There's this maple tree outside, and the leaves are starting to turn, real pretty, you know, and she looks at that, and she says, 'Look at the flowers. Look at the lovely flowers.' Then she turns my way—she's damn near bald—she turns my way, and she says, 'I just love spring. Don't you love the spring?' 'Sure,' I go. 'Spring. Love the spring. Real nice, Alma.' I had to get out of there. Christ Almighty, give me a shovel. I'll dig myself a hole and pull the dirt in after me. That got me, though. 'Look at the flowers,' she says.''

"I'll give you a shovel," said Elmer. "We've got about forty minutes to get this place in shape."

Elmer got a crowbar from the truck, and the three of them stood before the wooden vault. "Here goes," Elmer said, and he drove the crowbar under the lid. The nails complained, and water oozed from the wood like sap where he forced the iron in. He worked his way around the vault, gradually raising the lid, an inch here, a half inch there. Mark and The Crusher pushed, Elmer pried with the bar, the wet wood squealed, squawked, and the lid popped free. It lay on its back in the grass like a door into the earth, a ragged row of rusty nails, twisted and bent, staggered around the rim.

Bruised by green and purple mold, the gray coffin looked diseased. Mark imagined it new, shining and smooth. His mother's coffin had looked like a treasure chest. At the funeral he hadn't cried for his mother at all, but the thought of that rich, copper-colored casket sunk out of sight had troubled him for days.

Nobody spoke. They had made such a racket raising the lid that the silence now seemed huge. Mark wondered what was left of the woman inside. He thought, very quickly, of Egyptian mummies, of Lazarus and Jesus. He stared at the coffin, thinking it looked as flimsy as cardboard, thinking how thin was the membrane of

metal between himself and the corpse, and he knew
when they lifted the casket it would break in their hands
like rotten fruit.

The silence grew, and he heard, at its heart, a dull
bass beat, and, above the bass beat, the quiet seemed to
whisper and twang, to crackle and sing. He might have
been standing inside a power station. He knew this feeling. This was death. This was what happened. A quiet
so deep it disturbed the molecules of the air. He could
hear them vibrate and hum. He could feel them. He had
felt this before, at his mother's funeral, as he stood staring down at the lifeless body that seemed to be made
of translucent wax. He wanted to run, but his legs
wouldn't work, and then, as if the air had turned into
water, he heard the distant sound of Elmer's voice.
"Let's go," it said, and he found he could move after
all but slowly, as if underwater, as if he'd been shocked,
as if his limbs had been shot full of novocaine.

Slowly he moved to one end of the coffin. Elmer
nodded, and he watched his own hand reach inside the
wooden box and grasp the corroded metal handle. The
Crusher hugged the other end of the casket and grunted,
"Ready? Heave!" Mark strained at the handle, and then
they had her up and out of the box and were shuffling
sideways. It was lighter than he had expected. Maybe
she's nothing but dust, Mark thought, and the handle
broke off in his hand. The casket dropped, Elmer said
"Shit," and Mark slipped, fell, and skidded against the
casket.

He sat up. He was all right. Then he looked at his
hand. It was green, and his arm was coated with mucus,
and the side of his shirt was wet. And then, as if he had
fallen on a hornet's nest, he was up on his feet and
turning in circles, tearing at his shirt and screaming again
and again: "Get it off me!"

The Crusher grabbed Mark from behind and held
him, ripped the soiled shirt down the front, and, using
it like a rag, he scrubbed the fungus off Mark's arm.

The old man released him and stepped away. "There," he said. "You're okay."

"I'm all right!" Mark shouted. "I'm okay."

"It's only mold, Mark," Elmer said.

"I know it. I'm sorry." He was hot now not with fear but with shame.

The Crusher kicked the casket. "At least we didn't bust the son of a bitch."

"Thank God for small favors," Elmer said. "Why don't you take a break, Mark? We can handle this."

"I'm okay."

"I know. But go have a smoke, anyway."

Flushed with embarrassment, Mark carried his dirty shirt to the truck, plucked the pack of Luckies and the matchbook from the pocket, and threw the shirt on the floor of the cab. He lit up, inhaled, and was suddenly sick. He hurried behind a row of shrubbery, paused as if trying to remember something, then sank to his knees and threw up.

A song sparrow sang from a fence post. The silence was normal now. He could hear a tractor throbbing in a distant field. So that was the bass beat he'd thought was death itself. That was a good one, he thought, confusing death with a John Deere. He picked a few dusky blue berries off a juniper bush, chewed them, and the foul taste in his mouth was replaced by the tart, clean tang of wintergreen. He wiped his face with the red bandanna, walked to the grave, and took a long slug of water from The Crusher's thermos. They had already lowered the coffin and dropped the lid on the vault.

"You okay?" Elmer asked.

"I'm fine. Sorry to make such a fuss. Here, let me do that."

He took the shovel from Elmer and began flinging dirt on the vault. The clods of earth burst on the concrete lid with a hollow sound. Elmer knelt beside the grave and started assembling the brass frame on which the coffin would rest during the graveside service. Trying to atone for his hysteria, Mark worked furiously while The Crusher shoveled slowly but steadily, pacing himself. The grave was quickly filled, and they leaned on their shovels, panting and wet with sweat.

Elmer looked at his watch. "Twenty minutes," he warned. "Go get the grass, Mark."

Mark ran to the truck and hauled out the artificial turf. He draped the heavy carpets over his shoulders, struggled to the grave, dumped the rugs, and ran back for the other set. By the time he returned The Crusher and Elmer had carpeted the grave of Anna Marie and gathered the grass like green bunting about the base of the brass frame. They spread the second set over the mound of raw earth beside Milowski's grave.

"Now the tent," Elmer said.

They had it down to a system. Elmer raised the canvas on the poles while Mark drove the stakes and drew the guy-lines taut. The Crusher collected his tools and tidied up the gravesite. Then they all stood back to admire their work. The brass frame gleamed in the sunlight, and the artificial grass disguised the dirt. The pale green awning that protected the mourners from precipitation on gloomy days would shield them from the sun today. The tent was sometimes rented out for carnivals and church bazaars and, consequently, made the gravesite almost gay.

"Good," said Elmer. "Let's clear out."

For the next half hour their job was to make themselves invisible. Mark and The Crusher wheeled the second carriage out of sight. Elmer drove to the rear of the cemetery and parked behind a screen of evergreens. The Crusher pulled his battered pickup alongside, got out, and squeezed into the cab beside Mark. He poured coffee from a thermos and passed the cup.

"Here they come," said Mark, and they watched the funeral procession turn into the churchyard. The headlights of the cars burned dimly in the daylight, and the little flags on the fenders fluttered in the breeze. The heavy hearse eased up to the grave, and the doors flashed open. He could see Severson, the mortician, giving directions. The pallbearers crowded close.

"Hope they got some he-men to carry him," The Crusher said. "He ate like a pig."

The pallbearers rested the shining casket on the brass frame and stepped away. A parade of mourners filed up and huddled beneath the awning as if the sunshine were rain. Severson nodded. The minister stepped forward and began to read from a little black book.

"Wake me up when it's over," Elmer said.

The pleasant murmur of the minister's voice mingled with bird songs and the rustling of the nearby cornfield. Mark looked at the faint green stain on his arm. He spit on his fingers and rubbed, but it wouldn't come off. It would have to wait until he could shower. The sun warmed his bare chest, and his eyelids grew heavy. He bowed his head.

He was afraid he was going to dream. He had moved all his things to the basement in June, and, though sleeping was easy and cool down there, the dark was deep, and the first time he dreamed he was buried alive he was unable to find the light. He'd left the lamp burning from then on. Not all his dreams had been nightmares, though. His mother had visited him several times. They had laughed and reminisced warmly, and he had wakened from those dreams so gently he had felt as if he were floating on his back. Recently, though, she had scared him. He was following a dark, hooded figure down a spiral staircase, and, knowing who it was, he called to her again and again, trying to get her to stop and acknowledge him. Finally, she turned, and her face was a cold, flat mirror. Transfixed, he stared at his own image, and as he stared his features melted as if his face were wax and bared the skull, and his eyes clouded over until they were pale as milk, as mild and bland as the blind eyes of a statue, and he felt himself turning to stone. He woke from that nightmare screaming so loudly his father had come pounding down the steps to see what was wrong. "Go away," Mark had told him, still crazy with sleep. "Everyone I want to talk to is dead."

He was half asleep now, but he could hear singing or was it the wind? It was singing. They were singing about the river. The beautiful, the beautiful river. Shall we gather at the river that flows by the throne of God? And then he came wide awake as The Crusher said, "Mark? Elmer? Come on, you goldbricks, they're leaving. Time to get back to work."

The last few cars were pulling out. Mark and The Crusher lowered the coffin, disassembled the frame, and rolled up the grass while Elmer conferred with Severson. They struck the tent and were stowing it in the truck when Elmer walked over.

"Think you can finish up alone, Mark? Severson wants to talk business with me and Eddie, so I've got to go back to the shop. I can ride in with him, but that means you'll have to take the truck."

"Sure. No problem."

"Good. We'll come back for the other carriage tomorrow. Karl, maybe you can help him here, and then come on in for your check if you want."

"Don't worry about us. You just get your pencil out and practice up your penmanship."

"Greedy old bugger, isn't he?" Elmer said. "Okay, see you later then."

They waved him off and wheeled out the carriage they had hidden behind the church. They lowered the lid on Milowski's vault, and, as they swung the hooks free, The Crusher spat in the grave and said, "Bye-bye." They rolled the carriage onto the truck bed and locked it in place.

The air was growing cooler now, and they shoveled at a leisurely pace, working just fast enough to keep warm, the day's work all but over. The late afternoon light slanted across the cemetery, and all the stones threw shadows on the graves. "Good riddance," The Crusher said, loading his spade with loam, "to bad rubbish." The dirt hit the vault with a solid thump.

"I don't think," Mark said, "I've ever seen anyone take more satisfaction in his work."

The Crusher laughed. "Well, this one was special. Couldn't have happened to a nicer guy. Normally, you know, you don't take much pleasure in putting people under, and sometimes you feel pretty bad if it's a young one, say, or someone you grew up with." He sighed. " 'Let the dead bury the dead,' the Good Book says, and sometimes I feel half dead myself. Hell, who knows? Maybe you'll be dropping the lid on me this time next year."

"Baloney," Mark said. "You're stronger than most guys my age."

"That may be, but I'm running out of pep. Anyway, what's the point? Half my friends are gone, and the rest of them can't even go to the can without a nurse to show them how."

"But you've got a lot of younger friends."

"Yeah, but it's not the same. And then I miss the old lady, too. The winters get awful long without her."

"How long ago did you lose her?"

"Five years next month. We used to get snowed in, you know, and we'd play a lot of gin, and, I don't know, it was fun. I never cared much for solitaire, myself, and it seems like the bed never really gets warm anymore. I used to call her my hot water bottle." He laughed. "She hated that."

Mark watched a nightcrawler ooze from a clod at his feet. "Well, even if you do kick off," Mark said, "I won't be here to bury you. I've had enough of this. I think I'll try to get a job as an orderly next year. I'd rather be helping people stay alive, even if I'm only giving enemas to old men. This just gets too depressing."

"I know what you mean. It's a lonesome kind of a job. But then somebody's got to do it."

They smoothed the dirt over the double grave and set the sod back in place. Then they arranged the flowers that would melt back into the earth with the first rainfall. As they walked to The Crusher's pickup Mark clanged the blade of one spade against the other. They rang like a small bell. "Well, anyway, it's been fun, sort of. I liked the hard work, and Elmer's a good guy. And I sure have enjoyed working with you."

"The same to you, kid." They laid the tools in the bed of the pickup. "The first funeral we worked together, I told Elmer, you got a good one there. A hard worker and a smart kid who don't act it." They shook hands, and The Crusher got in. "Best of luck with the books, now. And you come see me whenever you're back in town."

"Thanks," Mark said. "I will."

They nodded good-bye, the pickup coughed and roared, and Mark stood watching until the old man disappeared.

Proud that Elmer had trusted him with the truck, Mark drove the gravel road carefully, gearing down and descending slowly into the valley. When he reached the bridge, he turned off on the dike, drove out to the dam, and parked. The marsh was wild with waterfowl, and as soon as he cut the motor his ears were filled with their gabbling. He could hear swallows twittering, too, and the creak of insects and frogs. Excited, he picked his dirty shirt off the floor and got out. He slammed the door, and a pair of wood ducks shot out of the channel. The wind off the water chilled his bare chest. He sucked in his breath.

The shoreline was mostly muck and reeked with a sour odor, but the water ran more swiftly through the channel. Mark knelt on a wash of gravel there, soaked his shirt, and scrubbed his forearms clean. He wrung out the shirt and wiped his face. Then he sat back on a piece of driftwood and smoked, watching the water turn to wine, watching the sun go down.

He was about to leave when he felt them, heard the rush of their wings, and there they were, ghostly and strange as angels in the half-light but nonetheless real, row after row of snow geese skimming the cattails and flooding above him, close enough to touch. Paralyzed with excitement at first, as the final row passed over him, he reached up, felt feathers. The startled goose honked, veered off, and there was a thunderous beating of wings as the whole flock ascended, then coasted down on the dark water, far out.

No one was going to believe this, he thought, but he hurried toward the truck. He wanted to get back to the shop in time to tell Elmer. Coming up the path, he felt something crunch beneath his boot. He looked down. Skin and bones. What was it? He turned it over with his toe. Carrion beetles scurried away. A muskrat, most likely. He ran to the truck.

When he turned the key the motor groaned and quit. "What now?" Mark moaned. "What is it now?" He flicked on the lights; the battery was good. He kicked the accelerator and tried again. Then he read the gas gauge. "Damn it," he said. "Goddamn it!" he shouted. "Goddamn it all to hell anyhow!"

Now he was going to be late. Now his father would worry, and Elmer would think he was dumb. First that rotten casket. Now this. He would have to walk to the nearest farm and hope that someone was home, and even if he could beg some gas and a ride he was going to be late.

He got out of the cab, slammed the door, and then, instead of walking away, he sat down on the running board. The wind off the marsh was cold, and he crossed his arms and rocked a little. He wasn't going anywhere. He was beat. Defeated and ashamed, he sat in the dark and listened to the small birds and animals disturb the dry weeds. He thought of Milowski and Anna Marie, the carcass he had stepped on, his mother and Jesus, and he knew he was going to die.

Because that's life, he thought. Either you were somebody decent or you were a bastard and then you died.
You had a heart attack and went down like a cow in a
slaughterhouse or you got cancer and they cut you to
pieces. Then what? Nothing. Worms and beetles and
mold.

His mother had taken two years to die, and the morning his father had called him downstairs to tell him she
was dead, he was glad. First there was a lump, and the
doctors removed it. Then she went back, and they took
her insides out. And then there was the morning she
had called Mark and his brother into her bedroom and
said she wanted to show them something. She had
thrown back the blanket and said, "I wanted to show
you this because people will talk, and I'd rather tell you
myself." She had gone on talking, but her voice was
only a murmur because Mark had never seen a woman's
breasts before, and it was so different from what he'd
imagined, so strange and nice-looking, and the air in the
room began to vibrate and buzz, and he knew that his
mother was going to die because she only had one.
Where her other breast had been, her chest was flat, the
skin pinched by a lumpy, purple scar.

Later there were radiation treatments, prayers, and
other operations. She had lost her hair and gone blind.
The two of them had spoken little then, communicating
more and more by hand. He rubbed her back. She read
his face with her fingers, as if his features were braille.
She wanted kisses, but he was horrified by her breath.
Every afternoon that final autumn he had walked home
from school repeating, "She's dead. You know she's
dead." He prepared himself so well that when she finally
did die he couldn't even cry. He and his brother had
come downstairs, his father had put an arm around each
of them and told them and wept, and Mark had been
absolutely calm and wide-eyed. What he remembered
most clearly about that moment were the Indians on his
brother's pajamas.

Rotten with disease, his mother had screamed a lot that last year but slipped away peacefully in the end, dreamy with drugs and free of pain. On the final night she had smiled at the nurse and said, "I believe that Jesus is my savior," then turned her face to the wall.

Mark did not believe in Jesus or in medicine or prayer. He didn't believe in anything. Or did he? Those geese, maybe. And dirt. He believed in dirt.

As an experiment he had dug a compost pit in the garden in June, and he had been amazed by his results. He had dumped some garbage into the hole—coffee grounds, eggshells, bad bananas—and seasoned the whole mess with dead leaves and grass clippings. He'd covered this refuse with a layer of loam. Two weeks ago he had returned and sunk a spade in the compost pit. Instead of the sour slime he expected to find, he discovered nothing but earth—good, clean dirt. It was the only miracle he had ever witnessed, and he had talked about it for days.

That was the only afterlife he believed in, and what had he and The Crusher and Elmer been doing all summer? Sealing embalmed bodies behind cement walls, they were ruining the only form of resurrection there was. Unless you counted dreams, and how could you? What were they but chemicals gone crazy, a mishmash of wishes and buried memories. You might as well believe in UFOs. People said death was like sleep, but the dead didn't dream. Did they? If he dreamed his mother was living, did she dream he was dead? No. It was just a blank. A black blank.

He was never going to sleep again. He would lie on his bed and look at the light bulb until his brain burned out. For now he would keep his eye on that low star. Star light, star bright, first star I see tonight. So bright, he thought, it must be a planet.

As he stared the star seemed to move and grow, and he knew, then, it was coming for him. Then the star divided into the twin headlights of a truck, and The

Crusher's pickup came grumbling down the dike, stopped, and the lights died.

The Crusher got out and walked over. "What happened, kid? We waited over an hour."

"I ran. Out of gas."

"Well, that's nothing to cry about, for Christ's sake."

"Who's crying?"

"You are."

Mark wiped his cheeks. "Oh, no," he moaned. "I didn't mean it. Mean to. I mean. I just ran out of gas, but first that lousy casket, and then the truck wouldn't go, and I was so tired I felt so stupid I just sat down, and I started to think."

"Well, it wasn't your fault you ran out of gas. What the hell? It's Elmer's damn truck. He should have checked it before you left. Look," the old man said, "you got goose bumps. You must be freezing. Here. Put this on." He held out his jacket, and Mark pulled it on. It was smelly and warm, and the wool scratched his bare back. "What were you thinking about that made you feel so bad?"

"I don't know. That casket. And all those people we buried this summer. My mother."

"Oh, yeah. That would do it. I remember your mother. She was a good woman."

"I've been dreaming about her all summer. I've had a hard time sleeping."

"Yeah? You never said anything."

"It seemed too stupid."

"That can happen, though. You ask Elmer sometime. And Vera. After she died she kept coming to me in the night and crying. She kept me awake for a year. Oh, boy. One night I remember I dreamt I was buried beside her, and I kept trying to lift the lid off the vault all night long. I had whiskey for breakfast that morning, I'll tell you."

"Really? Really bad, huh?"

"I'm telling you. They stopped after a while, though.

Oh, she'll still visit me now and then, but now it's kind of nice. We're younger, most often, and maybe it's after a match, and we're out on the town, and she seems just as real. I like it."

"Do they mean anything?"

"What?"

"Those dreams. Do they mean anything?"

"Oh, I wouldn't know about that. I never put too much stock in them. Just kind of take them as they come, you know."

They listened to the waves run against the shore. The wind off the water was cold.

"Crusher?"

"Yeah?"

"Do you believe in life after death?"

"Like in the Bible, you mean? I don't think so. Nope. I believe in life before death. Come on, kid. You're too young to be brooding about this stuff. You got your whole life ahead of you—school, a good job, women and drinking, a family. You ought to leave this kind of thing to old farts like me. Tell you what. Let's drive into town, and I'll treat you to supper. Then we'll fill my five-gallon can and come back here and try to bring this old pig back to life. What do you say?"

"Okay," Mark said and got to his feet.

"Good," The Crusher said, clapping him on the back. "Let's go. You ain't dead yet. Not by a long shot."

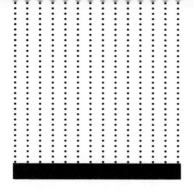

DON'T STICK
YOUR ELBOW
OUT TOO FAR

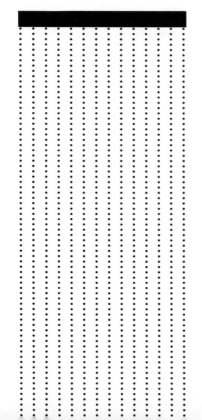

Back in high school I decided Iowa was nowhere, so I went East to college and, after graduation, moved to Boston, where I found a job as an editorial assistant. The hours were long and the pay was low, but, by doing free-lance work on weekends and living in a miserable apartment, I managed to pay off my college debts and save a thousand dollars. For the first time in my life I had enough money to buy a car. Then I got the good news that I'd won a fellowship to graduate school. Except for Sandy, the woman I hoped to marry someday, I hadn't made many friends in Boston, so deciding to go on to grad school was easy. Sandy, ironically, had grown up in Sioux City. When I quit my job—this was the summer of '75—we agreed to synchronize visits to our folks. I would buy a car while I was home and drive her back to Boston, where we planned to live together until I had to leave for school.

Initially I thought I'd find a car right there in Boston, but I barely knew a radiator from a carburetor, and the slick city dealers made me nervous. It seemed a lot smarter to take my bankroll back to Iowa, where at least I spoke the language, where the accents would be German and Norwegian rather than Irish or Italian. If all else failed, I figured, I could always call on my mother's brother. Uncle Otto was a character, but we were friends as well as relatives, and he had sold cars for years.

My flight took me as far as Minneapolis, where I stayed overnight with a friend, and the next morning I bought a bus ticket to Pocahontas. I rode that gritty Greyhound all day long, boring through the rolling fields and small towns of southern Minnesota and out onto the rich, flat farmland of northern Iowa. I'd been living in cities for so long that the scenery, such as it was—deep green, corn and beans—seemed exotic at first. But long before the bus dropped me in Pocahontas I remembered why, back in high school, I'd been so eager to get away. The geography was monotonous, and the people were so much the same, so predictably wholesome, they looked as if they belonged on a billboard: DRINK MILK.

I'd never set foot in Pocahontas before. My father was a conservation agent, and we'd moved all over the state when I was young. He kept dreaming of a better position. Pocahontas was only another dot on the map to me, but to him, closing in on sixty at the time, it was not only his latest but his final hope for the perfect situation. My parents met me at the gas station that served as the town's depot and drove me out to their new place in the country. For once, my father's expectations appeared to be justified. He liked his new job, and my mother was in love with the farmhouse they had found. They walked me over their property with pride, pointing out the woodlot, showing off the view, bragging up their garden. I was happy for them.

The next day I split firewood and mowed the extravagant lawn. Manual labor felt like a luxury. I enjoyed the calm of the countryside all afternoon, but the silence that surrounded the house after supper oppressed me, so I hiked into town for a little noise and neon. A beep and a flicker were all Pocahontas had to offer. I strolled Main Street once and stopped for a cup of coffee and a wedge of homemade pie topped with a scoop of vanilla. It was a pleasure to be served by a waitress while I sat, instead of elbowing strangers at a stand-up sandwich bar.

By the time I'd chased the pie with a second cup of coffee, I had a passing acquaintance with half the cars cruising Main Street. The old sense of suffocation returned as I watched the moving picture of traffic screened by the restaurant window. It was a dull show. Friday nights are the same all over Iowa. The kids bring their boredom to town and circle from drive-in to Dairy Queen, trolling for trouble—sex or a scrap—any escape from the narrowness of their lives.

I'd pretty much managed to avoid this weekend ritual when I was growing up. While my classmates slaved on their parents' farms or sold their summers to the railroad in order to buy the cars they needed to join the Friday-night parade, I'd played the piano, or taken to the woods, or brooded over a book. Sitting there in the restaurant, though, I realized I'd only postponed my participation in that ceremony. For all its mindlessness, it *was* a ritual, both sexual and social, and finally, it seemed, unavoidable. Hadn't I come home to buy my car? Despite the sophistication I thought I'd earned, I still felt threatened by the Cougars and the Firebirds, the Mavericks and the Mustangs cruising past the window. Iowa was part of the Wild West once upon a time, and a vestige of the old violence survives in the cars that prowl the small towns after dark. And so I sat there, feeling superior and insecure, twenty-four and still without wheels.

I paid, wished the waitress good night, and walked out into the open spaces. After all the dog dung on Beacon Hill, the odor of cow manure on the breeze smelled clean. It cleared my head. I decided to call my uncle Otto and see if he had a line on a good used car. In the meantime, I enjoyed the walk. Frogs twanged in the ditches, and wind rustled the waist-high corn all around me. At the pond below my parents' place, I stopped to appreciate the stillness and the stars. Then a carload of kids roared by. One of them stuck his arm out the window and gave me the finger as they disappeared, the racket of their radio drifting back with the dust they'd raised.

My folks thought calling Otto was a wise idea. Otto had a John Deere dealership in Granger, and used machinery was his specialty. Mom had his number squirreled away. I put through the call, smiling as I dialed. "Hello, Otto Heller," I said. "This is Brian."

"Butch!" he said. "Where are you? Is anything wrong?"

"No. Why should there be? I'm fine. I'm here in Pocahontas."

"Well, I'll be. It's good to hear your voice. I thought you must be in trouble, we haven't heard from you for so long. What's the matter? Did you break your pencil?"

"I was just too busy getting rich out there. I saved a thousand dollars. That's why I called you."

"Good. I can use it. How long you home for?"

"Just long enough to say hello and buy a car. I won a fellowship to study up in Ithaca this fall, and I'd like to drive back in style. I was hoping you might know where I could find a bargain."

"So when you coming over?"

"How about Monday? I was going to check the car lots over here, but I'm pretty dumb when it comes to anything mechanical. Can you afford the time to help me out?"

"You're my nephew, aren't you? I'll take the time."

"Terrific. I appreciate this, Otto."

"Sure. I'll look around town, see what these horse traders are hiding. It should only take a day. We'll expect you to stay overnight."

"I'll be looking forward to it."

"Okay. Don't spend all your moola before you get here."

I hung up, pleased at the prospect of seeing Otto again. My childhood memories of him were all happy. He was crafty, and a bit of a weirdo, but he had a heart as big as a beach ball. And he knew cars better than anyone else I could think of.

Early Monday morning I packed my duffel bag, said farewell to my parents, and stumbled down to the Greyhound. I was the only passenger out of Pocahontas, and with nothing for scenery but farmland so perfect it seemed artificial, I let the humming diesel lullaby me all the way to Granger.

Granger looked like Pocahontas. It was smaller than I'd remembered. I hiked out past the elevator, across the tracks, and down the highway to the metal Quonset at the edge of town.

The interior was dim as a tavern. I leaned in the doorway, trying to see straight. In the far corner, a welding rod sputtered and flashed. Front and center, a combine was laid up; inside the machine, somebody muttered and hammered metal. Otto stood at the greasy counter, shuffling a parts book the size of a Gutenberg Bible. He was dressed as I remembered him, in a dark green uniform. His combat fatigues.

I said "Uncle!" and he hustled out from behind the counter to meet me. He was delighted. "Well, well, well. Butch! How you been? You look skinny. Couldn't you find anything to eat out there?"

"Just tea and cakes," I said. "I see you don't disagree with Lois's cooking yet. Where's the cigar?" He looked the picture of himself, all five and a half feet of him, but his stage prop was missing.

"I gave it up," he mourned. "Had to. Either give up the weed, the doctor said, or go on a diet, and how could I disappoint Mama? Boy, but you're a sight for sore eyes. Come say hello to Harlow."

"That's quite the car you picked out for me," I said as he walked me over to the combine.

"I hoped you'd like it," he laughed. "Impress your

friends. Hey, Harlie!" he hollered. "Guess who's here."

Two hands and a head appeared at the top of the hopper, Kilroy fashion. This was my cousin Harlie. "Brian," he said and nodded and grinned. Then he ducked back down in the combine. He'd always been a quiet one.

"I'll be back after coffee," Otto told the machine.

Harlie hammered in answer.

"The Greasy Spoon?" Otto offered.

"Just the thing," I said, and followed him into the sunlight, across the highway to Millie's Cafe.

Otto had a gift for conspiracy. Millie's Cafe was only a highway diner. Millie, whoever she was, was long gone, and the coffee they served there tasted like tar. But when I was a kid a trip to the Greasy Spoon with Uncle Otto was better than the county fair. How he managed to make so much out of nothing, I'm still not sure. Secrecy, anticipation helped. Otto spoke a kind of code. To most people, Millie's was only Millie's; to us it was the Greasy Spoon. I wasn't Brian; I was Butch. Whenever my parents planned a trip to Granger, he'd promise over the phone to take my brother and me to the Greasy Spoon, and our expectations would grow as we waited for the weekend. Then all day Saturday he'd hint about what went on at the Greasy Spoon, use it as the setting for the stories he told, treat it like a secret he reserved for trusted friends. After supper he'd drive us down to the shop and walk us over to the cafe, where he'd set us up with soda pop. We nursed our drinks like whiskey, and we were satisfied.

Otto led me to a booth in back. We cleared the table and ordered coffee. Overhead, a fan the size of an airplane prop stirred the heat. Otto leaned toward me and lowered his voice. "Now, Butch, above all, remember you've only got two hundred dollars."

"What? I told you I saved a thousand."

He glanced around as if I'd blurted out classified information. "You don't want them to take all your money, Butch. All your hard-earned capital. Do you?"

"Well, no," I admitted. "But I thought it would take that much to get anything worth driving out of the lot."

The waitress brought our coffee, and Otto kept mum until she left. "Listen," he said, "you tell them you got a thousand dollars, how much you think your car's going to cost you?"

"Oh."

"That's right. I see how you won all those scholarships." He sipped his coffee while I meditated on what my money had cost me.

"Okay," I said. "I've only got two hundred dollars."

"Good. Because that's what I told these fellas. If you want to spend all your money, I'll sell you my car. Then I'll know you're getting your money's worth. But a used car is a used car. There aren't any guarantees in this business, Butch. You can't afford a new one unless you borrow, and you don't want to do that."

"I don't know," I said.

"Let me tell you. My father gave me three pieces of advice: 'Stay away from doctors, stay away from lawyers, never buy a car on time.' He might have been wrong about doctors, but the rest of it is true. You don't want to put yourself in debtor's prison for a car. All you want is something to court your girlfriend with and hold up all the way to New York State and maybe give you transportation while you're there. Wheels. Right? Am I right?"

"All right, Otto. I only wish you were still selling cars yourself."

"No, sir. When Hudson quit, I quit. All these other buggies are just Brand X as far as I'm concerned. But never mind about that. We'll set you up okay. Now, I want you to hurry over to my neighbor, Arnold Nelson. You want to remember the name, now. There's a Plymouth over there needs work. We can get it for a hundred and a half. Try her out. See what you think. Meet me at the shop when you're through, and I'll drive you over to Zimmer's. Charlie's got a Buick. More car, more money. Two hundred, and he doesn't budge. Don't say yes or no. Just thank them for their time. I'm not sure either one of these is the car for you. I've got another idea we'll try out after lunch." He smiled to himself, but he wasn't ready to let me in on it yet. "Let's go," he said and hauled himself out of the booth.

As we crossed the highway, Otto laid down a last commandment. "Don't tell them you'll be back, because you never know. Then I'll be in Dutch, and I have to live here." He shook my hand and wished me luck.

I found the owner of Nelson's Good-as-New Autos in the office, behind a stack of papers and computer printouts. A thin man in a white shirt and tie, he reminded me of a minister. "So you're Otto's nephew," he said. "What can I do for you?"

"Otto says you've got a Plymouth I should see."

"Oh, yeah. Uh-huh." He went over to the wall and contemplated a rack of color-coded keys.

"You're pretty well organized here," I said. "Computers and everything."

"With the business we do, young man, you have to be efficient. We serve the entire tri-county area, you know. And lately we've been getting customers from Minnesota, too. Johnny!" he hollered into the shop. "I need the keys to P17. That Plymouth Olsen brought in." He got an answer I couldn't hear, went to his desk, and discovered the keys underneath a pile of papers. "Here we are," he said. "Follow me."

The car lot covered a couple of acres, and he guided me through the labyrinth of gleaming automobiles. "So you're Otto's nephew."

"Can't deny it."

"You know what we say about Otto? He's a real Heller." He chuckled at his own joke, then stood on tiptoe until he spotted my car in the far corner of the lot. When we reached the car he opened the door on the passenger's side for me. "There you are." He shut me in, got in on the driver's side, and turned to look at me.

"You understand about this car, now, don't you? We haven't touched it yet. That's why I told Otto we'd let it go for two hundred. If we'd already done the reconditioning it would cost you five. It's not really ready for the road yet, but I think you'll be impressed." He turned the key, and the engine moaned. His foot flapped at the gas pedal, and he tried again. The engine grunted and gave up. "Maybe needs a new battery," Nelson muttered. All the car would say was click. Click, click. Embarrassed and giggly, I looked out at the nearby cornfield and remarked how well the crops were coming along.

"Yes," he said, "it looks like another bumper year for the farmers. The weather's been wonderful. Just wonderful." He got out of the car, and I thought he was going to walk away and leave me there, but he stuck his head back in the window. "Come on," he said, "I'll show you the engine."

I eyed it as critically as I could, but the motor looked more or less like any other to me. I think I was less impressed by the spare tire in the trunk than Nelson expected me to be.

"Of course it needs a little work," he said. "As I say, we haven't put it through our renewal system yet. But at the price it's a bargain. Just ask Otto. Now look here." He steered me over to a navy blue Ford. "Here's a dandy for five-ninety-five. Can't go wrong. This one's ready for the road right now." He raised the hood and opened the trunk. The paint job was fresh and appealing, and the charcoal interior looked rich. I climbed in and turned the wheel this way and that, and just then Otto showed up.

"Otto," said Nelson. Otto said nothing. He circled the car, then spoke to me through the window.

"Let's go, Butch," he said, and I slid out from behind

the wheel. I turned to thank Nelson, but he was already retreating toward the office. I had to run to catch up with Otto.

"Computers!" he spat as I came up. "I knew Nelson had gone to the dogs the day he installed that crap."

"What? Otto, what happened? What's wrong?"

"Wrong?" We were standing next to an old corn picker. Otto smacked it with the flat of his hand, and the sheet metal rumbled like thunder. "God almighty! I send you up there to look at a car, and soon as I turn my back he's got you sitting in a six-hundred-dollar wonder."

"Well, the Plymouth wouldn't even start," I said, defending myself more than Nelson. I was smarting as if Otto had slapped me. "The Plymouth wouldn't even start," I argued. "And what about that front fender? At least the Ford's a decent-looking car."

"Car? What car? I didn't see any car. Did you see a car?" He smacked the machine again and hurt his hand. He held it, and I didn't answer. "Butch," he said, calmer now that he'd hurt himself, "we won't even call that pile of parts a car. Scrap metal. Junk. That's all that thing's good for. Come on, let's go over to Zimmer's."

He took my arm and walked me to his pickup, explaining that Nelson's Good-as-New cars were good for nothing, that his workers painted over the rust and threw a new spare in the trunk and sold them to suckers, that the only hope you had with Nelson was to get the car before he'd messed with it, that Nelson was a good-for-nothing, backbiting horse's ass, and he, Otto, must have left his brains in bed to think he could send me up there alone, to even imagine that Nelson, that horse's hinder, would do anything other than what he'd done, which was try to sell me a glorified manure spreader.

Humbled by Otto's indignation, I realized I'd been rescued. He turned off Main Street and parked the pickup in front of Zimmer's garage. "Well, I'm glad you're on my side," I said.

"You're no dummy, Butch. You'd figure all this out yourself. But you can't afford the time and money it takes to learn these things. Besides," he grinned, "I enjoy this. The main thing you got to remember in this business is this: What were car dealers before there were cars?"

He was Chinese, too, this German-American uncle of mine.

"Horse traders," he said. "And a horse trader's only a cut above a horse thief, and they used to hang horse thieves. The moral of which is this: Never trust a car salesman farther than you can throw a horse."

Zimmer's garage was a greasy, wooden building. The tulips growing in the tractor tire by the door looked ludicrous and sad. Charlie Zimmer was a big, chunky man who seemed genuinely glad to meet me. He gave us the keys to the Buick and told us to take her for a run.

The Buick might have been bright red once, but now it just looked sunburned. I kicked a tire and stooped to look under the car, but Otto touched my arm. "Come on," he said. "Charlie gets insulted if you look them over in front of him."

So I drove out south of town, fighting the wheel while Otto ticked off troubles. "Shocks," he said as we rocked along. "Needs new shocks. Muffler's going, but you could get by." He snapped the radio on and off. "There," he pointed. "Pull over."

I turned off on the gravel, and Otto inspected the car. The grimy engine showed signs of eating oil, he said, and even I could see the water bubbling from a pinhole in the radiator. The tires were slippery smooth. "Bald as a baby's butt," Otto said. He drove us back to town. "What do you think?" he said.

"Not much."

"Me either. You could do worse, though. I think you're just afraid to scare your girlfriend with that pretty pink. At least we can call this a car. But the price is too steep, and Charlie won't come down. Tell him it's a bigger car than you had in mind."

So I lied to save Charlie's feelings, and we shook hands all around. As we walked out to the pickup the noon whistle blew. "Lunch," Otto said. "Let's go see Mama. She'll be happy you're here."

And so she was. All hugs and kisses and how have you been. She showed me her new refrigerator. "I nearly died," she said. "Otto bought it for me. Brand new. A birthday present." Otto nodded, suddenly shy. I knew it was hard for him to buy anything that wasn't a bargain. Aunt Lois looked as worn out as her appliances, and everyone held Otto responsible. You'd look that way, too, the aunts told each other at family reunions, if you had to live in a pawnshop. So the refrigerator was a token of true love, and I was so embarrassed I just said, "Very nice," and switched the subject.

Harlie rumbled up in a multicolored pickup, and his older brother Andy came in from the garden. Lois loaded the table, and I tried not to watch Otto eat. I recounted my adventures of the forenoon—Otto interrupting to remind me we weren't going to call that junker Nelson tried to sell me a car—and I was so depressed when I finished the story that Lois felt the need to serve me a second bowl of strawberries and ice cream.

"Buck up, Butch," Otto said through his dessert. "We ain't begun to fight."

"What about the Mennonites?" Lois asked. "Have you tried them yet?"

"That's just what we're going to do, Mama. Where's the Harmony paper?"

"Mennonites?" I asked.

"Mennonites," said Andy. "Over in Harmony. Otto's always robbing them."

"You keep out of this," Otto said. "You don't know what you're talking about."

Andy pushed back his chair. "Where you going?" I asked.

"Away from him. Fishing. See you later." He slammed the screen door behind him. Harlie grabbed a sandwich, grinned good-bye, and followed Andy out the door.

"Kids," Otto said. "Think they got it all figured out. Butch, we're going to try Harmony because they're Mennonites over there, and they take good care of their stuff. They're like me, stay close to home and work with what they got. I've bought good cars from them before, and I got a hunch that's where we're going to find yours."

Lois brought the paper, and Otto read the want ads with a pencil clamped between his teeth. He circled several ads and went off to the telephone.

Lois asked about my life out East, and I launched into a monologue about noise, crowded sidewalks, and the price of apartments. I didn't mention jazz, booze, or sex. I stuck with work, and Sandy's background, and how I'd won the fellowship. Otto returned halfway through our conversation and relaxed in his easy chair. By the time I finished my travelogue he was snoring. His midday naps were famous in our family, so I didn't take offense. I just said, "Hey, Uncle! What about those Mennonites?"

He jumped and blinked. "Right," he said. "They're out there waiting for us. See you at supper, Mama." He grunted and wheezed and shot up out of his chair.

"Get a good one!" Lois called as we walked out the door.

We drove north out of town. Otto asked me what I planned to do with my graduate degree. I told him I expected to be a professor some day, and he glanced at me, his eyebrows raised. "No fooling," he said. "That would be different. Never had one of those in our family. Any money in it?"

"Not much," I admitted. "The pay is pretty average, I guess. But I'll enjoy it."

"Well, you've always been one for the books. Say! Is this the Ph.D. you'll be shooting for?"

"Afraid so," I said, almost blushing.

"I once had a guy explain these higher degrees," Otto chuckled. "B.S., the guy says, everyone knows what that is. And M.S., that's more of the same. Ph.D.? That's piled hip deep."

I gave him a sick smile.

"Hey!" Otto yelped, slapping my leg. "Ha! Just a joke. Don't take it so serious."

"Sorry," I said. "It's a flaw in my temperament."

"Temperament, schmempermint. You forget how to laugh, you're really in trouble. No, I think teaching college would suit you to a T. A perfect match for your peppermint." He grinned at me, and I smiled back. "Just get the job done," he said. "Get that degree. We don't want one of these perpetual students on our hands. Sooner or later, you know, a guy's got to get out there and make a living."

"Look, Otto, I'm doing all right. We're going to buy me a car, aren't we?"

"Don't get me wrong! We're proud of you, Butch. Oh, there was a time there," he confided, "when you had us a little worried. That long hair and all. Thought you might end up a beatnik. But like you say, here we are today going to get you a car. And you're doing what you want. That's important. No, we're proud of the way you've stuck with it. I just wish my boys would do as well."

"They're doing okay. Aren't they?"

"Maybe you can tell me. That Harlie, that boy's almost a genius. That's what the counselor at the high school told me. And mechanical? You saw that pickup he was driving. He put that together himself. Started with just a bunch of odd parts. But do you think we could get him to go to college? No, sir. 'Harlie,' I told him, 'I'll pay your way, give you twenty-five dollars a week, and buy you a brand-new pickup.' I thought the pickup would do it, but that boy won't leave Granger. Can you imagine?"

"Sounds like quite a deal to me. It's hard for some kids to leave home, though, I guess. I was eager to get away, myself, but then Harlie's always been kind of shy. Maybe he has to work up to it, build up confidence."

"Yeah, he's a shy one. I guess that's it. But he's a good boy. Lois worries about him. She can't get him to take a bath to save her soul. She says it's his form of rebellion. I don't know. There's worse sins than that, I suppose. That other one, I don't even want to talk about him."

"Andy?"

"Yeah. He tried three or four schools, that one did. Got his butt booted out of them all. All he wants to do is go fishing."

I had to laugh. I liked Andy. "He's all right, Otto. He's probably just trying to find himself."

"You think so? I can't see how you find yourself by catching crappies."

I laughed. "I don't know, Otto. I spent a lot of time in the woods, myself."

"He can catch fish, I'll say that for him. He won't starve."

We were in Harmony now, a town of tall trees, trim lawns, and look-alike houses. "Read me the first address there," Otto said.

The car belonged to a widow in her seventies who insisted on reciting the story of her husband's life. If even half of what she said was true, he'd been a man of heroic proportions. But his car wasn't much. It looked as if it hadn't been driven since the day he died. Otto listened to her humbly, accepted the keys as though it were a privilege, and told me to drive around the block because, he said, you have to look out for people's feelings.

At the second address, across town, we found a maroon Chevrolet. The owner was a teacher at the high school. He was asking one seventy-five. I drove it out on a gravel road for the Otto Heller checkup. Otto was well pleased. "Butch," he said, "what we have here is a regular car, a genuine automobile. It's a little rusty, and it uses oil, but this is a real machine. We'll just give the guy a little test."

I was almost as excited as Otto, and I was relieved. "And for under two hundred," I said, "I've got a car."

"He'll go one and a quarter, but don't jump too quick. We've found one car, now we only have to find one more."

"What? What's wrong with this one? I'm tired."

"Takes it out of you, doesn't it?" Otto laughed. "No, sir, I'm not buying your car for you. I won't be responsible. We got to burden you with a choice. Otherwise, if the car goes bad, I'll have to take the blame. I won't have it. No, sir. Besides, cars are like women. You wouldn't want to marry the first pretty one that came along. You need to compare. And comparing the good with the bad is no comparison at all. Right? Am I right?"

"All right," I groaned. "Uncle. You're the boss."

"No, I'm not! That's just what I'm trying to tell you. That's why I'm insisting we find another car. Now let's see what the teacher has to say for himself. I'll be disappointed if he tries to bluff us. A Mennonite would sooner lose money than lie to your face. Especially if he knows you know what he is."

"What makes you so sure this guy's a Mennonite?"

"You can tell. They got a look to them."

The teacher was waiting for us in the driveway. I'd forgotten his name, but naturally Otto remembered. "Jim," he said, "we were out looking all morning, and yours is the first real car we've seen."

"I sure can't complain," the teacher said. "I only wish I could get another one just like it, new."

"I believe you," Otto said. We'd moved close to him, and Otto was looking up into his face. "I trust you folks over here, and that's why I feel I can ask you, Jim, if you know of any trouble this car might cause my nephew here." He lowered his voice. "Is there anything you want to tell us?"

"Well," the teacher said, "it does use a little oil. Say a quart every five hundred miles. But, honestly, that's all I can think of."

"I believe you!" Otto said and shook the man's hand enthusiastically. We thanked him, but Otto told him we weren't the kind to make a snap decision. Neither was he, the teacher said, and urged us to look around.

Otto drove back to Main Street. He was as gleeful as though he'd already closed the deal at fifty dollars under the asking price. "Now *there*," he said. "That's a Mennonite for you. Tell the truth, even if it hurts."

I was impressed. "Uncle," I said, "I'm beginning to suspect you know people even better than cars."

He accepted the compliment with a nod. "That's the only reason I'm in business. The stuff you buy and sell just lies there. People are the fun part." We rolled up against the curb in front of a large car lot. "Now this is Gordon Graham Cracker."

"What?"

"Graham. Graham's the name. I just call him that for fun."

"Is he Mennonite?"

"True blue. Come on, I'll introduce you."

Graham's showroom sparkled, and the shop was nearly as clean. Graham, himself, was big, bald, and wore a bright white shirt and dressy slacks. "Otto Heller," he said when he saw us, "what brings you over?"

"My nephew Brian. He needs a car, and there's nothing but nags in Granger. Butch, this is Gordon Graham—" He caught the Cracker just in time. "This is Gordon Graham."

"Pleased to meet you," the dealer said. "What kind of car did you have in mind?"

"I'd like something shiny that runs like new and will last forever. And I want it for two hundred dollars or less."

Graham laughed. "You're related to Otto, all right. What did you tell him, Otto? I run a bargain basement over here?"

"The truth, Gordon. The truth and nothing but. I said you're solid and sell good cars, and I never knew you to lie in your life."

Graham smiled wryly and polished the top of his head with his hand. "Let me think," he said. "Two hundred and under. I've got a Falcon out back for one fifty. You want to look at that?"

"If you want to show it," Otto said.

"Just a minute." He fetched the keys from the office, and we sauntered out back. Graham started the Falcon, and I walked around it a couple of times. The engine hummed harmonically. It looked all right to me. I joined Otto and Graham, who were hunkered down in the shade.

We sat there for a good fifteen minutes before anyone mentioned the car idling in front of us. Otto mopped his face with a handkerchief and remarked on the heat. Graham commented on the crops. Otto told Graham about the tomato-growing contest he had going with his brother-in-law, and Graham went on about the variety of roses his wife was raising. They asked about business, traded family history, exchanged the current gossip concerning county politics. Finally Otto told Graham half the story of my life and finished it off with the news about my fellowship.

"Well, congratulations," Graham said.

"Thanks," I said. "I hope I'm not getting in over my head."

"Now the school Butch has to get to, Gordon, is out

there in New York, and we're wondering about this car. Can you guarantee it'll get him all the way from Iowa to New York State?"

Graham glanced away, then looked at us with irritation. "Otto, you know better than that. I can't offer any guarantees. Not with a hundred-dollar car."

Otto made a face—a mask, I guessed, to disguise the fact he'd just realized we could get the Falcon for less than he'd expected. "Sure, Gordon. I know that. But I'd appreciate your opinion. How about it? Can she make it to New York?"

"How should I know? Why don't you try her out?"

"I'd rather take your word for it."

Graham ripped up a handful of grass and fiddled with it. "You know anything about cars?"

"Not much," I admitted. "They cost money."

"Then I wouldn't send you to New York in this car. If you knew enough to make minor repairs, it would be different. But this would be like selling to a girl."

I could feel Otto watching me. You bastard, I said to Graham in my mind. "No," I said aloud, "I really need something I can trust."

"Then this isn't the car for you," Graham said, getting up. He went over to the Falcon and shut the engine off. "I thought you just wanted something to drive around town. This would make a nifty street car." He patted the car on the roof. "But I'd never sell it to a girl, and if you can't do a little work yourself, it's practically the same. Sorry I can't help you."

"That's all right," I said. Baldie. "Thanks for trying."

"We'll just keep looking, Gordon. Thanks for your time. I sure enjoy doing business with people I can trust."

"Any time, Otto. Nice to meet you," he told me and hurried off.

Otto put his hand on my shoulder. "By golly, Butch, but I'm proud of you! That Graham Cracker calls you a girl, and you just sit there and take it like a man. We got the truth, too," he chuckled. "You can come to work for me any time you want."

"No thanks," I said. "I'd be a wreck in three days. Look, I'm still shaking."

Otto laughed. "You're all right, Butch. You're okay."

We meandered out through the car lot. The prices painted on the windshields were all over a thousand dollars. "Let's go buy the Chevy," I said.

Somebody whistled and hollered Otto's name. A man in his thirties, in a blazing orange sport shirt, came hustling through the obstacle course of the car lot. "Hi, Billy," Otto said. "What can I do for you?"

"You mean what can we do for each other. I hear you're looking for a good, cheap car."

"That's right. For my nephew here. Butch, this is Billy Polk. He works for Gordon."

"Yeah, Gordon tells me you wanted something a cut above that Falcon, and I happened to think of this Galaxie we're getting on a trade-in. It's eight years old but a very solid car. Belonged to Max Reichel. You know him, Otto."

"Don't believe I do."

"Sure you do. Delivers LP gas here in town? His wife's the organist down at Gordon's church."

"Oh, sure. I knew his dad. How much you asking?"

"Well, Gordon sold a Galaxie last week for two seventy-five, but I told him this one's in better shape, so he said we better go three and a half."

"I think we ought to take a look, Butch."

I agreed. I'd lost my spirit in the skirmish with Graham, but I was curious. I could hear myself saying: Yeah, the original owner was a Mennonite organist. Besides, I figured, Otto had to be onto something if he was willing to admit we had more than two hundred dollars.

"They haven't brought it in yet," Billy said, "so we'll

have to drive over to Reichels'. They were going to leave it here tonight when they pick up their new car, but I don't think they'll mind if we drop in on them. The papers are already signed. Come on, I'll chauffeur you."

The Reichel place was a model home. The front yard lay smooth as a carpet, and the house wore a fresh coat of paint. The gas truck was parked in the shade of a maple, and up near the house a man stood with a hose in his hand, washing a car. A lovely, palomino car, looking cool and clean in the heat.

"Hi, Max," Billy said as we walked up the driveway. "How about a drink of that?" Billy introduced us, Max turned down the water, and we all had a drink from the hose. It was good and cold.

Max was as soft-spoken as Billy was noisy. The three of them talked while I circled the car and tried to contain my excitement by running through Otto's checklist. Good rubber. No rust.

"If you want to take her out," Max told me, "the keys are in the ignition."

"Thanks. You drive it out, Otto. I'll drive back."

I sat up front with Otto while Billy babbled enthusiastically from the backseat. "Can you beat this for luxury? You've even got air-conditioning. All you have to do is hook it up."

"Too expensive," Otto said. "We don't care about the doodads, Billy."

"No, you've got a real solid car here. Rides nice, doesn't it?"

We didn't encourage him. I thought he'd know better than to try to sell Otto, but when we turned off on the gravel, Billy began again. "Max says she gets better than fifteen miles a gallon. I think you'd be real happy with a car like this."

"Brakes need work," Otto said. We got out, looked under the hood, and traded places. It was fun to drive, smooth and responsive.

Billy was quiet, and Otto must have felt we'd convinced him that he couldn't hustle us, because Otto began to question him. "How long you been a car jockey, Billy?"

"Seven years now. Five on my own and these last two with Gordon."

"Gets in your blood, doesn't it?"

"Yeah, I like to sell. And then I like the merchandise, and that makes it easy. Hell, I've had a car ever since I was a kid, ever since I got my license. What I didn't like, when I was on my own, was all the paperwork."

"I know what you mean. That's half the reason I got out."

I ran the car up the driveway, and Max came out of the house. "What did you think?" he said.

"I don't see why you're getting rid of it," I told him.

"I wouldn't, if the family didn't want a new one so bad."

Otto had hopped up on the front fender and was telling Billy the story of my life. I'd heard it before, so I helped Max clear his belongings out of the trunk. We carried his tools into the garage, and when we came back Billy was saying, "Tell you what I'll do, Otto. I'll let it go for three twenty-five. But that's as low as I can go."

"Good enough," Otto said and jumped off the fender. He bellied up to Max. "Max, I just got one question for you, and I know you'll tell me the truth. I knew your dad. What I want to ask you is this: Would you send your son to New York in this car?"

Max backed off, but he didn't flinch. He smiled. "He's only eight years old, so it's a little early to be sending him off on his own. But you don't have to worry about the car. I'd have the brakes checked first, but I wouldn't be afraid to try it."

Otto shook his hand. "All right," he said. "Butch?" We walked off a little way and went into a two-man huddle, as though this were a game of sandlot football and we had to come up with a play. "You've got your two cars now, Butch, and I can't decide for you. This one's a lot of car for three hundred dollars, but that's two hundred more than the Chevy, and they're both used cars. No guarantees. It's your choice." And he walked away.

I kicked a few stones around the driveway and gazed off over the fields. Inside five minutes my mind was made up. There was a moment when I wondered if the Ford weren't too good for me, but then I saw myself tooling down the freeway with Sandy beside me. I wanted that palomino car. I walked over and ran my hand along the roof.

"What say?" Billy said. "You want to take her home?"

"I do," I said. "I'll take it."

Everybody smiled. "You won't be sorry," Billy said. "Let's go sign the papers."

"And spend all my money."

"Right. I'll meet you there."

Otto and I got into my car. "Just a minute," Max said. "You've got the key to the church." He took it off the ring and handed the car keys back. "Good luck."

"Thanks, Max," I said and backed out into the street. I drove over to Graham's as carefully as if I'd just bought a brand-new Cadillac. When I parked in front of the lot, I realized we hadn't said a word on the way. I looked over at Otto, and he grinned, and I grinned back, and we both broke up.

Billy was already in the office, filling out forms. When he'd finished, he brought them over and tried to explain them. Then Graham walked in. "Is that the Reichel car out front?"

"Not anymore," said Billy. "I just sold it."

"For three fifty?"

"Three and a quarter."

"Where you taking that car?" Graham asked me. "New York?"

"I hope so," I said and knocked twice on the wooden desk.

"They've got an inspection out there, you know."

"Inspection? What do you mean?"

"Inspection. A state car inspection. If you're living out East, your car has to pass this inspection or you can't drive. So I don't even know if we can sell you this car."

There was a long silence. I felt panic and defeat, but then Otto said, "Come on, Gordon. This is Iowa, and Butch has an Iowa license. You wouldn't be in business long if your cars couldn't pass some sissy inspection."

Graham grunted and left the room. Billy seemed unsure of himself, but finally he said, "Sign here," and I did. Then I wrote out a check, and we all thanked each other.

I told Otto I'd meet him for supper, and he took off for home. I pulled into a station, spent another ten dollars on gas, and headed south out of town. Hot afternoon air billowed in through the window. I drove one-handed. Then I saw the signs along the fence line. Put out by a shaving-cream company years before, they were badly faded, but I could still make out the message. DON'T STICK YOUR ELBOW I could remember watching for them when I was a kid and just learning to read. OUT TOO FAR They floated like buoys in a sea of green corn. IT MAY GO HOME You had to wait for the rhyme. IN ANOTHER CAR I laughed and put both hands on the wheel. Half a mile ahead a mirage of water shimmered on the highway; when I'd covered the distance to the water, it was still a half-mile off. I chased it all the way to Granger, singing "King of the Road" at the top of my lungs.

When I drove up in front of the house, Otto's entire family came out to admire the car, and then we went in to supper. Supper turned out to be a sort of victory celebration. I told the whole story, and when I reached the part about how Otto had put Graham on the spot and Graham said he wouldn't sell me the Falcon because I was a girl, there were shouts of laughter.

"I've never seen that Graham Cracker act so stubborn," Otto said. "When we came in to close the deal with Billy, he wasn't going to let Butch buy the Galaxie, either."

"Yeah, what was that about inspections? Do I have to worry about that?"

"Don't you know what happened? That inspection stuff was just a lot of horse manure. Graham Cracker didn't want to sell you that car."

"But why not? That's what he's in business for."

Otto leaned back in his chair. If he'd had a cigar, he would have taken a long draw. "Because," he said, "that's a six-hundred-dollar car out there."

"Are you serious? He said three fifty himself."

"Sure, he said three fifty, but he'd never seen the car until we drove it in. All he knew was what Billy told him. Billy sold Reichels their new car, Billy took the Galaxie on the trade-in, and Billy, bless him, is not too bright. Why do you think he's working for Gordon instead of selling for himself? So when Gordon saw the car, he knew he'd made a boo-boo, and that inspection stuff was just his way of trying to wiggle out of it."

I sat and looked at Otto. Then I reached across the table and shook his hand. Everybody laughed.

"Now," said Otto, "you want to go out after supper and sell it for six hundred? Then we can go buy that Chevy tomorrow and you'll be getting it for free, plus a little profit for your trouble."

I laughed with admiration and astonishment. "I think I'll keep the Galaxie," I said. "But I feel sorry for Billy. I hope he won't be fired."

"Are you kidding? He just sold Reichels a brand-new car. Naw, used cars are peanuts. They're glad to keep them moving. They didn't lose any money on this deal." He grinned. "They just didn't make a whole lot."

Supper left an afterglow of goodwill. Andy had brought home a mess of crappies, and he and Otto and I took them out to the garden and buried one fish at the foot of each of Otto's twelve tomato plants. Fish, Otto explained, were his secret weapon in the contest with his brother-in-law. He and Andy razzed each other, and I was pleased to think I had something to do with their friendliness. When the fish were all buried, Otto took up the old story of how his family had weathered the Depression by plowing up their yard and planting potatoes. "That was right here in Granger," he said. "Forty years ago. You know, I went away two or three times, but I always came back. I like a small town. Look at the fun we had today."

Lois called Otto in to clean up for choir practice. Andy and I poked around in the garden until his parents left for church. Then we sat down on the front steps and watched my car change color in the sunset. The conversation came and went.

"Have you thought ahead, Andy?" I asked. "Made any plans? Your dad seems worried about you."

"Yeah? What did he say?"

"Oh, he just said you seemed at loose ends. He said you got kicked out of school. What happened?"

"Nobody kicked me out. I quit. Three times. I was never that interested. The trouble is, I like to fight. I'd go drinking and punch out some dude, and that got me in Dutch with the school. It got so college seemed more trouble than it was worth."

I looked at him. Andy was built like a linebacker, all arms and chest. "You like to fight, huh?"

"Yeah, it makes me feel good." I waited for an explanation, but he didn't offer any. "I don't do it much anymore, though. Harlie's the one who ought to go to college. He's real smart. But he works in the shop for two bucks an hour. He's crazy."

The conversation came and went, and we were at ease

with the silence. Suddenly Andy said, "Tell me about your girl. What's her name? Sandy?"

"Sandy. What do you want to know?"

"Is she beautiful?"

I laughed. "I don't know."

"I bet she's beautiful."

"She's better than that. She's handsome. Come on. Let's go down to the Greasy Spoon. I'm buying."

We drove downtown and cruised Main Street a few times before parking in front of the diner. At Granger's only stoplight, a teenager in a jacked-up Mustang challenged me with a long stare and a blast from his tailpipe, but I just laughed and waved him off. The pink neon sign at the diner said MILLIE'S, blinked out, then came back CAFE. MILLIE'S. CAFE. MILLIE'S. CAFE. We drank a couple cups of creosote and watched the June bugs batter the window.

Andy wanted to know about Boston. I told him the subway was more fun than a roller coaster. I tried to describe the carnival atmosphere of Haymarket Square. I mentioned the foreign accents that seasoned the talk in the streets. Cobblestone squares and concerts by the Charles. And all the noise, the continual clamor, my claustrophobia. And how at that crowded cocktail party, surrounded by highly distinguished drinks, intimidated by the dry martinis and exotic wines, I kept watching the woman with the honest laugh. And how after a while she walked over, stuck out her hand, and said, "Hi. I'm Sandy. I'm from Iowa. Vanessa tells me you're from Ohio."

Andy seemed to miss the point. He'd sure like to try someplace like that, he said. He'd thought of buying a trailer, had to get out of the house, but he was sick of Granger. A decent job was practically impossible to find, people watched your every move, and he'd had it up to here with being known as Otto's boy. Everyone thought Otto was such hot stuff. They ought to try living with the ornery bastard, he said. Mr. Know-It-All. He said he was going somewhere where no one had ever heard of Otto Heller. He said he was thinking of Denver, Seattle.

"All right," I said, "go ahead. That's better than sitting here hating everything in sight. But be sure to come back in a couple years, see how the place has changed."

"Are you kidding? This place will never change."

Early the next morning I said good-bye to Lois and Andy and Harlie and followed Otto's pickup downtown to the office of Oliver Lund. We had to insure the car, and Lund was the local agent for Farmers' Union. Otto said we shouldn't buy from them because they were Communist, but he liked Lund anyway. He was always good on claims, and he'd sent some business Otto's way.

Outside Lund's office, Otto and I shook hands. "Do us proud out there, now," he told me.

"I'll try," I said and got in.

Otto ran his hand along the fender. "This is some car, Butch. Your girlfriend's going to kiss you when she sees this car."

I laughed and backed out and headed down the highway to Sioux City, where Sandy was visiting her family. She didn't exactly kiss me when she saw the car. She walked around it warily, then stopped and caressed the door. "It's beautiful!" she laughed. "Where in the world did you find it?"

We stayed two days with her folks. Then we packed up the car and took the four-lane out of town toward Pocahontas and Chicago, Albany, and Boston.

Fifty miles out of town the water pump went out. The hot light winked on, and the car was spouting steam when I pulled over. I got out and kicked the car until my foot hurt and I ran out of curses.

"I knew it!" I hollered at Sandy. "I knew I was getting too cocky. This is just to remind me I'm a girl." I told her what Graham had said when Otto pushed him, and she got the giggles. "It's not funny!" I barked, but it was, and my tantrum dissolved in laughter.

"Come here, you big sissy," she said, and she wrestled me down in the ditch. Then I was on top, I had her pinned, and I bent down and kissed her, both of us giggling, while cars hissed past and honked like outraged geese.

We filled the radiator with water from the ditch and crawled into Holstein. The pump was replaced in less than two hours, and that was the only major repair the Galaxie needed until she cracked a piston three years later, and I put her out to pasture. I've had three cars since—all of them used, all three paid for with cash—but the Galaxie was my favorite by far.

We live in Minnesota now. Black River. I finally got my degree and was lucky enough to land a job at the U of M in Duluth. Eskimo U, my friends from Cornell call it. I don't care. We like it here. Sandy's a social worker for St. Louis County and keeps getting promoted. My situation is just about perfect. The commute to Duluth is easy, and I schedule my classes so I only have to go into town three days a week. I'm on the local library board, we support the high school hockey team, and we drink at the Northern Lights. There's always something to do. We pick agates in the spring and berries in the summer, watch the hawk migration every fall, and ski through the long, white winters. We've got a ramshackle house with a splendid view of Lake Superior. Once in a while an ore boat plows by, but mostly it's just local traffic and the empty, amazing horizon. Whenever the jack-pine culture wears thin, we drive down to Minneapolis and take in a play. It's nice to have reliable transportation, but I drive a lot less than I thought I would back when I bought that old Galaxie. Where's my car going to take me? To Boston? Seattle? Here in Black River the highway and Main Street are one and the same.

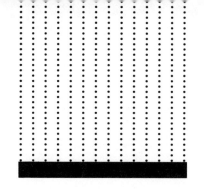

HAPPINESS

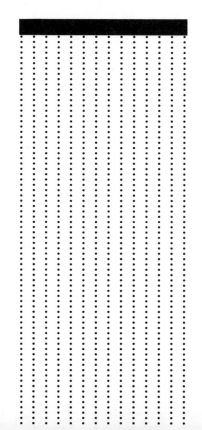

I

The trip on which we almost drowned was Dick's idea, but he didn't have to argue very hard to get Bud and me to go along. We had four days for Thanksgiving break. "Plenty of time," Dick said. "We drive up Thursday, canoe down Whiskeyjack to that little creek we found last summer, camp right there. No need to bust our butts. Then we've got two whole days to shoot some pictures, walk the creek, and generally putz around. You with me? We break camp early Sunday, and we're back in time for a good long snooze before classes Monday morning."

"It's going to be colder than a witch's tit up there," I warned.

"I know," he said. "That means no mosquitoes. No RVs. No fat fishermen. Just us." He let out a greedy cackle. "Gentlemen, I ask you to imagine birch trees. Listen to the wind in the lonesome pine. Inhale the sweet perfume of cedar smoke. Are you with me?"

We were with him.

The plan seemed sound, but we were surprised by the difference three hundred miles made in the temperature. Dick's ten-year-old Comet let in a lot of cold air, and the heater only worked intermittently. We didn't dare push the car much faster than fifty, so the drive, including bathroom, lunch, and coffee breaks, took all of eight hours. For the last four—from Duluth to Grand Marais and up the Gunflint Trail—we rode with our coats and mitts on. Bud finished reading *The Way of Zen* during the drive but said the next time he took a trip in The Vomit he'd have to bring tweezers along to turn the pages. Every half hour I beat on the heater and cursed. Dick laughed and called us pansies.

When we got out of the car at Whiskeyjack Lake we could see our breath. Dick hurried down to the water. Bud and I were still standing beside the car, sniffing the air and stretching, when Dick sang out from the shore: "You guys. You're not going to believe this."

Bud and I eyed each other. "What?" I shouted.

"The fucker's froze."

"What!"

"The lake. Come look. She's frozen at both ends."

We ran down to the shore. Whiskeyjack was eight miles long and roughly two across. A wide stretch of gray water lay open in front of us, but the east and west ends of the lake were white with ice. "Son of a bitch," I said.

Bud crossed his arms and tucked his hands under his armpits. "Guess we should have brought skates," he grinned.

"Damn it, MacMillan," I said. "I told you it was going to be wicked up here. Now what are we going to do?"

"Don't get excited," Dick said. "I'm thinking."

"That must be a novel experience," I said.

He smiled and knocked the rind of ice off a rock with the tip of his stainless-steel crutch. Dick had lost his left leg to cancer when he was fourteen. His classmates had bought him a color TV, and Dick had exchanged it for a canoe, the canoe that was lashed to the car, the canoe we had planned to paddle down Whiskeyjack.

"So," I said. "Any bright ideas?"

"We'll walk," Dick said.

"Through the bush? You're out of your gourd. It's four miles, minimum. And the first thing you've got to do is climb that cliff. Then you've got all that bog at the east end. You're nuts."

"I didn't mean over here, Peckerhead. I meant the Canadian side." He pointed a crutch at the far shore.

"Oh."

"We paddle across, leave the canoe, and walk the ridge down to the creek."

"Good," Bud said. "That'll work. There's an old railroad bed we can follow partway. Besides, if the going gets too tough, we can just park our carcass anyplace over there. It's all nice country."

"Okay," I said. "I'll go along with that. As long as you guys guarantee the lake won't lock up while we're over there."

"Naw," Bud said. "Not in three days' time." He laughed. "I don't think."

"Come on, Ray," Dick said. "What are you worried about? Say we did get stranded over there. Would that be so bad?"

I looked off across the lake. The distant shore was lavender and green. Back of that ridge, I knew, was another lake, and another ridge, and more of the same but all different, and rivers and rapids and lovely, rough country all the way to Hudson Bay. I took a deep breath of cool, spicy air. "You're right," I said. "Let's get cranking."

Coated with ice, the pebbles on the beach crackled underfoot as we loaded and launched the canoe. We took our caps and mitts but settled for jackets and left our coats in the car. "Go light, go light," Dick said. "We'll be moving around anyhow." Bud got in the bow, I sat in the center on one of the packs, Dick pushed off and hopped into the stern. Dick and Bud had run miles of white water together, so I naturally deferred to them. My back braced against the rear thwart, I enjoyed the ride while the two of them fought the choppy water. The crossing only took a half hour, but the light was fading fast when we reached the Canadian side.

We didn't bother to pitch the tent. Bud cut armloads of balsam boughs and built a green mattress. Dick gathered wood. I set up my cooking area, fetched water, and laid the fire. We had splurged on food for this trip. Our Thanksgiving menu included sautéed mushrooms, baked potatoes, sweet potatoes, steaks that draped over the edges of our plates, coffee, and pudding. Dick and Bud did the dishes in the dark, and then we all collapsed. I lay on my back in my mummy bag, my belly full, my body warm. The frosty air smelled like gin. When I closed my eyes I still saw stars. I grinned and drifted off.

We got an early start the next morning, but, without a real trail to follow, the hike was hard work. We stashed some of our gear beneath the canoe, but we were still overpacked for a trek through the bush. And though we all pretended otherwise, there was no getting around the fact that Dick was a lot slower in the woods than he was on the water. With the back and arms of a gymnast, he could make a canoe fly, but, determined as he was, he could only go so fast over rough ground. We worked hard, paused often, and reached the creek at noon. By the time we'd set up camp, we were all worn out and most of the day was gone, but I revived everyone with a thick chicken stew topped off with dumplings. For the second night in a row, we gorged ourselves. Then we lounged around the fire—talking, smoking, sipping tea—weary but satisfied.

Saturday dawned clear and cold. The light in the ravine where we'd made camp was eerie, soft and green, and Dick spent most of the day taking photographs. The ravine was lined with the largest cedars any of us had ever seen. The trees filtered and transformed the light, giving it such a gauzy, mysterious quality that we spoke in undertones. Dick devoted the entire morning to a pool full of clouds and sky and the soaring tops of several cedars. Even I could see it would make an amazing shot, a view in which water, trees, and sky would be beautifully confused, the world turned upside down. Bud and I talked quietly while Dick worked, hopping around his tripod, ducking under the black hood of his big 4 × 5, popping back out, making adjustments, puffing on a cigarette, waiting for the light to change, alternately gloating and mumbling nervously. In the afternoon Bud and I walked up the creek, tracing the stream through a stand of birches to a small waterfall and then back through a tangle of willows and scarlet moose maples to the source, a spruce bog that lay less than a mile from the point where the creek emptied into Whiskeyjack Lake. The ravine drained by the creek held the same appeal as an island: it felt like a world that was small enough to comprehend. And for this one day, anyway, it was ours.

After supper we sat up late to mourn and celebrate our last night in the woods. Dick pulled out a pint of brandy he'd been hiding in his camera pack. We relived trips we'd taken in the past and dreamed up expeditions for the future. Dick wanted to run the Mackenzie River. Bud said he needed to see Hudson Bay. I confessed my reveries about Alaska. At our age, we figured, we had forty years to make these fantasies come true.

"The trouble is," Dick said, "you run out of gas."

"You get tied down," I said. "I suppose it's inevitable." I handed the brandy back to Dick.

"The trick is to keep your standard of living low," Bud said. "Avoid the middle-class traps."

"I don't think it's that simple," Dick said. He took a slug of brandy, shook his head, and buzzed his lips. "Good stuff," he laughed. "Most guys just change over the years. Look at my old man. When he was our age he spent all his spare time in the woods. Hell, he took my mom on a canoe trip for their honeymoon! But now he never goes. He's lost the urge."

"No offense," Bud said, "but I think your dad was tamed. You get married, pretty soon you want a family and a house, and there you go. It's the old domestic tug, the longing for hearth and home. We all feel it, and once you reach a certain age it must be practically impossible to fight. But if you buy the whole program you can kiss your life good-bye. Christ, you've seen it. Guys just a few years older than we are. Ornery, independent, full of weird ideas. They get married, and, bingo, suddenly Buffalo Bill is living in a split-level with a two-car garage, working some stupid nine-to-five job and looking for overtime. Instead of spending a year in Tierra del Fuego, he's talking about his pension plan and driving a carful of kids to Disneyland."

I laughed and laid another piece of wood on the fire. "Women are the devil, then; is that what you're saying?" I looked up at Bud, who was standing back in the shadows. Red reflections of the fire glinted off his glasses.

"It's not women," he said, "and it's not men. It's the combination. The social unit. Marriage as an institution. You take a male and a female who can both think for themselves, give them wedding rings, and they go loco. Suddenly they're playing house just like the TV wants them to. Buying everything in sight. It's like they start living *down* to other people's expectations."

I tossed my cigarette in the fire, gazed into the flames, then sank back on the balsam boughs. Bud raved on, and I smiled. If there was one thing the three of us shared besides a liking for the woods, it was the conviction that the way most people lived was pathetic, criminal, and cracked. The question of how we should live our own lives fueled half our conversations.

Bud moved in from the darkness, bent over the fire, and rubbed his hands. He was tall but round-shouldered, with a smooth, boyish face and a way of going unnoticed in large groups. But he had the most intriguing mind I had ever encountered. Bud could move from music to physics to poetry and back so fast he left me feeling both delighted and scared. He didn't read books as much as he ransacked them, and once he'd adopted an author's best ideas, he gave the book away or tossed it in the trash. Bud hated the very idea of property. He lived by a rule he called the Backpack Principle. Whenever he'd accumulated more belongings than he could fit in his backpack—once every two or three months—he started throwing things. "This is what it all comes down to," he was saying now. "Warmth. That's what Thoreau says. Clothing, food, and shelter. Which are all just different ways of keeping warm. You wouldn't think a guy would have to work forty hours a week to keep warm! And you don't. I read this book about Australia once. Know what the aborigines work? Four hours a day. But we're civilized. We work eight." He laughed, a yelp that sounded as if he'd been hurt.

"Here," Dick said, offering the brandy from where he sat. "Have a little warmth."

Bud took a quick nip and passed the bottle to me. "The most valuable thing in the world is time. Isn't it? Outside of warmth? It's all we have. But we cash it in for junk—stereos, electric knives, dishwashers—and then try to cram a year into a crummy two-week vacation. I can't stand it. I won't live like that. I'll kill myself before I'll live like that."

"Don't you think suicide is just a touch extreme?" Dick said.

"What's the difference? You work all year for two weeks of freedom, you must be brain dead anyhow." He ducked his head and drank some coffee. "That's why I say, of all the lousy options available, teaching still looks like the best bet to me. At least you get your summers."

"But that's a sad-ass reason to choose a line of work," I said. "On the basis of how much time off you get. Jesus. The job itself ought to offer some satisfaction."

"You'd think so," Bud said. "But name a job that doesn't have monotony built in. Look, here's the problem. Human beings aren't meant to do the same damn thing day after day. Up until about a week ago, historically speaking, we were hunters and gatherers. Put up a hut today, go fishing tomorrow. Plenty of variety. But what do we do? Stand on assembly lines or sit in an office all day while the old bod is screaming to be out chasing deer or harvesting wild rice."

"Roots and berries, roots and berries," Dick grunted, hunching his back. "That's the life for me."

We laughed. "Well?" Bud said. "Isn't it? Why the hell else do we come up here all the time?"

"To cut the crap," Dick said, "and get down to bedrock. To leave the billboards behind. Because the farther you go from the end of the road, the fewer assholes you find per square mile."

"I like the quiet," I said. "I love it when the silence gets so deep you can hear your own heart thump."

"And there's the chance to test yourself," Dick said. "To see if you can survive without sidewalks and vending machines."

A breeze burst through the trees and fanned the fire. I felt for a cigarette, held the tip to an ember till it caught, took a deep drag, and passed it on to Dick, who handed me the brandy in return. "Mostly," I said, "I keep coming back just because it feels right. I feel good out here, even when the bugs are bad or the sky is pissing rain. Right? Even when the country's trying to kill you off you feel like you belong. The first time you guys brought me up here I realized I'd been homesick all my life without knowing why. This country is what I was missing." I paused. The fire popped and sighed. "But I can't see myself living like this for any length of time. I mean, to be honest. I like books and movies and hot showers. Part of the pleasure of every trip into the boonies, for me, is sharpening my appetite for all those things."

"I hear you talking," Dick said. "I've got a sizeable

hanker right now for a piece of that banana cream pie they sell down in Schroeder."

"Well, I'd like to try it," Bud said.

"The banana cream?" Dick said.

"That, too. No, I mean living up here. For a good long stretch."

"How?" I said. I didn't like the way these conversations went. I always came off as the hesitant skeptic.

"I don't know," Bud said. He turned around to warm his back and spoke to the trees. "Save up some money. Build a cabin back in the bush, come out to work a few months a year."

"That's just a pipe dream, Walker."

"Is it?"

"Come on," I said. "What are you going to do, live like a trapper? You like to talk too much. I mean, I hate to say this, but I'm afraid these trips we take are only high-class versions of the two-week vacation. They're escapes, aren't they? This is dreamland. Reality is back out there. Face it. To think you could actually make a life out here is just a romantic fantasy."

Bud turned and smiled down at me. Light and shadow flickered over his face as if he were underwater. "Sabo, when are you going to learn? It's all dreamland, man. You think shopping malls are real? You think freeways are the truth? Passing fancies. And don't go calling me romantic. People who use that word as an accusation are just chicken-shit defenders of the status quo."

I crossed my hands on my chest as if I'd been shot. "You got me," I moaned.

"I'll tell you one thing," Dick said. "I sure as shit do not want to go back to that other reality tomorrow. I could use another week or two out here."

"Me, too," I said. "But I'm afraid we'd run a little short on food. Unless Davy Crockett here goes out and snares a deer."

"I don't know about that," Bud grinned, "but I could

always hike into Grand Marais and pick up a box of Bisquick." We all laughed. Grand Marais was sixty miles away.

"Here," I said, pointing to a spot beside the fire. "Why don't you have a seat? These boughs are better than a sofa."

"Naw." Bud backed away. "You guys are sitters. I'm a stander." We laughed. It was true. Bud was always on his feet. He even ate standing up. When we gathered around the fire at night he never settled down but hovered in the background restlessly, moving in and out of the light, as if he might vanish into the woods at any moment. "Anyhow," Bud said, "I feel the sandman calling. I better sack out if we're going to take off early."

"Good thinking," Dick said. "One last smoke and I'll be with you." He frisked himself for cigarettes. "Goddamn. I'm out. Can I bum one, Ray?"

"Sure," I said, but I only had two left, myself. "Piss-poor planning," I said. I lit one cigarette and tucked the other away for morning. Dick and I sat gazing at the bed of coals, murmuring contentedly, passing the cigarette back and forth as if it were marijuana. We finished the brandy. I took a final drag on the cigarette and flipped the butt onto the coals. It smoldered, flared, and turned to ash. "This was a great idea, Dick. The best Thanksgiving I ever spent."

"Didn't work out too bad, did it?" He hauled himself up on one crutch. "Good night now, kid. Time for me to hit the hay."

I stepped out of camp to piss. My belly was warm from the coffee and brandy, but the night air felt frigid. I shivered, zipped up, and turned to look at the camp. I could see the dark shape of the tent and the coffeepot perched by the dying fire. A pale wisp of smoke wavered up into the darkness and disappeared. I put my hands in my pockets, walked over and stood looking down at the twinkling embers.

I thought how lucky I was to have found a pair of

friends like Dick and Bud. They were both characters, and I felt certain they were going to do something unusual with their lives. I knew people grew apart, but I couldn't imagine a future that didn't include the two of them. I wanted to grow bald and fat with these guys. I could see us in our old age, sitting around getting soused and talking over old times. And this would be one of those times, I thought, and felt odd, as if I were already standing somewhere in the future instead of right there by the fire. That was why the three of us kept coming back: we were creating memories, and we knew it. I looked up at the narrow river of sky visible through the treetops. It was filled with stars. I felt small but not insignificant. I must be drunk, I thought, and laughed out loud.

With the toe of my boot, I pushed the charred ends of wood onto the coals. Then I went into the tent, stripped, and slipped into my sleeping bag. The nylon was so cold against my bare skin that I gasped, but the down bag warmed up quickly. Dick and Bud were breathing heavily. A gust of wind rushed through the trees and rustled the tent flaps. Closing my eyes, I envisioned the pool Dick had photographed that morning, and, leaning out over the water, I looked up the long, spiral trunks of the cedars and beyond the green tops until I fell, finally, into the blue.

2

The next morning we ate breakfast, did the dishes, and packed up quickly. Once we were set to leave, Dick and I shared the last cigarette, and the three of us stood around the fire, sipping coffee and looking over the campsite.

"Well, it's a great spot," I said.

"Just so nobody else discovers it," Dick said.

"I think we're safe," Bud said. "You can't see the creek from the lake, and it isn't on any of the maps. Man, that cigarette smells like incense. I hate the fuckers, but they sure smell fantastic out here sometimes."

"Well, take a good whiff," Dick said, "because this is it. We get stuck out here, we'll be smoking leaves and bark."

Bud emptied the coffeepot on the fire, and we helped each other put on our packs. "Ready?" Dick said.

"Ready or not," I said.

Dick led the way out of the ravine and onto the old railroad bed. We moved along smoothly for a mile. Then we left the level railroad bed and struck off up the ridge. The climb was steep, and our enthusiasm was gone by the time we hit the top of the ridge. We had to make our way through the brush now—skirting patches of bramble and thorn, squeezing through clumps of balsam and spruce.

Laboring under the weight of the Duluth pack, I hiked along carefully, watching for roots and rocks. I was tired. I wanted a smoke. The sky was overcast and the air was cold, but I was sweating under my wool jack-shirt, and my thighs burned. Every few steps I glanced up. Ten yards ahead of me, Dick was choosing our route along the ridge, pausing to study the slope or whack at a branch, then swinging off on his crutches.

I stopped and turned slowly, like someone with a stiff neck, to check on Bud, who was coming along behind me, bent forward under the other Duluth pack. His brown hair looked black on his forehead, and his ruddy face was streaked with sweat. Bud raised a hand and dropped it, smiled grimly, and kept on coming. I tugged at the straps of my pack to ease the pressure on my shoulders, turned, and moved off again. I was hungry. We hadn't eaten anything since breakfast, and it was almost one o'clock. Bud had called for lunch at noon, but Dick had insisted we push on until we reached the canoe. Sometimes Dick overdid the macho-man routine, I thought. We could have stopped long enough for a little trail mix.

"Pines ahead!" Dick hollered.

I looked up. Standing on a hump of raw granite, stocky as a tree stump, Dick was pointing down the slope. "That stand of Norways," he said. "That's where we came up."

"Good going," I panted. "I was beginning to think you were taking us all the way to the Yukon."

"O ye of little faith," Dick grinned. His chest heaved, and his red union suit was damp at the neck. "You ought to know by now," he breathed, "you can always count on MacMillan's internal compass." He wiped his brow on his sleeve, braced himself to take the slope, and started down toward the pines. He slipped once, but caught himself.

Watching from above, I said, "You okay?"

"*Don't fa-all,*" he sang sarcastically. "Fuck you."

"Sorry," I said, and angled down the slope behind him.

There was very little undergrowth beneath the big pines. Dick swung along quickly through the half-light, and I followed, still feeling the weight of the pack but otherwise going downhill as easily as if I were strolling down an avenue. The forest floor was cushioned with brown pine needles. The wind made white noise in the treetops, and the air was fragrant with elusive odors—musky, herbal, slightly sweet. What an aroma, I thought. Bottle that, and you'd be rich. Call it *Borealis. Essence of the North. Muskeg.*

Dick stood waiting below the pines. I blinked as I came out into the daylight. "Not too bad, eh?" Dick grinned.

"Fuck," I sighed. "I love it. Some of those babies must be three feet thick. Think what this country looked like before they logged it off."

"I know." Dick pointed through the scrub and balsam. "There's the canoe."

I saw the dull gleam of aluminum and, through a clearing in the trees, a patch of dark water. "And the lake stayed open, too." I could hear waves breaking.

"Yeah," Dick said, "we lucked out. The wind must have kept her open. It's blowing pretty good."

We watched the treetops pitch and sway. "Damn cold, too," I said, "once you quit moving." I raised my collar and buttoned my jackshirt.

"It ain't August," Dick said. "Where the hell is Walker, anyhow?"

"Here he comes." I raised a hand as Bud came out of the pines.

"Where you been, boy?" Dick said.

"Enjoying the scenery. Isn't that sweet in there?"

"Hey, guys," I said. "I just felt a raindrop."

"Oh, great," Bud said. "That's all we need. A good soaking."

Dick held out his hand. "That wasn't rain you felt, Ray. Look." A white flake sparkled on the arm of his red union suit and dissolved as we watched.

"Snow," I said. "Holy shit."

We stood without speaking, our arms extended, while flecks of snow gathered on our clothes and collected in our hair.

"Merry Christmas, boys," Bud said.

"We better have a look at that lake," Dick said.

We hurried down to the shore and dropped our packs. Balancing on roots and rocks, we peered out from under the branches of balsam and spruce. The clouds were heavy, low, and white. Snowflakes flickered in the wind. The waves came rolling down the lake, slapping the rocks at our feet and spitting spray, tossing and foaming far out.

I whistled.

"Whitecaps," Dick said. "What do you think, Bud?"

"That nature is bigger than we are," Bud laughed. "I don't know. Looks like three-foot swells anyhow. We've been through worse."

"When?"

"That time we rode down Long Lake in the rain, for one."

"Yeah, but we were running with them then," Dick said. "We have to cut across these bastards."

"I know. But we're at an angle from the landing. I think we can quarter into them."

"Ray?" Dick said. "What do you say?"

"It looks awful rough to me. But you guys have to judge. You know what you can handle."

"If we stay here," Bud said, "we could get good and stuck. There's no telling about that snow. It might just dump a foot." He and Dick exchanged a look. Bud shrugged.

"Okay," Dick said. "Let's hit it. Sorry about lunch, you guys."

"That's all right," I said, turning back for the canoe. "If we'd taken time to eat, we'd have been stranded here for sure."

"You can buy me a piece of pie in Schroeder," Bud said.

Bud and I carried the canoe down to the shore, eased the bow into the water, and swung the length alongside the rocks, where I crouched and held onto the gunwale with both hands. The empty canoe jerked and bounced in the choppy water.

"You take the stern, Dick," Bud said. "You've got a stronger J-stroke."

"Finally," Dick said. "Finally you admit the truth." He pounded his chest and bellowed into the wind. We all laughed wildly.

Bud dropped into the canoe, and Dick handed in the packs. Bud slung the bulging Duluth packs between the thwarts and stacked the camera pack—a homemade, fiberglass box the size of a suitcase—on the pack nearest the bow.

"Can't you stick it under the seat?" Dick said.

"Not without spending ten minutes trying to get it to fit. Fuck it. Let's go."

I handed Bud his paddle. He grabbed hold of a tree root, and I eased into the canoe, where I sat riding high on the rear Duluth pack.

Dick stood on shore, adjusting his suspenders and buttoning his jackshirt.

"Come on," Bud said. "It's getting worse. We're going to bang a hole in this sucker before we even get started."

"Don't tell me you're nervous," Dick teased. He turned his fisherman's cap around so the bill wouldn't catch the wind.

"Goddamn it, MacMillan," Bud yelled. "Let's go! Let's go!"

"Coming, sweetheart," Dick said. He threw both crutches and his paddle into the boat. Then he grabbed the gunwales, vaulted lightly into the stern, settled himself, and pushed off. The canoe rocked up and down the first wave, slipped over the next, and we were away.

I was relieved to be clear of the thrashing water along the shore. The canoe slid through the glassy waves, and the motion felt fluid and free. There was nothing like it, I thought. The canoe surged ahead as Dick and Bud pulled on their paddles, then it seemed to hesitate and slip to the side as a wave rose up and rolled away under us. Bud shouted, "Whee!" and I grinned. I was worried about the crossing, but I had confidence in my friends, and, anyway, there was nothing I could do about it now. I was a passenger. I looked up the shore at an arm of land that reached into the lake. It ended in a jumble of boulders where a small cedar tree tossed in the wind. A fountain of spray shot high in the air and showered the tree. I pointed, and Dick said, "I see it, I see it. Once we clear that point, the shit's going to hit the fan."

We were out a good hundred yards. I looked across the lake. Through the veil of snow I could just make out the landing where there was a break in the shoreline, a clearing in the trees, and the blocky shape of a cabin. Dick kept the bow of the canoe lined up with the landing, cutting through the waves at a forty-five-degree angle. Two miles, I figured.

We nosed into a heavy wave, and drops of cold spray spattered my face. Bud yelped and turned halfway around in his seat, laughing and gasping for air. He was drenched. "Jesus Christ, MacMillan."

"Sorry," Dick laughed. "We're overloaded. It's like trying to steer a damn barge. Move more to the left. Woops." The canoe swayed like a hammock. "Ray, pull that camera pack down. It's riding too high, and so are you. Hunker down if you can. That's it. Good gawd," he said, and leaned on his paddle. The wave crested and passed. "Okay, good. Everyone set? Here we go."

Slowly, steadily, we moved out into the lake. We lost the protection of the point and felt the full force of the wind. The snow thickened. Then we were out in the whitecaps, the waves were suddenly huge, and the canoe seemed to lug down. Dick let out a groan. I turned and said, "You all right?"

Dick shook his head. "It's a bitch. We're standing still!" He grunted and hauled on his paddle.

We slid down the back of a wave like a bobsled going downhill, and our momentum carried us halfway up the next wave. Then we stalled, with the top of the wave still poised above us. "Now!" Dick yelled. Bud plunged his paddle into the wave, wetting his arm to the elbow, and we inched up over the crest. The canoe rushed into the trough.

Oh shit, I thought. We could be in real trouble here.

We topped the next wave, the bow hung in the air, then smacked the back of the wave, and we hissed down the slope.

There was a lull. The next three waves were smaller. Dick shouted, "Bud? You think we can hack this?"

"No choice!" Bud yelled over his shoulder.

"Turn back?"

"Hell, no! We're almost halfway. We'll swamp if we try to turn in these bastards."

"We could run with them, ride them down to the east end."

"Ice!" Bud shouted. "You forget the ice?"

"Oh, God," Dick groaned.

"We're committed," Bud said. "Big one," he warned.

The wave came on like a car. As we climbed up the side, the crest curled, broke, and boiled around us. Bud looked as if he were sitting in the surf. I watched, wide-eyed, as water slipped over the side and soaked the packs at my feet.

"Shipped a little that time," Dick said.

"A little!" I said.

Down and up we went, and again water entered the boat, though only half as much this time. I looked away, up the lake. The water was gray in the distance and looked like paint, but near the canoe it turned purple and black. I realized I didn't know what water was. Liquid, I thought. H_2O. It was odd not to know what water was, but I felt any minute I might find out. This much I knew: the waves came in patterns—two or three nasty swells, then one or two monsters, then three or four breathers. I tensed when a big wave approached, wished the canoe over the top, then relaxed, breathed, and prepared for the next big breaker.

The water in the bottom of the boat was over my ankles now, and I wanted to bail it out, but there was nothing I could use. I thought of the coffeepot, buried in the Duluth pack, out of reach. I made a mental note: in future, wire some sort of bailer inside the canoe. Even a cup would help, I thought.

A dark wave rose out of the others, translucent toward the crest and smooth as quartz, with froth at the top and bubbles dribbling down the side like a trickle of sand down a dune. A word went off inside my head, whispered hoarsely: *leviathan*. The canoe sailed up the side of the wave but trembled and swayed, and I

thought: *Wrong! Wrong!* Our angle was way too flat, and
three feet of water still hung above the bow. Bud leaned
over the side, sank his paddle into the wave like a har-
poon into a whale, but the canoe still came to a stop. I
felt the aluminum shudder. Dick sputtered and gasped.
"I can't hold it!" he cried, and the bow turned back
toward the trough. Parallel to the wave, we slid back
broadside, the crest curling above us. Froth and cold
water poured into the boat.

I leaned to the left to avoid the icy water coming over
the gunwale. Shit, I thought, this is it! But then we were
lifted, the wave sank away, and we slid down sideways
into the trough. The next one will swamp us for sure,
I thought. All I could hear was the seething water. It
sounded like seeds, like grain being funneled into a bin.
For a second or two, the canoe sat dead in the water,
stock still between waves. Then Dick shouted, "Draw!
Draw left!" Bud rose, reached out, and pulled the bow
to his paddle. He did it again, and then the wave lifted
us up, the canoe sliced into it backwards, stern first, but
at a safe angle. We rose on the wave, it rolled away,
and we sat looking back at the shore from which we'd
come.

Dick yelled, "Bud! Turn around! You're the stern!"

Bud swiveled around in his seat, so that now, instead
of staring at Bud's brown back, I was looking him in
the face. His face was white except for a red patch high
on each cheek. His clothes were soaked down the front,
his hair drenched, and his glasses, like mine, were
blurred. Bud sat up straight, looking past me at the
coming wave. He hauled his paddle through the heavy
water, then leaned on it, using it like a tiller, and steered
us over the swell.

I was appalled at the amount of water inside the canoe.
I felt as if I were sitting in a bathtub. I hated the icy
water, but I tried to sink lower to give the canoe better
balance. Most of the weight was back toward the stern,
but the stern had become the bow, and the canoe was

riding low in front, right where we took the brunt of the waves. We only had a few inches of freeboard left, and the water inside the canoe flowed back and forth as we tilted up and down. Another two inches, I thought, and we're going down. I tried to bail with my hands, but the effort was so pathetic I quit.

Bud said, "Forget it. Hold still."

"I wish I could help," I said. "I wish we'd brought another paddle."

"I know," Bud said. "Just sit still."

My fear was gone. I felt clean, cold, wide awake. I lived from wave to wave. Looking over my shoulder, I saw we were more than halfway to the landing, and I took some comfort from that. We had come that far. We had done that much. But I fully expected to die. I could swim fifty yards in a pool, but that meant nothing out here in the waves, in heavy clothes and boots. Say the canoe swamped but didn't sink, say I managed to hang on somehow. What good would that do, with the water colder than snow?

I looked up at Bud and said, "Been nice to know you."

Bud smiled tightly, nodded, and worked. When he pulled on the paddle his body shook.

Any minute, I thought. Very soon. One bad wave. Or the next. I was glad and surprised not to be too afraid. I tried to imagine how drowning would be, and I thought it must be a cold kind of burning, and I thought it was probably white and then black. It would be quick, anyhow. Better than rotting from some damn disease. I saw headlines and felt how awful my parents would feel, how wild and angry they'd be. What a waste, they would think, and how foolish. But, really, it was a good way to go. It wasn't some stupid car crash. I gazed back at the Canadian shore—the long, low hills barely visible through the flickering screen of snow—and my chest heaved. If I could choose a death, I thought, it would be this one, here, in this place. I only wished I could go down with a little more dignity, working to save myself and my friends, instead of squatting passively in the canoe going backwards across the lake with my hands in my lap like a withered old man in a wheelchair.

The canoe rode so low in the water now that it no longer floated but wallowed through the waves. Still Bud paddled and steered. I was glad I couldn't see Dick and the spray splashing over the bow. The water was up to my waist. Water flowed back and forth inside the canoe, and water flowed by outside.

Although I was ready to die, I was troubled by regrets and odd thoughts. I remembered the plates in Dick's camera pack, the film exposed but undeveloped, and I was disturbed to think no one would see those pictures now. And how was it, I wondered, I'd lived to be twenty years old without making love? Why had I been so damn shy? I hated myself and suddenly wanted, wildly, to survive. I hadn't prayed in years, but I tried it now but got no further than *Dear God* because it didn't make sense, I didn't believe it, and so I prayed to the water, *Water, let me live.*

At that moment, I noticed a raven overhead. It appeared to be flying in place, as if held by a string. Then the wind caught it, the raven tilted and sailed out of sight into the snow downwind.

I glanced at Bud and saw that he'd seen the bird, too. But Bud was laughing! I stared, and I thought, That son of a bitch. He's enjoying this! As if to prove it, Bud began singing: "Row, row. Row your boat. Gently down. The stream. Merrily, merrily. Merrily, merrily. Life. Is but. A dream."

"You're crazy," I shouted, "you're nuts!" But I was suddenly insanely happy myself, and I helped Bud paddle by singing along. We might have been a pair of drunks walking home after hours.

We shipped water and Dick screamed, "Will you watch it! What the fuck is going on!"

We quit singing, but Bud still wore a cockeyed smile.

I watched Bud's face, feeling more for him than I'd felt for any woman yet. I watched him strain with the paddle as if by watching so closely, with so much care, I could lend him my own unused strength, and, after a time, Bud said, "We're going to make it."

I noticed then what I hadn't before, that we were out of the whitecaps, and, though the waves were still big, we were angling into them well. The canoe sat so low I still had to hold my breath now and then to help it over the swells, but I turned cautiously and looked over my shoulder. I could see the landing and the yellow cabin, and the windows in the cabin, and not just the windows but individual panes of glass. I felt a surge of hope and killed it. I couldn't allow myself to believe we'd really make it. I looked back at the Canadian shore, which had nearly disappeared in the snow. Snow lay on Bud's shoulders like fur. A puffy flake landed in my eyelashes, and I blinked.

Then Bud yelled, "Dick! Don't quit! We're not there yet! Get up!"

I turned. We were only twenty yards out. Dick had dropped his paddle and sprawled over the bow. His back rose and fell. "I'm too tired," he groaned. "I'm whipped."

"Fuck you!" Bud snapped. "How do you think I feel? Come on, you pussy. Paddle!"

"Dick," I said. "Come on, Dick."

He lifted his head, palmed a drink from the lake, picked up his paddle, and went back to work.

I could hear the waves break as we came in close to the beach. There were rocks and trees to my right. The canoe still rose and fell, and the water inside poured back and forth. The waves looked like flint. Bud grunted, pulled back hard on the paddle, steered, and the bow scraped up on stones. The waves washed heavily against the side of the canoe, so that we tilted and swung alongside the shore. Bud swore and steadied the canoe, bracing it with his paddle.

"Out," Bud said, and I stood up stiffly. Water ran off my legs, down the inside of my pants, and I stepped out into the lake. The icy water was over my boots, but the stones beneath my feet felt good. I held the canoe while Bud got out. Then we each grabbed a side of the bow, and together we hauled the canoe halfway out of the lake. The stern, where Dick lay stretched out, his head on one arm, his other arm in the surf, still rocked in the waves.

"Come on, Dick," Bud said. "Get your ass out."

"Hell, no. I like it here."

"Come on, dumb shit. We've got to get warm."

Bud waded into the lake and helped Dick out of the stern. I hoisted the sopping packs out of the water and up the shore, then dragged the canoe a few feet higher. The three of us stood and looked at each other. Bud's lips were purple, his skin a delicate blue. Dick was dead white.

"Fire," I said. "We have to have a fire."

The landing was open and bare, but I saw a supply of wood stacked against the wall of the cabin. Glad to be of use at last, I ran up to the cabin and tried the door, but it was locked. The wood looked like pine. Good, I thought: fast and hot. The first layer was wet, so I tossed it aside. Then I carried an armful of dry, golden stove lengths down to the beach where Dick and Bud stood waiting. I jerked the axe from the pack and split the halves into quarters, the quarters to pieces. Working fast, I warmed up enough to realize how cold I was, and it scared me. My feet, my legs, and my butt were numb. My hands felt thick and clumsy. When I had split enough pine, I went over and cracked a dead branch off the bottom of a balsam, then crunched the twigs into a tangled nest and built a tepee of pine over the kindling. Kneeling in the snow, I glanced up at Dick and Bud, who stood waiting patiently, looking not at me but at the unlit fire.

I fumbled in my jackshirt and found my matches. The

safe had kept them dry, but the first one I struck flared up and went out in the falling snow. I touched a second and a third to the kindling, but the twigs were damp and refused the flame. I said, "Shit, shit." I could feel Dick and Bud watching. I looked up. Neither spoke. Bud hugged himself and shifted his weight from foot to foot. Dick stood hunched like a heron, staring at the fire that wouldn't start. He was white, he shook, and his teeth chattered. Water dripped off his nose. "Goddamn it," I said. I got up off my knees and ran to a birch tree beside the cabin. I took out my jackknife. "Sorry," I said. I slit two circles around the trunk, connected them with a vertical slash, lifted the bark with my knife, worked my fingers underneath, and peeled it free. Crushing the bark in my hands, I walked back and stuffed it under the tepee. Then I stood for a second, squeezing my fingers under my armpits, trying to warm my hands. I knelt, struck a match, and touched the flame to the papery bark. It caught. Black smoke curled away from the flame, releasing a bittersweet odor, and the fire spread through the twigs and grew. The pine crackled, orange flames feathered off the wood, and I had to back away from the heat.

"Attaboy, Sabo," Dick smiled.

"Magic," Bud said. He stepped over the burning pyramid and stood directly over the fire.

"You'll burn your balls," I said.

"Who needs them?" Bud said. But the flames licked his leg, and he stepped away.

The three of us stood close to the fire without speaking and worked our fingers. We rubbed our faces and felt our ears. We turned our backs to the fire, then turned again. We murmured and sighed, as if we were eating an excellent meal. The snow continued to fall, but it seemed harmless here, out of the wind, even beautiful. It drifted down so softly that the hiss and crackle of the fire sounded loud. Steam rose off our clothes as they began to dry. I fetched another two armloads of wood and piled on the chunks without bothering to split them.

"That's it," Dick said. "Build her up. Big mother-fucking bonfire." The fire snapped and roared. Dick stood close, and his face reflected the flames, but he still shivered.

"Well," Bud said at last, "wasn't *that* an adventure?"

Dick rolled his eyes and said, "Fuck you."

"I thought we were finished," I said. "I could feel us going down."

"Me, too," Dick said. "We had way too much weight for swells that size. Christ, they must have been four feet! I've never seen such a sloppy job of loading in my life."

"My fault," Bud said. "I rushed it."

"Forget it. Doesn't matter. We made it."

"Skin of our teeth," I said. "You guys must be washed."

"More or less," Dick said. "I don't know what it is, but I just can't seem to get warm."

"Give me the keys," I said, "and I'll go get the coats."

Dick dug for the keys and handed them over. "Start her up. Maybe if we run the fucker for an hour we can get half an ounce of heat."

I walked uphill to the Comet. My clothes were still damp, but I felt warmer, anyway. The car shuddered to life on the third try. I got the coats and the army blanket out of the backseat and left the car idling.

We held our coats to the fire to take off the chill, then pulled them on. I handed the blanket to Dick, and he draped it over his head like a shawl. The three of us stood and looked at the fire as if we were watching TV. Then Dick said, "Guys. Guess what." He drew his right hand from his coat pocket and held up most of a ciga-rette. The end was ragged, and the paper was stained three different colors.

"What a find!" Bud grinned.

"Sacred tobacco," I giggled.

"Mr. Sabo," Dick said, "would you do the honors?"

I held a match to the dirty cigarette. Dick inhaled, coughed, laughed, inhaled again, and held the smoke in his lungs. "Not bad," he breathed. "Not *good*, but not too damn bad, either."

I took a drag. The smoke scratched my throat, but my lungs, deprived all day, welcomed the nicotine rush. I felt light-headed and happy as we stood there in the falling snow, passing the butt back and forth, blowing smoke rings and laughing. Even Bud took a toke. When the cigarette burned his fingers, Dick dropped it in the fire and said, "All right. Let's go get some more drugs. That's all I need, food and drugs." He kicked snow on the fire, and a geyser of smoky steam shot high in the air.

We hauled up the packs, heavy and dripping, and dumped them in the trunk. Bud and I emptied out the canoe, carried it up to the car, and eased it onto the roof. Dick lashed it down. Then he crawled in back, saying, "You drive, Ray. I'm too tired to hold the wheel."

I adjusted the seat and mirrors, gunned the engine, and started slowly out the side road, then turned down the Gunflint Trail. The snow had been falling for two hours, but there wasn't more than an inch of white on the blacktop. The flakes were heavy and wet and melted the moment they hit the windshield. The tires hissed through the slush.

I stopped at Moosehead Station for cigarettes and coffee to go. The old man behind the counter took my money without uttering one word. Outside, I stood for a minute, the coffee cups warming my hands, the bitter fragrance rising to my nostrils, and looked around at the deep green trees frosted with snow. I shivered and went to the car.

The Comet's heater only worked in fits and starts, but the coffee helped. In the backseat, Dick slurped and grunted with satisfaction. No one said much, and I knew Dick and Bud were back on the lake, as I was, reliving the crossing, even as the trees flowed past and the car climbed and dipped and swept around curves, spraying wet snow from the tires.

3

An hour later, we topped the big hill above Grand Marais. Through the thin scrim of snow, I could see the small town spread out below, a few lights burning like early stars, the arms of the harbor reaching into the lake, and Lake Superior—as large as today, yesterday, and tomorrow—filling the whole horizon. The water was dark, and then there were layers of gray and the different whites of the sky. I took my foot off the gas and touched the brake as we started the long descent. "Want to stop in G.M.?" I asked.

"Schroeder," Bud said. "Dick owes me a piece of banana cream."

"Yeah," Dick said, "what the hell. It's only another half hour."

So, when we reached the foot of the hill, I turned right, out of town. We climbed through the trees, and dropped again, and the lake came storming in on our left.

"Look at that," Dick said.

"Wild!" Bud said. "Beautiful."

I glanced at the lake and drove on into the flimsy snow. The highway crossed Cutface Creek, curved around the bay beneath the cliff, and then we were out on the straightaway, and the driving was easy.

When we pulled into Schroeder, it was nearly dark, and the windows of the Kom-On-Inn were blazing. The cafe was empty. We slipped onto stools at the counter, and a middle-aged woman in white came out of the kitchen. She had a nice figure and a plain, kind face, but there were circles under her eyes. "Hi, fellas. Nasty weather, isn't it? Coffee?"

We ordered cheeseburgers and American fries, and

the woman went off to cook our food. We took turns washing up, then sat at the counter smoking, drinking coffee, and eyeing the homemade pie. The woman brought our food and stayed to talk. The tag on her uniform said "Joyce."

"You boys aren't from around here."

"No," I said between bites, "we go to Wausaukee State. But we get up here whenever we can."

"We spent Thanksgiving on Whiskeyjack Lake," Bud said.

"I saw you had a canoe. You didn't get caught in this weather, I hope."

"Afraid we did," I admitted. "Just a couple hours ago. We almost bought the farm."

She shook her head. "We get these big storms in the fall all the time. You wouldn't catch me out there this time of year."

"We're experienced," Dick said. "We know what we're doing."

"When we don't forget," Bud laughed. "This was dumb. We just got in too big a hurry."

"Well, I'm glad you made it," she said. "You better be more careful next time."

We ordered pie. Dick and Bud had the banana cream. I decided on blueberry à la mode. The pie was perfect. I felt warm all the way through for the first time in hours. The room was bright and cheerful, and the stainless-steel equipment—the coffee maker, the milk machine—gleamed like brass on an altar.

The woman talked about the coming winter, isolation, loneliness. Her voice was tired, warm and low, a little sad but friendly. "Of course we'll get some skiers on the weekends now, but otherwise it'll be pretty dead until well into May. You get your truckers coming through, and local people, friends and neighbors. But it isn't much. Awful quiet up here once the snow starts coming down."

"But that's exactly why we like it," Dick said. "It's a great place to get away from all the creeps."

"You don't live here," the woman smiled. "We've got our bad ones, too. Besides, the older you get the more you need other people. A lot more than when you're young."

"You're not so old," I said.

"Thanks. But I'm older than you, and I'm telling you, you get lonesome after a while. I've spent half my life looking out that window. Sometimes I'd like to move down to the Cities."

"Why don't you, then?" Bud said.

"Oh, well. I got three kids. And my husband grew up here. He'd never dream of leaving."

"Then maybe you should run away with us," Bud said. "Right now. What do you say?"

She laughed. "Thanks for the offer. I've just been talking. I like it here well enough. The summers are gorgeous—cool and bright—and you get all kinds of people coming through then. It's just that the winters drag on so long. You guys want more coffee?"

"No thanks," Dick said. "We've got to get going."

"You don't have to worry. This snow isn't supposed to amount to anything."

"That's good to hear," Dick said, "but it's a long drive, anyhow." He stood up and dug for his wallet. "I got it, guys."

"Bye, now," the woman called as we went out the door. "Careful on those roads."

Outside the cafe it was chilly and dark, but the snow had nearly stopped. I could hear the Cross River cascading over the rocks and rushing out under the bridge toward Lake Superior. The car was cold, but the heater kicked in when I started the engine, and we all cheered. I backed out and turned down the highway toward Duluth.

Bud slapped his belly. "Great meal."

"Good stuff," I agreed. "And that waitress. Joyce. I thought she was awfully attractive. I wanted to love her up right there. On the counter."

Bud looked at me and laughed. "You too? Same here."

"Are you kidding?" Dick said. "You guys would fuck a snake." He was wrapping himself in the blanket. "I mean, she was nice enough, but that was one plain-looking lady. Not to mention the fact she's old enough to be your mother."

"So call me a motherfucker," I laughed.

"She looked awfully good to me," Bud said. "I think I know why. We damn near died back there, but we survived, and she was the first woman we saw. So we felt this rush, the life force surging up like sap. *Elan vital*, the French philosophers call it."

"What bullshit," Dick said. "*Elan vital*. Vidal Sassoon. You guys can wake me up when you start talking English." He stretched out on the backseat, farted, and said, "*Sacré bleu!*" We all laughed, then settled back in silence. Before long, Dick was snoring.

I grinned and shook my head. "I guess you could say Dick doesn't have a whole lot of patience with philosophic speculation."

"Mr. MacMillan," Bud said, "is an eminently practical fellow. That's why we're pals. He keeps me from floating away like a hot air balloon. Old Dick's got his feet on the ground. Foot," he corrected himself, and we both laughed lightly.

"Well, he wields one hell of a paddle," I said.

"The best."

It had started snowing again, but the flakes were fine and dry and blew right off the windshield. I lit a cigarette and cracked the wing vent. "Were you scared out there?" I said.

"Not really. A little nervous at first, but I got over it."

"How? I just about shit when we went broadside."

"A moment to remember," Bud chuckled.

"Yeah, and the next thing I know, you're *singing*, for God's sake."

"Might as well enjoy yourself. Hey, you joined in."

"I was out of my mind."

"So was I. That's what saves me in a spot like that. I get outside myself. I split. It's like I'm watching a movie, and I'm also *in* the movie. I do what I can, but part of me—the important part, I think—is way off watching, wondering how things will turn out. Know what I mean?"

"I think so, but that wasn't how it was with me. There was one point, though, when I just got very calm. I was ready to die. I didn't feel too bad about it, either."

"Good for you," Bud said. "No one should be scared to die. Pain, okay, I can understand the fear of pain. But not the fear of death. Because death is either nothing, in which case your problems are over, or else it's something pretty interesting, and you're finally let in on the mystery."

"Yeah, but let's wait until the time comes, okay?"

"What do you mean, 'until the time comes'? Who says you're going to live to be seventy? I've never understood that. People act like they're owed threescore and ten. Like it's guaranteed."

"It's the normal life span, isn't it?" I said. I stubbed out my cigarette.

"Normal for who? The kid who gets hit by a car? My uncle who had a heart attack at forty-two? You're talking averages. Averages are statisticians' fantasies. They work for groups but not for individuals. There's a certain uncertainty principle." Bud laughed. "You can predict how many in a given group will croak by such and such a time. But nobody can say when you, yourself, are going to die."

"You know not the day nor the hour," I said.

"Right," Bud laughed. "The Bible still beats the statisticians on that one. But it's odd how people think

they've got this right to old age. They're so convinced
of it they go around half-dead. 'Oh, I'll travel after I
retire.' Pie in the sky, man. Better do it now. Now is
all you got. But they're so sure they've got forever they
sleepwalk right through life. Which is the great thing
about danger, like today. It wakes you up. Did I tell
you that poem I found by this guy Machado?"

"No."

"It's about Jesus. Little poem to Jesus." He laughed.
"Goes like this: 'All your words were really one word:
Wake up!' "

I laughed. "Great poem."

"Great poem," Bud giggled. "One of the few truly
religious poems I've ever read. 'All your words were
really one word: Wake up!' "

Dick sat up in the backseat. "What? What is it?"

"Nothing," Bud said. "We're just talking."

"Yakkety-yakkety-yak," Dick grumped and settled
back to sleep.

I grinned, looked over at Bud, and said, "This has
been a pretty amazing day."

"Not too shabby," Bud said. He leaned forward and
scraped some frost from the corner of the windshield.
"Anyhow, what I was saying was, I don't get scared
much anymore. I get thrilled, but I don't get scared."

"Boy, I do."

"Well, I guess I'm different. Most people seem to feel
their lives are important. To themselves, if no one else.
I feel more like a leaf in the wind. Just along for the
ride. It's fun. Nothing to be scared of."

I looked at Bud in the dim light from the dash.
"You're a strange one."

"I know it. Don't let it bother you."

"It doesn't bother me. I just can't take my life that
lightly."

"I'm not saying you should. I'm just saying how it
is with me. Think of this. Think of yourself as a kid,
eight years old or so. Are you doing it?"

"Yeah," I said, "okay."

"How do you feel?"

"You mean about that kid?"

"Yeah."

"I don't know," I smiled. "Amused. Embarrassed by how dumb he is. Proud of how hard he's trying. A little sad, I guess."

Bud nodded. "Now," he said, "do you think you'll feel any differently about yourself right now when you look back in ten or twenty years?"

I felt my mind tilt and slide. A thrill shot through my solar plexus, as if the car had flown over a dip in the road. "No," I smiled, "I suppose I'll feel about the same."

"There you are. If you can't take yourself seriously when you remember who you were, why should you feel any differently about yourself right now? All you have to do is shift your perspective. Remember who you are. Life is not the big deal we make it out to be."

"You got me," I laughed. "You asshole."

Bud grinned. "Amused melancholy," he said. "I think that's about as weighty an attitude as we deserve."

I felt a chill on my neck and closed the wing vent. We rode in silence for a time. The snow came and went in little flurries. I crouched, once, over the wheel, peered up and saw stars in a big patch of clear, black sky. And then suddenly there was a deer on the road, in the other lane, angling toward the car. I looked straight ahead, tromped on the foot-feed, and clutched the wheel with both hands. For one long, floating moment the deer seemed to be running right at the fender. The car and the deer were both drifting—smoothly, slowly—and I waited for the crash. Then we were past and shooting on down the road. I glanced in the mirror and saw the deer standing on the shoulder in the swirling snow, and then it was gone. I looked straight ahead and sagged at the wheel, feeling the blood pulse at my temples, my chest expand, my fingers tingle. I turned to Bud. "Did you see that?"

"Wonderful. Was it real?"

"I don't know! I was absolutely sure we were going to smash."

"We can't," Bud laughed. "We're golden. Nothing can touch us today."

"But that was incredible!"

"Everyday magic," Bud said. He cocked his cap to cushion his head and leaned against the window. "Okay, Sabo. My life is in your hands. Wake me when we hit Duluth."

"Sweet dreams," I said.

"You too."

"I'm driving, you idiot."

"So? You can dream with your eyes open, can't you? I do it all the time. That's the best part about driving."

"Daydreaming, you mean."

"I guess that's what you call it," Bud yawned. "Though it's night now, of course."

I smiled. "Well, I'm not supposed to, anyhow. I'm supposed to pay attention here."

"It's up to you," Bud murmured. "I'm gone."

I drove on into the night. The snowfall glittered in the headlights, quit, came back in clouds, then cleared again. Now and then a gust whipped a white scarf across the windshield, and I was momentarily blind, but the traffic was light, the highway dry, and I felt quite safe, though I drove for several seconds on sheer faith. I focused on the road and the dark evergreens going by, and I watched for the incandescent eyes of deer. Birch trees, whiter than white, lined the road for several miles, and the headlights flickered and flashed off the trunks like a strobe light. I grew dizzy and forced myself to stare straight down the highway. I felt giddy, transparent, almost clairvoyant, and, as the snow flew by like bits of light, tiny stars speeding out of the black, I thought of the car as a capsule rushing into the future.

But of course I was not clairvoyant. Otherwise I would have known, and should have been able to guess anyway, that Dick and Bud and I would all eventually marry and drift apart, that the three of us, like other men, would be forced to take jobs we disliked, succumb to duty and dull routine, and gradually, as the years went by, admit the lives we had made were not the ones we'd imagined. That much I might have guessed. But I didn't. Nor did I foresee that Bud would actually keep his word and, one sunny September morning a dozen years later, shoot himself in the head. Nor did I dream that, four years after Bud's suicide, the cancer that had taken Dick's leg would return to claim the rest of him. There was no way for me to know that I alone would remain to remember this trip when the three of us nearly drowned, and, with no one to verify my memories, I would feel, sometimes, as if it had never happened, that I'd made it up or dreamed it, that it was all as ethereal as that deer on the highway, though now and then a memory would blow up like a gust of snow, and I would forget where I was and be back in that green ravine, watching Dick work and hearing him chuckle wickedly over his camera, or be out on the lake and see the pure glee in Bud's eyes as we rode the waves and water broke over the bow, and I would wonder, then, how it was that I hadn't known at the time, as I drove down the shore through the snowy night, with my funny, vulgar friend asleep in the back of the car and my other, suicidally brilliant friend asleep at my side, that I was as happy then, right there, as I would ever be.

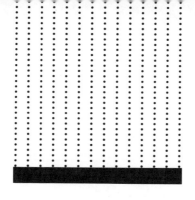

VERY

TRULY

OURS

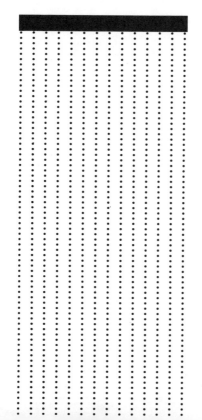

My Granddad Hackbart was a big old bastard, six feet tall and heavyset, with a chest like an overstuffed suitcase. He was fat, but he didn't look fat. His hair was thick, and he brushed it back in a silver pompadour. His forehead was high, his cheeks were pink, and his eyes were a scary blue. He was a handsome man, but it didn't do him any good, because everybody in Bessemer knew he was cranky and drank like a large-mouthed bass. When my Grandma Hackbart died, there wasn't a widow in town who would even consider him. He couldn't take care of himself, he wasn't ready for the nursing home, and he only had a small pension, so the son of a bitch moved in with us. He took my room. I was eight years old when Granddad came to live with us, and he was still in the house when I left for college. I grew up with him. Granddad was family, and I hated his guts.

He could be nice enough when he wasn't drinking, but that was damn seldom, and he was meaner than a barbed-wire fence when he was in a mood. Granddad was forced to retire early because of an accident at the mine, and he walked with a limp. He complained about his job all the time when he was working, but he wasn't any happier after he took retirement. He didn't seem to know who he was or what to do. I suspect that having him around the house all day drove my grandma into her grave. He used to hit her. Once, when I was little and staying overnight with them, she said something at dinner. He came right over the table and slapped her. Hard. She was a haughty woman, but she didn't deserve that. Christ, today we'd prosecute. But that was a different time, the Iron Range was tough, and people kept their troubles to themselves. I remember, when I was in high school, I asked my dad one time why Granddad used to hit Grandma. He looked at me a long time, and then he said, "Because he loved her." He paused, and I was about to object at the top of my lungs that belting someone was a pretty lousy way of showing love, when my old man added, "And she didn't love him." I can still feel the chill that gave me. By the time Granddad retired he'd softened some, but I'm still convinced his presence in the house hastened Grandma's death. He was downtown, drunk, at the Hardhat Bar, the night she had her stroke, and I think he felt guilty about that the rest of his life. But naturally he only used his guilt as another excuse to hit the sauce.

Once Granddad moved in with us, he started in on my mother. Nothing physical—he wouldn't have dared—but he whined and bossed her so much that she finally just ignored him. Ma did what she considered her Christian duty. She washed his clothes and made his meals, but she barely spoke to him. She'd communicate through my dad or one of us kids. "Tell Granddad supper's ready." He'd be sitting right there. There were sparks almost every night between my dad and Granddad, too. If he'd made himself useful now and then, that would have been one thing. But he hardly ever went out of his way, and when he did take up some chore you could count on him to drop it halfway through. He read magazines. He watched TV. He sipped whiskey in his room and walked downtown for coffee.

Basically, he spent his retirement waiting around for the first of the month, when his pension arrived, so he could go out and get plastered. He liked to hunt, and I have to admit that he was a wonderful companion during deer season—he'd warm up then, and tell terrific stories, and show you things—but the rest of the year he was a giant pain in the ass.

When Granddad first moved in, we kids thought it was going to be fun to have him in the house, but he cured us of that notion in a hurry. Mostly what it meant was that we had another grown-up to order us around. He was always hissing at you to be quiet, even when you had something interesting to say. He'd give you a whack without warning, for no apparent reason. And the worst thing about him was that he was a pincher. Squeeze you like a pliers. He'd pinch your leg or arm or get you by the back of the neck. He left bruises, for Christ's sake. I was in junior high before I could get him to quit that shit. He grabbed my arm one day, and I kicked his bum leg until he let go and dropped in a chair, wincing and blinking back tears. That was a frightening, triumphant moment for me.

As Barb and Steve and I grew up and Granddad got weaker, we were more like equals. We squabbled all the time. Now and then, when he ran short of cash, he'd rob our piggy banks. To get him back, we'd raid his room and steal the dimes he saved in empty cigar tubes. His room was right across the hall from the one I shared with Steve, and it stank of perspiration, whiskey, and cigar smoke. One day Steve and I emptied two entire cans of Right Guard on his room. We sprayed the place so thoroughly he had to sleep on the living room sofa for two nights in a row. And then there were the music wars. Granddad had a red-and-white plastic hi-fi he'd picked up at a garage sale. He called it his Victrola. The trouble was, he only owned one record, a scratched-up 78 with a green label. It had a schottische on one side and "The Beer Barrel Polka" on the other. He'd lock his door and play that sucker until our eyes were bugging out, and we'd have to crank up the rock and roll on Steve's radio in order to retaliate. You could stand in the hallway with "The Beer Barrel Polka" in one ear, Elvis in the other, and go completely crazy from the noise. We could get more volume, but we always lost those battles because sooner or later my old man would come pounding up the stairs to ream us out and confiscate the radio. We finally silenced the Victrola, though. One day when Granddad went downtown, Steve stole "The Beer Barrel Polka," and we used it for slingshot practice. That green label made a perfect bull's-eye. Granddad never did figure out what happened to his one and only record, but he had suspicions, and he called us scummy scabs for weeks. That was his worst curse, a poison dart he'd saved from his days on the picket lines. I can hear him now. "Mavis, how in hell did you and Hank manage to produce a couple of scummy scabs like these two?" More and more as time went on, my folks were forced to settle scraps between us kids and Granddad. It must have been exhausting.

By the time I hit high school, I could hold my own with Granddad physically, but he could still sting me with an insult. He liked sports, and I'll say this for him: I think he came to every hockey game I ever played. Growing up poor, Granddad never had the chance to participate himself, but he was nuts about hockey. He watched the pros and college teams on television. He subscribed to *Hockey News*, and he read every word of every issue, moving his finger across the page as if the print were braille. He and his buddy Benny Suderman used to ride the booster bus to away games. They took a flask along and had a high old time. The attention Granddad paid me was hardly flattering, though, and I would have gladly done without it. I'd be eating breakfast the morning after a game, reading about myself in the paper, feeling sore and satisfied, and he'd come into the kitchen, sit down across from me, light up a cigar, and watch me. I'd say, "Can't you take that turd in the bathroom where it belongs?" I knew what was coming. He'd blow a cloud of smoke my way and start in giving me the works. "Ya, I suppose you think you're pretty smart, scoring them two flashy goals, hah, Lenny? Suppose you think we ought to be calling you Boom-Boom Hackbart now." "Come on," I'd say, "lay off." "That was a pretty good first period, all right. But where did you go the rest of the game is what I want to know. Taking a little snooze, hah, Boom-Boom? I have to tell Benny, 'No relation of mine. I never seen the kid.' That last goal they got, you barely touched the guy. What kind of chickenshit check was that supposed to be? You score two goals, you're on the ice for four of theirs. Four goals against! Even a dumb old man like me can cypher two from four. And what do we lose by, Mr. Boom-Boom? Two lousy goals. What a tweetybird." I'd have to leave the room.

Aside from that sort of insult, though, he couldn't touch me. By this time Granddad was far from being a tyrant. He wasn't even a worthy competitor anymore. We treated him like a pet, some half-trained bear we kept around the house for laughs. But by my senior year his drinking was getting out of hand, and he became a terrible embarrassment. Kids gave me a hard time about him at school. "Hey, Hackbart, I saw Axel pissing in Mrs. Pelkey's flower bed last night. When you going to get the old boy toilet-trained?" That kind of thing. He'd become a town character. Clowns are fine as long as you're not related.

He'd always been a daily drinker, Granddad. He'd start in the early afternoon—sip some whiskey, nurse a beer, keep himself tuned up just right. But my final year at home you could sometimes smell the whiskey on his breath at breakfast. He got paranoid about his drinking, too, and that was odd, because we'd never bothered him about it. But now he kept a flask or half-pint in his pocket all the time. We started finding bottles in peculiar

places—behind the paint cans in the basement, in a flow-
erpot on the porch. He even tried to disguise the smell,
dousing himself with aftershave and chewing Double-
mint until you thought he'd get arthritis of the jaw.

Whiskey was his favorite—Seagram's 7—but he
couldn't always afford it. Toward the end of the month,
he often had to get by on beer. He kept a case or two
in his room at all times, but my senior year he developed
a ridiculous fear of running short. That winter a blizzard
buried Bessemer the first week in December. We already
had a foot of snow on the ground when this monster
storm blew into town. School was let out early, and by
the time we'd finished supper the streets were drifting
shut. For a veteran of so many Minnesota winters,
Granddad was acting strangely nervous that night. He
kept tuning in weather reports and pacing the living
room. About eight o'clock we noticed that he'd disappeared. Ma got worried, made us check his room, the
basement, and garage, but he was gone. She finally sent
us out into the storm. Steve and I started downtown,
and we were halfway there when we spotted him. He
was coming down the center of the street, wallowing
along like someone wading through a marsh. Granddad
had that bad leg anyhow, and the snow was up to his
thighs. He'd been to the liquor store, bought himself a
case of beer, and he was having a hell of a time getting
it home. He'd throw that case out in front of him, then
thrash his way up to it, hang onto the case and rest, then
throw it out in front of him again. Steve and I plowed
over to him through the drifts. The wind was amazing,
and the snowflakes stung. "You crazy old bastard!" I
shouted. "What the hell are you doing out here?" He
leaned on the cardboard case and fought for breath, his
eyebrows frosted, his face pink and wet. "What does it
look like, dumb shit? I bought some beer. Who knows
how long this blizzard's going to last?" "Jesus, Mary,
and Joseph," Steve said. Steve is built like my old man—
thick and strong—and when he gets mad he looks just

like him, like a bomb about to go off. He hoisted the
case of beer onto his shoulder and stomped away
through the snow. I grabbed Granddad by the arm and
hauled him along toward home. He came quietly
enough. The force of the storm was terrific, and I think
he was a little scared to discover how weak he was. Ma
read him the riot act once we reached the house, but he
didn't seem to mind. By this time he was willing to put
up with plenty of hollering, not to mention the hazards
of a blizzard, as long as he was assured of a certain supply
of booze.

Granddad really went over the edge that winter. His
benders at the first of the month, when he was flush,
weren't just entertaining toots anymore but deadly
drinking bouts. He'd vomit, piss his pants, drink until
he blacked out. He got to be a real worry and an awful
source of shame for the entire family. We'd get calls
from the neighbors in the middle of the night. "Sorry
to wake you, but Axel's lying out here in front of our
place. Thought you'd like to know." My old man
couldn't handle Granddad by himself, so he'd wake me
up—midnight, one a.m.—all apologetic. I'd throw on
some clothes, swearing and still half asleep, and follow
my dad out into the cold. We'd find Granddad passed
out somewhere down the block, sleeping in a snowbank,
snoring at the stars. Or he'd be sitting there singing,
slurring out the words to "Solidarity Forever" or some
old dancehall tune. We could haul him home between
the two of us all right, but then we had to get him up
the stairs. Two hundred pounds of dead drunk. I hated
him, and I hated my old man for not being harder
on him.

The climax to Granddad's drinking, though, the real
topper, came the following summer. I was working
nights, loading boxcars, and I almost slept through the
excitement, but the racket finally brought me downstairs. Granddad had started drinking early that day, but
for some fool reason he decided to mow the lawn after

lunch. That was a silly move in the first place, because the grass was half dead from the dry spell we'd been going through. And of course he didn't get very far. He just cut a couple swaths and then retired to a lawn chair with his jug. That was the last Ma saw of him before all hell broke loose.

Nobody knows exactly what happened, but there's no doubt that Granddad went a little off his nut. It was one of those rare days on the Range when the temperature climbs into the nineties, and maybe Granddad got a touch of sunstroke. Or maybe all that alcohol finally blew a few circuits in his brain. My dad said, afterward, he thought it had something to do with the early strikes. Granddad was just a young guy then, and apparently he screwed up one night, fell asleep when he was supposed to be on guard, and, as a result, several miners got beat up by a goon squad. My old man said no matter what he did—and he did a lot, even serving as a steward later on—Granddad never quite got over that. And so, that afternoon when Granddad got his wires crossed, he was back there in the teens, trying to redeem himself. Whatever it was, he certainly disturbed the peace. We had a shed out back where we kept tools and lumber, and Granddad lit that thing on fire.

One minute everything is calm and drowsy. The next minute my sister's yelling, "Ma! The shed's on fire!" Ma looks out the window—sure enough, there's tar-black smoke and two-foot flames. She can't believe it. But she quick rings the fire department and calls the mine for my old man. By this time I'm downstairs. I'm still half naked, but Barb is screaming at me, so we rush outside, and there's Granddad, stumbling around with a gas can and hollering about the Pinkertons. "We got 'em now! Scummy scabs and Pinkyboys. We got 'em trapped down there. Fry their ass, by God." He's out of his mind, back in the 1916 strike, and he thinks he's set the shaft on fire. "What you think of old Axel now? I done the right thing this time, ain't I?" "Beautiful,"

Ma says. "You're my man. You done just right. I'll take that gas can now." "Oh no you don't," he says and swings away. "I got more work to do!" So that's when I tackled him, and Barb and Ma managed to wrench that gas can out of his hand. Barb was in her swimsuit, I remember, because it was a two-piece suit, and there'd been a row about that. People were calling them bikinis, though they were really very modest, and she'd had a big fight with my old man. I'd been on her side, and she'd won, but now here she was, sunburned salmon pink, all oiled up with lotion, wrestling with Granddad while I tried to hold onto his legs. He kicked and roared, but pretty soon he was just whimpering and talking out of his head. Then the fire truck shows up. They got there quick, thank God, and put the fire out all right, but not before it took the shed, blackened the backyard, and ate up half an acre of woods.

My dad arrived about the time the guys had the fire down to smoke and ashes. Most of the neighborhood was there by then, watching and worried and trying to help. People get nervous up north whenever the woods go dry, and with good reason. We were just lucky there wasn't any wind that day. Granddad had threatened the whole community, and my old man was absolutely mortified. I don't think I've ever seen him so upset. He had Granddad thrown into the hospital that afternoon, and they kept him there for several days. The doctors said there was nothing really wrong with him except that he was drinking enough to numb an elephant. They dried him out and sent him home, but my dad was still pissed, and after I left for college my folks decided to ship Granddad off to the nursing home in Hibbing. They made him stay there for a month. The nursing home must have scared the funny-business out of him, because Ma wrote to me shortly after that experiment and reported that Granddad was back in the house and behaving like a perfect gentleman.

So Granddad underwent a reformation in his late old

age, but I wasn't there to appreciate it. Besides, he'd
been such a royal pain when I was growing up that I
didn't give a damn. I was glad to be out of the house,
away from Bessemer, on my own. But I guess he really
did lead a different life in those final years. For one thing,
the first winter I was away Granddad's buddy Benny
Suderman died. Benny didn't have any family, and he
left his house to Granddad. This was a little old bachelor
place at the end of our street, set back in the woods.
Granddad had his own house at last, and I understand
that he was happy there. He'd fix his own breakfast and
lunch and then come over to my folks' place for supper.
Being a property owner seemed to inspire him. He took
good care of his place, grew a respectable garden, and
scraped enough money together to buy an old pickup.
He got hold of a riding mower, too, and for several
years he had his own small business cutting lawns. I
only heard about most of this, because I was still so
bitter I didn't bother to visit him when I went home.
But Steve and Barb, who stayed on in Bessemer, both
developed a fair amount of affection for him. Steve and
Granddad became regular fishing partners. And Barb
says Granddad was so good with her kids that she
counted on him as her backup babysitter.

I'd never have believed these tales of Granddad's trans-
formation if it weren't for the last time I saw him alive.
This was the summer Granddad turned eighty, just a
couple months before he died. I was in law school then,
recently married, and I'd brought Ellen back to Bessemer for a quick visit. It was fun to see family and friends
and check out some of the old haunts, but it was a sad
time, too, because I realized I'd outgrown the place. The
talk was all about the mines, fishing, hunting, snow-
mobiles. A small world. I knew I'd always think of
Bessemer as home, but it was pretty plain I didn't belong
there anymore. My old pals treated me with that odd

combination of deference, resentment, and amusement
people up there normally reserve for strangers. So by
Saturday night, our last in town, I was feeling fairly
melancholy. At supper that evening Granddad invited
us over to his place. He said he had something to give
me. I was surprised, since he'd barely said a word to
me the whole time we'd been home, and I was going
to turn him down, but my old man frowned at me in
such a way that I said, "Okay, maybe later."

"Good," he said. "I'll be watching for you. Bring
your missus, too."

I didn't really mean to go, but, after Granddad left,
my folks insisted. My dad said, "He's been planning
this, Lenny. He's been talking about having you over
ever since you said you were coming home."

"Oh, yeah? What's got into him? We're hardly bosom
buddies."

"He's getting old," Ma said. "He's different. You
must have noticed how quiet he's got. You take Ellen
over there. It's not going to kill you."

"All right," I said, "we'll go. But I don't see why
everybody's sticking up for him all of a sudden. I remember when he used to make life pretty miserable
around here."

"He's eighty years old," my dad said, as if age excused
everything.

I didn't want to argue. After coffee and some conversation, Ellen and I walked down the street to Granddad's place. It was a chilly evening, so cool we had to
put on jackets just to walk four blocks. The air was
crisp, and everything was glazed with moonlight as we
walked up the path to Granddad's little house. "My
goodness," Ellen murmured. "It looks like something
out of a fairy tale."

"Yeah, right," I said. "This is the troll's house." I'd
told her all about Granddad.

I knocked on the door and stepped back. I rapped
again, harder. Ellen and I looked at each other. I heard

an owl hoot, but there was no sound from inside the house. I was going to knock one last time when the door suddenly opened.

"Lenny," Granddad croaked. "Come in. You, too, Helen."

"Ellen," I corrected him.

"Yeah, come on in." He swung the screen door wide. "Awful nippy for August, ain't it? I lit the stove, so it ought to warm up in here before long." He stood in the center of the room and waved at the walls. "You never seen my place before. Look around."

There wasn't all that much to see. The house was basically one room, the kitchen area indicated by yellow linoleum, the "living room" set off by a worn maroon carpet. There was a bathroom the size of a closet. The bedroom, closed off with a curtain, was little more than a lean-to stuck onto the house. It had a slanted ceiling and was overwhelmed by a bed, a single chair, and a heavy, battered dresser. The whole place was furnished with the sort of stuff you see at garage sales. There were stacks of magazines and newspapers, and the house had a musty, sour smell.

"Pretty fair setup," I said. "More space than you had in the bedroom back home, anyhow."

"I think it's very nice," Ellen said. "I love the way it sits back here in the woods."

"You should see it in daylight," Granddad told her. "I know it's nothing fancy, but I've sure enjoyed being on my own." He pointed around the room. "TV, Victrola, place to eat and sleep. What else you need? Here, take a seat." Ellen sank down on the sagging couch. I took a straight-back chair at the table. "We'll have some whiskey," Granddad announced.

"I thought you gave it up," I said.

"I'll still have a sip after dark. Besides, I got company." He pulled a quart of Seagram's from under the sink and poured an inch of amber in three jelly glasses. Watching him, I saw how he had aged. He was stooped

and unsteady, and his hands trembled as he poured the
drinks. When he had screwed the cap back on the bottle,
he used a red crayon to mark the level of the whiskey.
There was a whole series of hashmarks running down
the side. He turned and saw that we'd been watching
him. "Got me a system," he grinned, "to keep me from
going all to hell." He set my glass on the green-and-
white checked oilcloth, then delivered Ellen's drink. All
of this took time. He was wearing bedroom slippers,
and he dragged his feet across the floor. He got his own
drink, but before he sat down in his easy chair he made
a small speech.

"Since you two didn't see fit to invite me to your
wedding, I'd like to toast you now. Health and happiness," he said, raising his glass. "And lots of babies,"
he leered at Ellen.

We drank, and Ellen made a face. Whiskey was not
her favorite, but she'd always been a sucker for old
people, and she was making a special effort to be kind
to Granddad. "I don't know about the babies," I said,
"but we'll take the health and happiness."

"We would have invited you," Ellen said, "if we'd
known you wanted to come. We thought Chicago
would be too far for you."

"I could have come with Hank and Mavis," Granddad
said. "But never mind. I know how Lenny feels. We
ain't always got along so good."

I looked at him over the rim of my glass, acknowl-
edging the truth without speaking.

"Anyways," Granddad said to me, "I wish you luck
and no hard feelings. I'm glad you made it home and
come to see me this time, because I don't think I'm long
for this world."

"Oh, don't say that," Ellen said.

I said, "What are you talking about?"

"Just what I said. I'm getting tired. I've about come
to the end of the line. I don't know if anybody told you
this, but I took a fall here last winter. I been having

these little spells when I blank out and don't know where I am. Had to sell my mower. Don't hardly dare to drive the pickup anymore. And Hank and Mavis are talking about the nursing home again. So I'm just facing facts."

"But you look pretty good," I lied. The silver hair had finally gone white and thin. His skin was not only wrinkled but pale and scaly. It crossed my mind that he might be contemplating suicide.

"Well," he said, "I don't feel so hot. That's why I asked you over here. I'm telling all the kids if there's anything they want, now's the time to speak up. Benny give me this house, and it's meant happiness to me, so I learned from that. I'll pass this place to Hank and Mavis, seeing as how they put me up for so long. But I got some little stuff around here, and I thought you kids ought to have it. So if there's anything you fancy, you just say so."

"You're talking crazy," I said.

"Hell I am." He looked at me a long time. Those blue eyes that used to scare me were blurred and milky now. "I'm eighty years old. Only sensible to make a will."

I looked around the room to humor him, but what was I supposed to claim? Geraniums in coffee cans? The antlers on the wall? Then I noticed his deer rifle hung above the door.

"Sorry," Granddad said. "That's already spoken for. Steve gets the .30-.30, and Barb wants the pickup. But there's some other things. How about my rod and reel?" He pointed at his metal fishing rod leaning in the corner. I'd admired it since I was a kid.

"Sure," I said, "thanks. I'd like that. When the time comes."

"When the time comes." Granddad smiled and drained his drink. "Good. Then there's just one more item of business here. But first let's have another drink."

He got the bottle and filled me back up. "How about you, Helen?"

"No, no." She covered her glass. "I've still got plenty."

"Ellen," I said, irritated. "Her name is Ellen."

Granddad, refilling his glass, didn't seem to hear. Ellen glared at me and whispered, "Let it go."

Granddad left the bottle on the old cable spool that served as his coffee table and hobbled back to the kitchen. He rummaged around in the cupboard, mumbling to himself, and returned with a five-pound coffee can. "You want a cookie with your whiskey? Mavis made them. They're damn good." Ellen took one, and Granddad set the can at my elbow. "Go ahead," he said. "Have all you want. That's what they're there for."

"Seagram's 7 and sugar cookies," I laughed. "Hell of a deal."

"That's right," Granddad said. "I live like a king with Mavis around."

He disappeared behind the curtain to his bedroom. Ellen and I exchanged a look. I rolled my eyes and shrugged. "You be nice to him," she hissed. I heard a drawer slide, and then Granddad came back out, pushing aside the curtain like a tent flap.

"Here now," he said. "I told you I had something to give you. High time I got rid of this." He dropped a thick, heavy scrapbook on the table. "Go on," he said. "Open it."

The first page bore a title like an epitaph, printed awkwardly in crayon:

Leonard Hackbart
HOT ON ICE
1955–1961

I flipped through the pages quickly. There were team pictures and season schedules with the scores inked in. There were mimeographed programs, lineups with my name and number circled. And page after page of yellow newspaper stories, clipped from the *Bessemer Converter*.

I shut the book, looked up. Granddad was lighting a cigar with trembling hands. "Where'd you get this?" I said.

He blew out a stream of smoke. "Where you think, knothead?"

"You did this?"

"Who else?"

Ellen put her hand on my shoulder. "What is it, Lenny? Let me see."

I opened the scrapbook. "Here." I waved my hand at the book. "It's my whole life as a hockey player. Start to finish. It looks like all the ink that anybody ever spilled. It looks like every game I ever played in."

"You got it," Granddad gloated. "Every game."

"But where'd you get all this?"

"Saved it up. I had these papers put away I don't know how long. And then last winter, when I was laid up, I thought, what the hell. I had plenty of time on my hands, so I thought I'd make this book. You're welcome to it. I figured it might be fun."

"God yes," I said. "I'm happy to have it, but I can't believe you kept this stuff. You thought I stunk. You were always reaming me out."

"Well, you had a tendency to laziness. You needed hounding. But holy smoke," he said to Ellen, "could this boy skate. And handle the puck? Not a bad shot, either. Here, let me show you."

And so we sat there, Ellen and I on either side of him, while Granddad recalled the different seasons. I was astonished by his memory. He remembered moves and scoring plays from games that I'd forgotten long ago. It was eerie—as if, cheated of his own boyhood, Granddad had stolen mine. And sure enough, halfway through the scrapbook, he began to drift from my life into his. He went way back, telling tales from the turn of the century, when he'd been forced to quit school to help support his family. I remembered then what a ruckus he'd raised when, the summer of my senior year, I'd threatened to go into the mines instead of on to college. He'd literally thrown a tantrum, pounding on the kitchen table and pitching dishes at me while my mother howled and my dad roared at both of us. As Granddad spoke about the old days now, I had another whiskey, and, feeling my resistance to the old man slip, I suddenly saw my future. Just like that, I saw that I would specialize in labor law and mediation. It was a funny moment, out of time, just a flash, barely conscious; and then I was hearing him grumble again and hoot and cackle. This was Granddad at his best, the way he'd been during deer season, entertaining us with stories in the sauna out at our camp on Lost Lake, cracking jokes throughout the nightly card games. I could see that Ellen was absolutely charmed. She was leaning forward, both elbows on the table, her chin on her fists, her face lit up with interest.

"So I was young and green yet, and this old-timer, name of Hanu Maki, was teaching me to blast. I wanted to learn that blasting because it was dangerous, and where there's risk there's pay. So we set our charge, a dozen sticks of dynamite, and then got back behind the turn, where we'd be safe. Hanu touched them off, and the noise you can't believe." Granddad covered his ears and shook his head. "I thought I must be bleeding from both ears. You understand me? We are talking here not only dynamite, we are talking underground. The sound is trapped, you see, no place to go. So, blam, you got your first explosion, which is bad enough, but then, boom, she hits the wall, comes back the other way, and knocks you down again. You're down there in this echo chamber, and you just set off the atom bomb. My God, I thought I was a dead man. Finally that big boom fades away so my head is only ringing like a church bell, and I'm about to ask Hanu if he's still in one piece when Hanu says, 'Son of a bitch. Only eight went off.' I said, 'What?' I thought I must be hearing things. He says, 'Only eight went off. Now we got to go in there and find them other four.' And that's exactly what we found—four duds."

"You mean to say," Ellen said, "that he could tell how many sticks of dynamite went off just by listening?"

"That's it. All I heard was one goddamn kerblam, but he knew so well what he was doing he could pick out different sounds and judge the blast by ear." Granddad laughed. "Old Finlander. Hanu Maki. I learned a lot from him, but I was never half as good."

Ellen was enthralled. I enjoyed the story, too, but this was one of Granddad's classics, and when he moved on to other golden oldies, I let my mind float. With the oil stove going, the little house had grown quite warm, and I was happy just to sit and listen to the gravelly sound of Granddad's voice. I glanced out the window, but the outside world had disappeared. The window was a black mirror, reflecting half my face, Ellen's yellow hair, Granddad's hand holding the cigar, his face obscured by smoke. Granddad rambled on and on but finally began to fade. We revived him with questions, but soon he sank into silence again. The room reeked of cigar smoke. Ellen waved away wisps as if she were brushing at cobwebs. I said it was time to go.

"Already?" Granddad said. "But you just got here."

"No," I said, "it's time. We've got a long drive tomorrow."

"I guess I can't hold you, then. I'm glad you came, Lenny. You take a good long look at me. It's the last you're going to get."

"Don't start that again," I said. "Tough old toad like you, you'll live to be a hundred."

"No, no. I've decided. The time has come."

Ellen said, "What do you mean, you've decided? You can't decide these things."

Granddad looked at her. He tugged at his suspenders with his thumbs. "I'm glad I got to know you, Helen. Lenny's a lucky man." He turned to me. "You take good care of her."

"We'll take care of each other," I said and stood. I handed Ellen her jacket, slipped into mine, and scooped the heavy scrapbook off the table. "Thanks for this," I said. "I mean it."

"That's okay." He sounded tired, but he followed us to the door.

"And thanks for the whiskey," I added.

"And the cookies," Ellen said. "And all the wonderful talk." She gave him a hug, which seemed to take him by surprise.

When I reached out to shake his hand, he covered mine with both of his. "So long, Lenny. Don't forget about the rod and reel."

"Right," I said. "Good night."

"You hang in there," Ellen said. "We'll come visit you again."

"You do that," Granddad said.

We walked down the path and paused at the gate to look back. Granddad stood like a silhouette in the doorway. We waved, but he must not have seen us. He shut the door, and we turned away.

"I don't get it," Ellen said. "He's not at all like you said. He's a great old guy. Working class, for sure, but very gracious in his way."

"All right," I said, "but this was different. This was about the best I've ever seen him behave."

"He was wonderful! Making you that scrapbook. Telling all those stories. He was nice as pie."

"I can't explain it. He was like somebody else. I think you charmed the pants off him, that's what, paying him so much respect. We used to sort of laugh him off."

"I don't see why."

"You didn't know him then. He was a drunken sot. And a rotten mean old bugger, too. I've told you all about that."

"I know. It's just hard to believe after tonight."

We walked a few steps in silence. "Maybe it's death," I said. "It sounds as if he's been staring into the pit.

Maybe old age has finally scared the nastiness out
of him.''

"It's obviously on his mind," Ellen said. "Death, I
mean.''

"Yeah, he was talking pretty strange.'' I laughed.
"He'll probably outlive us all.''

"Look,'' Ellen pointed. We stopped. The moon was
big and round and caught like a kite in the branches of
a birch tree.

"Beautiful,'' I said. Ellen shivered. "You cold?''

"A little,'' she admitted. I put my arm around her,
she leaned against me, and we walked through the black
and silver evening back to my parents' place.

Two months later, my old man called to tell us Granddad had died. As I held the receiver to my ear I saw the
interior of Granddad's house and remembered how he'd
talked of reaching the end of the line. "It wasn't suicide,''
I said.

"No, no,'' my old man said. "Why would you say
such a thing? He died in his sleep. It was just old age.
That's what Doc Robertson said. But I'll tell you,
Lenny, it was awful odd how it happened.''

"What do you mean?'' I put my hand on the wall. I
could see all these tiny cracks and nicks in the plaster,
as if I were looking through a magnifying glass.

"It was like he just made up his mind.'' I was surprised
to hear a quaver in my old man's voice. "I don't feel
like talking on the phone,'' he said. "I'll tell you all about
it when you get home. You'll come for the funeral,
won't you?''

I told him I'd try, but it didn't work out. I'd gotten
behind in my classes, and I needed to hit the books hard
or I would have been facing a major disaster. And to
tell the truth, I didn't really care that much about going.
I was still young and dumb enough to think that funerals
were empty ceremonies. Besides, that final evening

Ellen and I had spent with him, nice as it had been, hadn't erased my lousy memories. So I played hooky from the funeral. I studied hard, got caught up, and by Christmas I felt I'd earned a break. I took a few days and went home. Ellen couldn't get time off—it was the bookstore's busiest season—so I made the long drive alone. The trip was exhausting, but I enjoyed it anyway, especially once I hit the spruce and jack-pine country north of Minneapolis. It was good to see some green against the snow.

The welcome that my parents gave me was peculiarly polite. As the night wore on, my old man grew quiet as a stone. We were drinking coffee in the living room when their resentment finally broke out. "You could have come to the funeral," Ma said. "He was your grandfather, after all."

"So that's what this is all about," I said. I felt vaguely guilty, but when my explanations failed to soften them, I got mad myself. "Look!" I said. "What's going on here? If I'd known it meant so much to you, I would have come. Okay? I'm sorry. I would have come for your sake. But not for him. Why should I break my neck for that old bastard? You want to know the truth? I hated his guts. He treated me like shit when I was little. He beat on us kids for no good reason, and you let him get away with it," I said, turning on my dad. "He drove Grandma to her grave and gave Ma fits. Am I supposed to forgive the son of a bitch just because he's dead?"

"Don't you raise your voice to me," my old man said. He's a short, stocky guy, and when he gets his hackles up he looks dangerous as a bulldog.

Ma glanced back and forth at us. "You two better settle this," she said. "I'll go do them dishes."

"Sorry," I told my old man, "but when people act deaf and dumb I tend to shout. I'm just trying to remind you that when Granddad moved into this house he drove happiness right out the window."

"I don't know what you're talking about," my old
man said.

"Have you got amnesia, or what? Christ, every time
I turned around you two were arguing. Ma wouldn't
even speak to him. What about those phone calls in the
middle of the night? How many times did you wake
me up to help haul him out of some damn snowbank?
Hah? How about the time he almost set the whole fucking town on fire? Don't tell me you've forgotten that.
Jesus. He never cared spit about us. He was a selfish,
mean old drunk."

"He was my father."

I was incredulous. I paced around the room, ranting
and waving my arms until I finally got him to admit
that Granddad had been something less than the ideal
house guest. But there were reasons, my old man insisted. He talked about Granddad's good behavior in the
past half-dozen years, and I realized I'd been railing
against the evil-eyed giant of my childhood, not the kind
old man I'd visited in August. I felt my anger ease. And
then, with a depth of understanding that astonished me,
my dad recited the griefs of Granddad's life: growing
up gut-hungry, going into the mines at thirteen, struggling through the early strikes, marrying a woman who
was beautiful but cold, raising a family so large he never
could get out of debt, getting hurt and forced out of
work before his time. "You think you'd act like Santa
Claus if you'd been through a life like that?"

"No," I said, "I guess not."

"Hell, you've had it easy. *Easy.* Both of us have,
compared to him. You think he wanted to move in with
us? He ate humble pie to do that. Your ma and me had
to bully him into it. He was stuck with us every bit as
much as we were stuck with him. The happiest I ever
seen him was when Benny left him that shack. He never
deserved the trouble he got. Never. He was ornery, I'll
admit, but the wonder was he wasn't worse."

"Okay," I said, suddenly drained. I dropped in an easy chair. "So tell me how he died."

My old man looked away. He went to the picture window and pulled the curtains. "It was the oddest damn thing," he said. "It looks like he just made up his mind and went to sleep."

"But that's how he was talking last summer. He said his time had come."

"I know! He said that sort of thing a lot last year, but we never took it serious. We just figured that's how old folks talk."

"That's what I told Ellen. I said he'd outlast us all."

"I never should have made him give up that mower," my old man said.

"What? Now don't go blaming yourself."

"No, but he seemed to sag so when I made him sell it. Then he took that tumble in January, and he was never quite the same. He got so quiet."

"Well, he was old," I said. "We should live so long."

"And go out with half the class. Listen, Lenny, it was the strangest thing. He took three days to do it. We never dreamed what he was up to. He told Mavis not to count on him for supper for a couple days. Said he was going out to the cabin. She thought, Where's the harm? He probably needs to pretend he's doing a little hunting. If I'd have been there, I wouldn't have let him go. It had got to the point where I didn't like to see him drive the pickup anymore, not with those spells he was having. He'd just blank out, you know. But by the time Mavis told me, he was already out there, so I figured, What the hell. But then when he'd missed supper for the third night running, I decided I better swing by his place and check on him. The pickup was there, so I thought I'd just run in. I knocked. No answer. So I went inside. Oh, Lenny."

"What?"

"He had it all planned out. There were papers and

things on the table. The place was spick-and-span. I
yelled out for him, but I knew what I was going to find.
There was like a buzzing in my head. I went into the
bedroom, and there he was, lying in bed, the covers
pulled up to his chin. I prayed he was sleeping, but I
knew better. I went over and touched him. Cold. Damn
dead."

"So you were the one who found him," I said.

"I found him, and I'd never come across anybody
who was dead before. Have you? It hit me hard. I sat
down in that chair beside the bed. I just sat there for a
while. Then I got up and looked around at things in the
other room, and I come home and told your ma, and
she called up Doc Robertson."

"And Doc said it was natural? He hadn't taken pills
or anything."

"Perfectly natural, Doc said. I asked him about that,
too. Doc said he just quit, just got into bed and gave
up the ghost. He said it's rare, but he still sees that now
and then."

"I'll be damned."

"But that wasn't what bothered me so much. What
really bothered me was all the trouble he went to. The
way he prepared everything. Because the whole house
was neat as a pin, and he'd laid out everything we could
possibly need. Insurance forms, registration on the
pickup, papers on the house. And then, you remember
how he always put away dimes in empty cigar tubes?"

"Yeah?"

"Well, he'd gotten all those out, and ranged them on
the table, too. There must have been fifty. It came to
over five hundred dollars."

"The hell."

"I swear to God. He left a note saying the money
should go to Barb and Steve's kids. And not only that.
He'd labeled damn near everything in the house that was
worth anything. What he'd done was, he'd gone to the
post office and picked up these mail tags and tied one

on each item and wrote who it should go to. He left
you something, you know."

I felt my scalp prickle. "His rod and reel," I said.

My old man nodded. "That steel rod with the Shake-
speare reel. We been keeping it for you." He got up,
went to the closet, and pulled the fishing rod out of the
dark.

I stood up to accept the rod. A red-and-white dare-
devil was attached to the leader and hooked to the reel.
A mail tag was tied to an eyelet. "To Lenny," it said,
and then Granddad had signed his initials, "A.E.H."

"That's a good outfit," my old man said.

I swallowed and nodded. "I always wanted one like
this," I said. I drew the rod back over my shoulder and
flicked my wrist a couple times. Then I brought the rod
down and held it out in front of me. I might have been
fishing off a bridge. I felt grateful, foolish, weird.

My old man grinned. "You can have his tackle, too.
He didn't label that, but you might as well take it."

"Thanks," I said. "I don't know what to say."

"Don't say anything. Just use it. And think of him
now and then when you're pulling in them whoppers."

I shook my head, went over and leaned the rod behind
the door. When I turned around my dad was opening
a desk drawer. "There's something else I want you to
see. The day after I found Granddad I drove out to the
camp to see if he'd actually been there." He turned to
me, holding a white book. "He'd been out there, all
right. He'd cleaned the place up and split a stack of
wood. I found an empty bottle. And this was on the
table."

He handed me the guest book we had kept at the
cabin for years. It had a pebbly surface. The word *Vis-
itors* was stamped in gold script on the cover. I held the
book in both hands and looked up at my old man. "He
wrote in it," my dad said. "Go on. Read it. It won't
take a minute."

I let myself down on the sofa and opened the book.

It was filled with the names of friends who had written brief comments about the fun they'd had at the cabin. I turned to the back of the book. Granddad had scrawled a letter there, using the book like an ordinary tablet, writing right through the vertical lines that divided the pages into separate spaces for dates, names, and addresses.

Dear Family,
   Been out here two days and weather has been great. Too cold for mosquitoes but warm enough to go without a jacket almost all the time. The leaves are real pretty. My favorite time of year. Had a sauna last night. Couldn't stay on the high bench, though, because I can't take that kind of heat no more. I am just too old and wore out.
   Nearly dark now and pretty soon I'll be going home. But I been sitting here thinking. I am feeling kind of funny. Would like to write down the story of my life but that would take too long, I never been much for writing as you know and besides my hand would cramp up. Still I want to say something.
   I lived in Bessemer all my life. The people I liked best, outside my family, was an old Finlander named Hanu Maki and Benny Suderman who give me his house. I went as high as 8th grade, then to work for Arrowhead Mining and stayed with that company my whole life until I took retirement. After that was self-employed in my own business. You know all this. I was a strong union man. I enjoyed music and liked to take a drink now and then. My hobby was following sports. Also liked hunting and fishing maybe fishing not quite so much.
   There has been a lot of hurt in my life nobody knows about because I never said nothing though certain parties called me a complainer. But that was only some things. Other things I never said because they was nobody's beeswax. But you people who thought I was an asshole you only knew the half of

it. Which means you're all half-assed or I'm only half
an asshole. Ha.

Anyhow nothing bad that happened to me matters
anymore. I been thinking things over here for two
days and I really only remember the good times.
Some of it is working and the union and some of it
is early days when I first got married to my wife. But
most of it is out here. Hank you hang onto this camp
and give it to your kids. Buying this place was the
best thing you ever done. Because just think of the
fun times and the memories. All them sauna parties
when everyone got naked and nobody give a damn.
That time I got Mavis drunk on vodka she fell in the
lake and we had to fish her out. Teaching the boys
how to hunt and how Lenny fell asleep on the stand.
Fish fries. Hank rowing all the way across the lake
and him so damn mad because he couldn't keep the
boat straight and the reason was he'd left the anchor
down. How about when Benny brought his dogs out
here to show us how to hunt good and proper so he
said but then the dogs got lost and we had to track
them way to hell and gone over on Featherstone Lake.
Always remember them times.

So it's been fun. True friends and laughter is the
most important. In the end that's all you remember.
Mavis I am sorry I was so hard to live with but that's
the way I am and thanks for putting up with me all
them years. Hank there's a leak in the back of the
sauna tank you need to fix. So long everybody.

> Very truly yours,
> Axel E. Hackbart

The body of the letter had been written with a weak
hand, but the signature was firm and fancy. I sat staring
at the loops and curlicues.

"What do you think?" my old man said. "What do
you make of that?" He was sitting on the edge of his
chair, leaning forward, his hands on his knees.

The back of my head felt hot. I swallowed and said,

"I'd like a drink. Is there any whiskey in the house?"

My dad looked annoyed. "Whiskey? I guess so. I stocked up for the holidays." He went to the sideboard, took down two glasses and a bottle of Seagram's.

"Perfect," I said. "That's the stuff."

He poured us each two inches. I stood, took the glass he offered, and raised it like a torch. "To the memory of Axel E. Hackbart," I said.

My old man looked startled, then smiled and raised his own glass. "Axel," he said. "My old man."

"Union man, miner, and mower of lawns."

"Husband and father," my old man answered. "Provider."

"Grandfather," I said, "and a mean old bastard."

"Drunkaholic," my old man said, "and a royal pain in the ass."

"Part-time pyromaniac."

"Sports fan, hunter, fisherman."

"Bitcher and moaner."

"Cheers," my old man said.

I touched his glass with mine. "Down the hatch," I said.

We drank, and then we stood there grinning, and both of us blinked and shook our heads, stung by the strength of the whiskey, by gladness, and by grief.

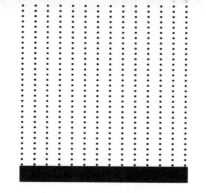

BLACKIE

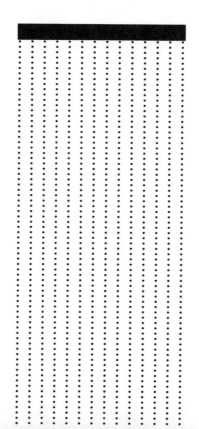

The dog showed up just as Jack and Abby were getting ready for Europe. Jack had started cleaning out his studio that afternoon. It was only a Wednesday, but Abby came home from work looking as if she'd barely survived a bad Friday, so Jack suggested they drive into town for dinner and drinks. After her first glass of scotch, Abby began to revive. Faculty politics left her pale and depressed, but, as the only woman in her department, she felt duty-bound to participate. "It's a good thing there's only a week left in the term," she said. "I'm so sick of St. Andrew's I could eat this glass." Jack listened to her rant, then gently directed the talk toward their trip. After dinner they stopped behind the liquor store and collected half a dozen cardboard boxes. When they got out to the farm and swung into the yard, Abby said, "Hey. There's a dog on the porch. Whose dog is that?"

"I don't know," Jack said. "Never saw it before." The dog was black, with a white throat, and, in the glare of the headlights, its eyes glowed like golden marbles. Jack tapped the horn. The dog stood up but didn't move off the porch.

"Is it Dietrichs' dog?" Abby asked as they went up

the walk, the cardboard boxes in their arms. "They've got a black dog."

"Naw," Jack said. "Theirs is pure Labrador. This one is something else. Go on," he growled. "Git."

The dog streaked away into the dark.

"You didn't have to be so mean," Abby said.

Jack said, "You want a stray dog hanging around?"

The next morning Abby stood in the kitchen door, her briefcase in one hand, her bookbag in the other, and raised her face for Jack's kiss.

"Have fun," he said.

"Ha. See you later."

Jack went back to the table, where he sat with his coffee cup, gazing out over the countryside. He loved this time of day. The air felt fresh as water. The oak trees on the ridge had already turned the dark green of summer, while the new shoots of corn in Dietrichs' field looked almost yellow against the rich, black soil.

Abby appeared in the screen door again. "Forget something?" Jack laughed. Her multiple exits were an old joke.

"No," she said. "Jack. That dog is still out here."

"No kidding?" He got up and went out on the porch. There was the dog, sitting by the mailbox, looking at them. "Uh-oh," Jack said.

"What are you thinking?"

"I hope somebody didn't drop him off here."

"What do you mean?"

"People do that sometimes. They want to get rid of a dog, but they don't want to kill it, so they just drive a long way from home and let it out at somebody else's place."

"Hoping you'll take it in?"

"Whatever. It's a weird practice. I hope this is just a stray. If we don't feed it, it should move on."

"Okay," Abby said. "It's a nice-looking dog."

"Not bad," Jack said. "Hey. Don't get any ideas. We're going to Europe, remember?"

"I know." She kissed his cheek. "Bye."

"Unless you'd rather stay home and make a baby," he called after her. "It's not too late to change your mind."

She turned and flipped him the bird. Jack laughed. When she'd driven off, he walked out in the driveway and picked up a stone. "Get out of here!" he hollered. "Go on." He stomped his foot and threw the stone. The dog slunk away down the blacktop toward town. It stopped once and looked back. "Keep moving," Jack yelled. "Nobody's going to take care of you around here." He turned and went back in the house. His coffee was cold. "Damn dog."

He poured himself a fresh cup and climbed the stairs to his studio. When Abby had been hired by St. Andrew's six years ago, they'd considered several farmhouses in the area, but this one had the best view, and Jack's excitement about the attic had made their decision. It had a full wood floor and, surprisingly, large windows on all four sides. With the landlord's encouragement, Jack had insulated the attic and installed a wood stove. He had been happy up here, lost in his work for days at a time.

Jack was a painter whose work didn't sell. At shows, in galleries, people stood in front of his paintings a long time but walked away without buying. His masters—the painters he was most anxious to see in the European museums—were Goya, Edvard Munch, and Hieronymus Bosch. He also loved Grant Wood. Jack had paid a high price for pursuing his peculiar vision. He sold about two paintings a year. At first this hadn't bothered him much. "I don't do interior decoration," he would say with a shrug. His confidence was so strong through his twenties, when he had supported himself as a picture-framer, that it bordered on arrogance. But now, in his thirties, Jack often suffered attacks of self-doubt. When he and Abby had married, she'd urged him to quit his job and concentrate on painting. He loved her faith in him, but, in the last year or two, her belief had been transmuted in his mind to a heavy blanket of guilt he had to throw off every morning before he could get down to work. So the grant he had won from the state arts board had come just in time. The award wasn't huge, but it was the first real money his painting had earned, substantial enough to pay for six months in Europe and rescue his self-respect.

They had talked about putting the money down on a house, but Abby was unwilling to resign herself to a career at St. Andrew's, and buying a house, she had argued, would tend to lock them in. So Jack had suggested they use the grant for living expenses while Abby took time off to write the book she had already researched, but she turned him down flat. She *would* be willing to take a leave, she said with a sly smile, in order to have a baby. That was the option they'd considered most seriously. They'd been postponing children ever since they'd married, saying their work took too much energy, they couldn't afford a family, they weren't cut out to be parents. But now they suddenly had some money, and time was running out. Abby was thirty-four. "My eggs are getting old!" she'd howled at the climax of one of their arguments, and then flapped her arms and squawked like a chicken. The tension that night was broken by laughter, but there had been tears, too, and long moments of silence, as they fought through the issue. Finally, around Easter, they had decided: no kids. They would go to Europe instead. Deciding had been hard but exhilarating, too, and once they'd made their choice they had been free to enjoy planning their trip, dreaming over maps, pumping their friends for advice.

Funny what a little money could do, Jack thought. He was so optimistic these days that he felt dissatisfied with most of the pieces scattered around the studio. He liked the self-portraits with animal skeletons. At least they showed a hint of humor. But then there were all those nocturnal landscapes: the prairie cemetery with roosting crows; the series of abandoned farms with ghosts; the one-room schoolhouse packed with hay, standing in the middle of a plowed field. "This looks like the work of a necrophiliac," he said aloud, and grinned. Time for a new phase. Time for a little joy, a little praise and laughter.

Humming to himself, Jack began to wrap and pack the canvases. The Kenwood Gallery in Minneapolis was taking five. His friend Frank Lambert, who taught in the art department at St. Andrew's, had agreed to store the rest until Jack and Abby returned. By noon all the paintings were ready to go. Jack filled the rear of his old station wagon, drove to the college and unloaded, then ate lunch with Frank and Abby. Later in the day he delivered the second load. When he got back to the farm, the dog was waiting on the porch. Jack groaned and banged his head gently on the steering wheel. As he walked up to the house, the dog came bounding out to greet him, but then, for no reason, suddenly cowered and crept off a few yards. "What a weird-ass dog," Jack laughed. "You keep turning up like a bad penny, don't you? Should we call you Bad Penny? Hah? Maybe we'll call you Bad Penny. Or Yo-yo." He shook his head and went into the house. If the dog didn't take off soon, Jack thought, they'd have to do something about it.

Without the paintings, the studio felt strange. "Might as well finish this," Jack said, and started clearing out the objects that had served him both as models and as totems—the snakeskin, the cow skull, the turtle shell, the feathers and nests of various birds, the antlers of a deer, the burl of an oak, the small skeletons of a dozen different animals. He considered each one carefully—appreciatively, reminiscently—then dropped it in a big cardboard box. When the shelves were empty and the box was full, he lugged it out to the scrap heap.

The scrap heap was all that was left of the grove. When Jack and Abby had first moved onto the place, it still had resembled a real farm. Killian, the landlord, had kept two horses in the pasture for his teenage kids, and, though the bottom of the weatherbeaten barn stood empty, the haymow had been heavy with sweet alfalfa. Jack had grown up in small towns in Wisconsin, and Abby had been raised in St. Louis, but after two years of gardening, canning, and making wood, they began to think of themselves as country people. Then Killian's kids had graduated, and he'd sold the horses. The following summer he tore down the barn. Then he burned the machine shed. "Think of it as progress," Killian told Jack when he'd protested. "High time I cleaned up around here. Besides, I'm not like you. My wife isn't about to support me, and I've got two kids in college now. I figure if I can get this place in shape, I might be able to sell off a few lots." And he had. Five houses had been built right down the road over the past two years. Killian had cut down the green grove of elms in an afternoon and bulldozed the trees into a twisted pile. As he'd gone on dismantling the farm, he'd added quantities of other junk—broken boards and windows, barbed wire, spools of rotten baling twine—until the whole heap looked like the aftermath of a tornado.

Jack made his own contribution now, tilting the big cardboard box, shaking out its contents. The dog darted in among the dead branches and emerged with the antlers. It lay down on the grass to gnaw the dry horn. "You pathetic creature," Jack said. "Why don't you get lost?" He turned the empty box over the dog and beat on the bottom like a drum. When he lifted the box, the dog ran off into Dietrichs' field.

Back in the house Jack washed the dishes and started supper. He decided on curried lamb. While he was browning the meat, the back of his neck felt strange. He turned. The dog was watching him, its nose to the screen door. It didn't whimper. It didn't make a sound. It stood there, trembling slightly, watching him. "You're beginning to bug me, Mister Bowwow," Jack said. "Am I going to have to get tough?" He waved the French knife. Then he put it down. He walked to the door, got down on all fours, and put his nose to the dog's nose. There was only the screen between them. "The food is for Abby and me," Jack said. "You ain't gettin' any. So go." He stared into the dog's eyes until the animal suddenly licked its chops, turned away, and padded out to the end of the walk, where it lay down, looking away from the house. "Jesus," Jack said. The frying pan hissed. He got to his feet, brushed his hands on his pants, and turned down the burner.

A few minutes later, Abby drove up. He heard the car door slam. She said, "Hello." And then, "No. Go away. Go on, now."

Jack went to the screen door. *"Bonsoir, madame!"* he called as she came wearily up the walk.

"Hi," she smiled. She pulled at the handle of the screen door, but Jack held it shut. "Come on," she said.

"What's the password?" he said. *"En français."*

"Fermez la porte?"

"Nope. It's already *fermée.*"

"Come on," she said. "Let me in. I'm pooped."

"Ouvrez," Jack said. *"Ouvrez."*

"Okay. *Ouvrez* the goddamn *porte.*"

Jack laughed, swung the door open, and kissed her cheek as she went by. She dropped her things on a chair. "Curry," she said. "Smells great. Should I make a salad?"

"Bien. S'il vous plaît."

She rolled her eyes. "You're going to drive me bonkers." She washed her hands at the sink. "I see the dog's still here."

"Yup. I couldn't get rid of him. Do you realize when you say, 'Go on,' your tone says, 'Come here'?"

"I can't help it," she said, rinsing the lettuce. "Poor dog. It's so skinny you can see its ribs. I think it's been abused, too."

"Why do you say that?"

"Because it comes running out like it wants to be friendly, but then it hunkers down as if it expects to get belted."

"You're right," Jack said. "I noticed that."

"You didn't feed it, did you?"

"No way. I tried to chase it off a few times. Otherwise, I ignored it."

"Is it a he or a she?"

Jack lifted the lid on the small saucepan. "Rice is done," he said. "It's a he. Don't tell me you didn't notice his pecker."

"Jack," she said. He grinned and patted her butt. "Do you know what kind it is?" Abby asked.

"I'd say a cross between a spaniel and something. A black lab? A collie?"

"He's a nice dog," Abby said. "If we were staying, I'd think about keeping him."

"But we're not," Jack said.

"That reminds me. Our passports came. They're in my briefcase."

Jack found the little flat blue books, opened them up, laughed at the photos, and thumbed through the blank pages. Soon the empty squares would be stamped with the names of foreign cities. "Fantastic," he said.

As they were cleaning up after supper, Abby hesitated. "What about these bones?"

"Forget it," Jack said.

"Okay," she said sadly, and scraped the bones into the trash.

He went over and put his hand on her shoulder. "Abby. If we feed the dog, he'll be ours. We'll be responsible. Then what? We'll have to find a new owner. It's not fair to the dog, and we haven't got time to be fooling around. Jesus. We've barely begun to pack."

"I know," she said, but sidled away. "We could place an ad in the paper."

"Sure, and by the time someone answers it, the dog will be gone. Besides, who wants a neurotic, full-grown mutt? You can't even get rid of puppies these days."

"We should call the humane society, then."

"Be my guest," Jack said, and followed her into the dining room. "But I doubt they've got a chapter out here. Just be patient. I bet you a buck he'll be gone by tomorrow. Come on. Let's practice our French."

"I can't. I've got thirty-five papers to grade."

"Don't tell me you're going to be one of those ugly Americans who expects everybody else to speak English." He popped the Berlitz cassette into the tape player.

"No, but this practice is boring. Look, I'm a smart person. I've got a Ph.D., right? I've decided as soon as I get to each country, I'm going to know, instantaneously, how to speak the language."

Jack laughed and punched the play button. A bass voice asked, "Have you anything to declare?" There was a brief pause, and then a baritone said, *"Avez-vous quelque chose à déclarer?"* Into the silence that followed, Jack repeated, *"Avez-vous quelque chose à déclarer?"* "No, nothing at all," came the reply. *"Non, rien du tout."*

"Jack," Abby said, "I really have to do these." She was spreading student papers on the table.

He punched the off button. "Okay, okay. I guess I'll have to do your talking for you."

"I'm sorry," she said.

"That's all right. I'll take this up to the kids' room." He unplugged the machine and started toward the stairs. "I miss you."

"I miss you, too," she said. "But Jack, we're going to have six months."

"Right."

"Honey."

"It's okay. I understand." He carried the machine up-

stairs to the spare bedroom. They had started off calling
this room the library, but that had seemed too preten-
tious, and so they'd simply referred to it as the spare
room until one day, as a joke, Jack had called it the kids'
room. It contained a rollaway and a nightstand, a box
of toys for their nieces and nephews, an ironing board,
a table, a chair, and books from floor to ceiling. The
winter clothes they'd been sorting through were strewn
across the bed.

Jack sat down at the table and plugged in the tape
player. "Where's the bus to the center of town, please?"
a familiar female voice inquired. *"Où est le bus qui va en
ville, s'il vous plaît?"* her partner translated. Jack repeated
the question and smiled. He felt he was getting to know
these people. He'd like to have them all over for dinner
sometime. The conversation, of course, would have to
be restricted to phrases on the tape. "I'd like a car. May
I have some razor blades? The central heating doesn't
work. May I introduce Miss Philips? Thank you, it's
been a wonderful evening." Jack checked his fantasy and
tried to concentrate on the lesson. Maybe he ought to
buy a different tape, he thought. His responses to this
one were growing automatic, and his mind tended to
wander. He leaned down and lifted a doll from the toy
box. He set her on his knee and spoke the French to
her. After a while, he held her against his shoulder and
patted her back, murmuring the foreign phrases into her
ear. When the second side of the cassette was finished,
he stood, held the doll upside down by her ankle, and
dropped her headfirst into the box. *"Merci pour cette
merveilleuse soirée,"* Jack said, and went downstairs for
a beer.

Abby looked up, pencil in hand. She was wearing her
reading glasses. "Oh, my god," Jack said, and struck
his chest. "It's the sexy librarian." He walked around
the table, leaned down, and planted a kiss on each lens
of her glasses.

"Damn you," she smiled, and reached for a Kleenex.

"How's it going?"

"Ugh. I'm about half done, I guess."

"You remember I'm taking those paintings to the Cities tomorrow."

"Oh, yeah. Lucky you."

"Don't feel bad. I'll toast you over the manicotti at Vittorio's."

"What a life you lead."

"It's true," he said. "Thanks to you." He blew her a kiss. Then he got his beer from the fridge and picked up Rilke's book on Rodin. He read until the print began to blur, then went up to bed. The sheets felt cool and sensual against his bare skin. He was almost asleep when Abby entered the room. "Finish?" he asked.

"Close enough. I've only got five left."

He listened to her taking off her things and turned to look. "Don't put on your nightgown," he said. "I want to feel you."

She slipped into bed and backed up against him. "Tired?" he said.

"Terribly."

He moved his hands lightly over her back. "You old smoothie," he said.

"Mmm," she hummed, and snaked her arm around to touch him.

Soon they were warm, and Jack threw off the sheets. "Up," he said. "On your knees. I want to come in from behind."

"Yes," she said, and reached back between her legs to guide him into her.

The moonlight lay in stripes across her back. Her face was in the pillows. He tangled his fingers in her hair and tugged. Then he placed his hands on her shoulders. "Okay?"

She turned her head to the side. "Do it," she hissed. "You know I like that."

He leaned all his weight on her, crushing her into the mattress, whispering obscenities. He felt like a king, like steel. Then he came, groaning as if he'd been wounded.

Breathing raggedly, he lay down beside her and touched her face. "Wonderful," he murmured.

"Um."

"You come?"

"Too tired," she said. "It's okay. I'm happy." She patted his arm.

"Sure?"

"Mm-hmm. Turn over. I want to spoon you."

He rolled on his side, and she pressed herself against his back. He laid his hand on her thigh and murmured, *"Avez-vous quelque chose a déclarer?"*

The bed shook gently as she laughed. "You're so romantic," she said, curling more tightly against him. She yawned. "And I'm so sleepy."

"Me, too," he said, and felt himself slipping down into darkness.

"Jack," Abby said suddenly, in a voice that sounded wide awake.

"Hunh? I'm sleeping."

"What are we going to do about that dog?"

"Starve him out. He'll be gone by tomorrow night, you'll see."

"Are you sure?"

"Sure, I'm sure. Come on. You need your rest." He reached back and patted her hip, then drifted off to sleep.

Jack woke with his head hanging over the edge of the bed. He looked at the floor and blinked. He turned on his side and peered through the blinds. The sky was pink.

Abby mumbled in her sleep, so he turned and hugged her. Resting his chin on her shoulder, breathing her fragrance, he stared at the white wall. Then it was on him, rushing through him like wind through a tree, the same disturbing blend of emotions that had haunted him for two years, whenever he woke up early—a mixture of grief, anxiety, regret, agitation, and other pangs he couldn't pin down. The disturbance took different forms, and Jack had given some of them names. There was The Muddy Canvas, the feeling that he had betrayed his talent and painted all the wrong pictures. There was The Lost Twin, the sharp impression that there was another life he ought to be living, another man he was meant to be. And there was My Life Is Running Away, when time became tangible, and he didn't have enough left, he could feel it running out like a mono-filament line some huge dark fish was dragging into deep water so fast he could hear it sing. But this morning the feeling was Where Are the Kids. He lay in the bed and hung onto his wife, listening for the children they didn't have.

"Ouch," Abby said. "You're hurting me."

"Sorry," he said, and let go.

She turned in the bed to face him. "How long have you been awake? What's wrong?"

"A while," he said. He looked away. "Where Are the Kids."

"That again." She put her hands on his shoulders. "Jack."

He shrugged. "I'm okay. It's fading. I get better as soon as you're awake."

She looked at him sympathetically, then turned her back. She lay still for a minute. Then he felt her stiffen. She threw off the covers and sprang out of bed. Naked, she turned and glared down at him, her fists clenched, her body shaking. "Ooh!" she said through her teeth.

"Abby," Jack said, "I'm sorry."

"Goddamn you!" She spun, snared her robe from a chair, and tore off to the bathroom.

Heartsick, Jack rose, dressed, went to the kitchen and started coffee. He hoped her shower would cool her off, but when she came down dressed for work, she was still steaming. "You bastard," she said. "You make me so mad! Why can't you be happy? I thought we agreed not to have kids. I thought we decided together. You want to have kids? Fine, we'll have kids. I'll quit my job, and you can go to work. Or, hell, I'll go on teaching, and you can raise the little meatballs. Whatever you want. *Just say what it is you want!*"

He stared right back. "Everything," he said.

"Well, you can't have everything!" she blazed. "Jesus, you—"

"Abby—"

"Abby, Abby, Abby. Goddamn you, I thought things were going great. You're painting full-time, you finally got some recognition, we're going to Europe. . . . No matter what happens, you have to find the dark side. No matter what we do, we're wrong. What the fuck is the matter with you?"

"I'm a sensitive artist," he joked.

"Oh, yeah? Well, you can stuff it, Mister. Next time I'm going to get me a mechanic."

He held out both hands, palms up. "Abby, what do you want me to do? I feel what I feel. You want me to lie about it?"

"No," she moaned. "I just want you to be happy!" Her voice caught. "I'm doing everything I can. I don't know what else I can do!"

"I'm happy," he snapped. "Will you relax? You're right, life is great, it could hardly be better. It's just that about certain things I've got these mixed feelings."

She turned and leaned on the table with both fists. "I am so sick of your mixed feelings! Why do you have to *dwell* on things all the time?"

"I'm sorry," Jack said. "I'm sorry I'm not your Simple Simon Smiley Face. But I'm not, and I'm not going to be. If you can't live with that, you better divorce me."

"I might."

"I know it," he grinned. "That's why I like you."

He stepped forward to take her in his arms, but she held up her hand like a cop. "Back off."

"Look," Jack said. "About the kids. I don't want them

any more than you do. And we did decide this together.
If we had a family you'd have to quit teaching or I'd
have to quit painting or both. And your mother had a
dozen kids, and my old man hates my guts, and blah
blah blah blah blah. I know all that, we've been over
that, but the fact remains. The urge to raise a family is
about as basic as the urge to fuck. Plus, from the time
you're two years old people are putting dollies in your
lap, and you're pretending you're ma and pa. You don't
just kill that instinct, erase all that conditioning. The
truth is, there's a real loss involved here."

"There's a loss with every breath you take," she said.
"So what?"

He ran his hand through his hair. "Listen," he said
quietly, "you and I have decided, for two dozen solid
reasons, to go against our instincts. I know as well as I
know anything that this is the right thing for us to do.
But I reserve the right to grieve. There are mornings
when I wish the little buggers were padding down the
hall and getting into bed with us. Don't you ever feel
that?"

"No."

"I don't believe you."

"I don't let myself."

"Well, you're stronger than I am, then."

"Okay," she said. "Sometimes I might feel something
like that. But you hog so much of the melancholy
around here I don't dare give in to it. We'd be swamped.
Somebody has to fight it. What I can't stand about this
is, I feel as if our not having kids is all my responsibility.
My fault. Sooner or later you're going to hate me for
it. You're going to hate me when we're old," she
moaned.

He risked putting his arm around her. "I'm going to
love your butt when we get old."

"No, you're not. I know you. You're going to brood
about this, and sooner or later you'll blame me."

"Okay, then," Jack said. "Let's have a baby."

She drew her head back. "What? You mean it?"

"Yeah, but it has to be a little one," he grinned, and measured two inches between his thumb and forefinger. "A Tom Thumb type. So I can carry him around in my pocket. And whenever he gets on our nerves, we can stick him in a matchbox and shut him away in a drawer."

She laughed and sniffed. "You're crazy."

"I don't want any kids," he said, stroking her hair. "I've already got a big baby."

She smiled and gently punched him in the stomach. "You promise not to hate me later?"

"Promise," he said. He embraced her, and they swayed, slightly, back and forth.

" 'Will you still need me, will you still feed me, when I'm sixty-four?' " she sang into his shoulder.

"You bet. You know I will." He patted her back. "You want a cup of coffee?"

"No," she said, and broke away. "Christ. I'm late. Good-bye." She wiped her eyes, snatched up her things, and headed out the door.

"I love you," he called through the screen.

"Yeah, yeah," she said. "So?" The dog danced around her in circles. "Go on, doggie. Shoo."

Jack opened the door and waved. Abby beeped the horn once and drove off.

Though the day had begun badly, it quickly improved. Jack fantasized about France as he drove to Minneapolis, and, because he was leaving it soon, the familiar landscape looked new. The white farmhouses, the cattle crowded in feedlots, the Minnesota River running broad and blue—everything seemed exotic. And when he delivered the paintings to the Kenwood Gallery, the owners handed him a check for six hundred dollars. They had finally sold a painting of his they'd had on exhibit for months. Ebullient, Jack celebrated by taking himself to lunch at a Lebanese restaurant. He checked out the show at the Walker Art Center and purchased a compact set of pastels. He shopped for and found the perfect backpack for the trip. Then he entered the alien, air-conditioned world of Twin Cities First International, where he bought fifty dollars' worth of currency from each of the first five countries he and Abby would visit. He stashed the wad of colorful cash in his new passport pouch, slung it around his neck, and slipped it inside his shirt. As he worked his way through the crowd of pedestrians on Nicollet Mall, patting the pouch from time to time, he imagined he was in Europe already. After dinner at Vittorio's, he drove the winding highway home, his mood matched by the glow of the apricot sunset. The radio played Bach, and fresh air rushed through the car. "I'm happy!" Jack shouted. "Abby, baby, where are you now?"

He was still so high when he got home that he wasn't even upset when he saw the pie pans on the porch. He showed Abby the items he'd purchased. Then he spread the foreign money on the table, and they sorted through the peculiar bills, exclaiming at the odd sizes and unusual hues. "It looks fake to me," Abby said, holding up a Norwegian note. "It looks like Monopoly money."

"I know," Jack laughed. "This proves what I've always maintained. Money isn't real."

He saved the check for last. Abby hugged him and shook her fist at the ceiling. "About time," she said. "They're finally beginning to wake up."

Jack poured whiskey. They toasted each other, their luck, and the continent of Europe. "Now, if we can just get through the next two weeks," he said.

"Jack," Abby said, "I have to confess. I fed the dog."

"I noticed," he said.

"You did? Well, don't go crazy, because everything is okay. The town constable is checking it out."

"The town constable?" Jack laughed. "I didn't know we had one."

"I didn't, either. Listen, I found out a lot more about

local government than I wanted to know. I feel rather intimately acquainted with the whole damn system." She laughed and leaned her head in her hand as if she were easing a toothache. "It was a real hassle, but I had to do something. I know you didn't want me to feed the dog, but when I got home he was chewing on this old piece of harness. He must have dug it out of the scrap heap. He was whimpering."

"Poor bastard."

"That's what I thought. I thought, 'I can't stand this. I have to do something.' So I called the humane society. Well, they said they'd like to help, but they aren't authorized to do anything in this county. They're only educational here. They said I should call the sheriff's office, so I call the sheriff. But the sheriff's office says they don't take care of stray dogs anymore, I should call the town constable. And they give me his name and number. Emil Hommerding."

"What?"

"Emil Hommerding. Can you believe it? These Germans. He's a farmer out here, over by Steuben. Anyway, I finally got hold of him and explained the situation and described the dog. He said somebody out his way had lost a dog like that. He said he'd check with them and call us back tonight. So I thought, with old Emil in charge, it would be all right to feed the dog. Don't be mad."

"I'm not mad," Jack said, "but I want to say something here. This is not our dog. If things get fouled up, this is your dog. You fed him, he's your dog."

"Okay, okay. I couldn't let him starve. You should have seen him go after that food."

"What did you feed him?"

"Bread and milk."

"Old Abby," Jack smiled, and went to the window. It was night, but there was a moon, and he could see the dog at the end of the walk, looking off down the road.

"Is he out there?" Abby asked.

"Yup. He's guarding the place. He looks like a statue. I guess you got yourself a watchdog."

"Well, don't worry about it. The owners will come for him tomorrow. Though I'm sort of uneasy about letting him go if they've been beating him."

"I know what you mean," Jack said. He turned from the window. "If he were your dog, what would you call him?"

She looked at the floor, smiled shyly, and said, "Blackie."

Jack roared with laughter. He went over and hugged her. "Abby Preus. I love you, you goof."

They grinned at each other, then turned and looked out at the dog, who sat like a dark boulder in the pale gravel of the driveway. "Blackie," Jack said, and they both laughed.

The constable failed to phone that night, so the next morning Abby called him, but there was no answer. She tried again at eleven. "Well?" Jack said.

"That was his wife. She doesn't know anything. He's out planting corn. She said he'll call us back at noon."

At one o'clock Abby called again. "Well, could I speak to him, please?" Abby rolled her eyes at Jack, then turned to the wall and said, "Mr. Hommerding? This is Abby Preus. I called yesterday about that dog. Yes, I was wondering when they'd be coming to pick him up. It's not? Really? Oh, shoot." She put her hand on the back of her neck. "Well, what should we do about this one, then? What? But I don't have a gun. Can't you— But the sheriff's office said you would take care of this. Yes. I see. We'll look for you Tuesday night, then. Thank you, Mr. Hommerding. I appreciate this. Bye."

Jack turned from the sink, where he was doing dishes. "What's the scoop?"

"Well, his neighbor's dog came back, so he doesn't know who ours belongs to. He said we could consider it a nuisance animal at this point. He said we could eliminate it."

"*Eliminate* it? That's the word he used?" Jack laughed. "This guy's been watching too many cop shows."

"I told him we didn't have a gun. So he finally said he'd come and take care of it. He didn't seem too happy about it." She crossed her arms and frowned at the floor.

"You don't seem too happy, yourself."

"Well, God, Jack. He's going to shoot the dog."

"What did you expect, hon?" Jack said gently. "The humane society would have put him to sleep."

"I don't know what I was thinking." She gave him a pained look. "I hate this."

"I know." He patted her shoulder. "I do, too. But it's the kindest thing."

She blew out a breath. "I suppose. Anyway, he said he has to stay in the fields as long as the weather's nice, but he'll get over here Tuesday night. I don't like his voice."

"He's probably perturbed that somebody actually asked him to do something." Jack chuckled. "Town constable. That must be pretty soft duty out here. Not exactly one of your high-stress positions."

"Just so this gets taken care of," Abby frowned.

"If he said he'll do it, he'll do it. Don't forget we're in the country. Things move a little slower out here."

In the afternoon they drove to Mankato for groceries. Jack insisted this was their last shopping run. "After this," he said, "we have to clean out the shelves. Finish off the soup and stuff."

"Mm-mm, good," Abby said.

In the checkout line, she plunked down four cans of dog food. "What are you doing?" Jack said.

"Come on, you old grouch. If these are his last meals on earth, they're going to be good ones."

When they got home, they stood on the porch and watched the dog eat. "What savagery!" Jack laughed. "Look at that. That's how I feel about lasagne."

"That's about how you look when you're eating it, too," Abby smiled.

After supper they walked down the road as far as the creek, and the dog went with them. Jack threw a stick, and the dog brought it back and laid it at their feet. He did this repeatedly. He still shied away from petting, though. When Jack called him Blackie, Abby said, "I don't think we should say his name. It makes him too special. It makes him too real."

"You're right," Jack said. "We don't want to get too attached."

They barely spoke during supper on Tuesday, but as the night wore on and they realized the constable wasn't coming, Abby's tender feelings turned to anger. "What's the matter with that man? His word doesn't mean a thing!"

She called the constable's home, though it was well after ten, and reported to Jack: "He's out in the barn." She threw her hands in the air. "He was out in the fields all day, his wife says, and now he's out in the barn."

"Busy man," Jack said.

"Yeah, well, he promised. How long is this going to drag on? I'm going to feel worse about that damn dog every day."

The constable didn't come the next night, either, nor the next, nor the night after that. Each night Abby called his home, and each night his wife said he was busy but promised he'd come the next day. On Friday Abby called the sheriff's office. Yes, they told her, it *was* the constable's job to perform such tasks. That night she finally got hold of the constable himself. She was courteous but cool. "I understand," she said calmly, "but we've been expecting you for a week now. We're very busy, ourselves. There are things we need to do, but we've been staying home nights because we thought you were going to show up. This dog is becoming dependent on us, and we're leaving the country in two weeks. Pardon me? Okay. Fine. We have to drive to the Cities tomorrow, but the dog will be here. He never goes anywhere else. Fine. Thank you." She hung up and told Jack, "He'll do it tomorrow."

As they drove away the next morning, Abby said, "Sorry, Blackie. You're a good dog. I'm sorry it has to be."

Jack reached over and patted her leg.

They got back from the Cities on Sunday evening. When Jack turned off the highway onto the blacktop and the farmhouse came into view, Abby said, "Ugh. I can't stand to look at the house since he cut down the grove. It looks like it's bald or something."

"I know," Jack said. "It's just as well we're leaving. This place has been ruined."

When they pulled up in front of the house, the dog came running out to greet them. "That lying son of a bitch!" Abby said. "I've had it."

They carried in a load of things, the dog barking and jumping around them. "Down," Jack said sharply. "Beat it."

Abby went right to the phone. Jack returned to the car for the suitcase. Entering the kitchen, he stopped to listen. Abby had one hand on her hip and was using her office voice. "I don't care, Mrs. Hommerding. He's always unavailable. Every time I call he's either out in the barn or out in the fields or off at some auction. I've begun to wonder whether you're even telling me the truth. I've begun to suspect he's sitting right there while you make up excuses. No? Well, it doesn't matter. You people have destroyed my patience. I only have one more thing to say to you. If this dog isn't taken care of right now, tonight, I'm calling the sheriff. I'm going to recount the full history of this little episode, and I'm going to explain, in detail, the degree to which your husband has been derelict in his duties. Do you understand me? I'm going to file an official complaint. I'll also be writing a letter to the editor of the *Free Press*. Perhaps you'll convey that information to your husband. Wherever he is. Good-bye." She hung up the phone and turned, her mouth set.

"Oh, Abby," Jack said. "I'm not sure that was such a good idea. You can't talk to people out here like that."

"Fuck you. I'm fed up with this aw-shucks, weather-talk runaround. It's just a screen people use. When we play along, we just get screwed."

"Yeah, but—"

"Yeah, but nothing. I don't see you rushing into the fray. If you thought you could handle this so well, you could have jumped in anytime, buster. I would have *welcomed* your assistance, believe me. But no. You think if you just ignore things they'll go away. If we'd done things your way, that poor dumb dog would be dying of starvation. So don't go telling me I'm using the wrong approach. I'm sick of these people taking advantage of us. The squeaky wheel gets the grease. It's as true out here as it is in St. Louis."

"Okay," Jack said. "I hope he doesn't shoot us instead of the dog."

Abby snorted. She opened the fridge, poured herself a glass of iced tea, and sat down with the paper. Jack opened a beer and went into the living room. The packing and the preparations were beginning to get on his nerves. He was worried about this constable. He was worried about getting everything done in the time they had left. He carried in some boxes from the porch and started pulling books off the living room shelves. He had been at it for a half hour when headlights flashed in the window, and a pickup pulled into the drive. Jack stood, and he and Abby glanced at each other. "That's him," Jack said. "You want me to talk to him?"

"I can handle this," she said. There was a knock, and she went to the door.

"You Preus?" the man in the screen door said. "You the party that called about the dog?"

"I am." She opened the door and stepped out on the porch.

The constable said something Jack missed. He went into the kitchen so the man would know Abby wasn't alone, but he still couldn't make out what they were saying. The constable wore work clothes and a seed-corn cap. A silver choke chain dangled from his hand. The constable's tone was accusatory, but Abby purred sympathetically, and before long the man's voice grew quieter, calmer. Jack relaxed and went back to packing books.

Five minutes later, Abby came into the living room. "Well, it's done," she said. "He took the dog."

"Good going. Good for you. Was he mad?"

"Oh, Jack." Her eyes were glistening.

"Abby, what's wrong? Was he mean to you?"

"No, but it was awful." Tears slipped down her cheeks.

"Here," Jack said, getting up off the floor. "Here, now." He put his arms around her while she trembled. "What happened? Tell me."

"Oh." She backed away, gulped for air, and brushed at the tears that kept coming. "It was so eerie! I knew he was mad at me, but he just kept smiling the whole time. His teeth were rotten. And he just kept smiling the whole time we were talking." She closed and opened her eyes. "Jack. He only had one finger on his right hand. The rest were stubs. I looked down at that awful chain he was holding, and he only had one finger!"

"He's a farmer," Jack said. "Machinery. Lots of accidents."

"I know, but—"

"What did he say?"

"He started off, 'You Preus?' Like that. 'You the party that called about the dog?' I said yes, and then he went into this long harangue. He said, 'First of all, don't ever talk to my wife like that. Nobody talks to my wife like that. She's a nervous person, and you set her off, talking like that. She came down to the barn yelling and crying. She got the cows all wild.' " Abby laughed and wiped at her cheeks. "He said, 'I've got forty fresh heifers, and now they won't let down their milk. Now I've got real trouble, and all because of that phone call.' " She took a shaky breath. "I said I was sorry, but being friendly hadn't gotten me anywhere. I said I'd been nice and polite for over a week and all I got was the runaround. He said, 'You don't understand my situation. I'm all alone out there. My boy got gored by a bull six months ago, so now I have to do everything myself.' "

"His boy was gored by a bull!" Jack said.

"I know!" Abby said. She put both hands on her forehead. "Can you believe this? He said, 'I've got the school-bus route, I'm trying to get my crops in while the weather holds. I've got a boy was gored by a bull, a nervous wife, and forty fresh heifers in the barn.' " Abby giggled, and Jack laughed, too. "I said I was sorry. I didn't know about that, but we had our own problems. I said all I knew was that the sheriff's office said this was his job. And then he said, 'It's not.' He said it's not in the regulations. He said he only does this as a courtesy."

"But he did it," Jack said. "He took the dog?"

"It was easy. He put the chain on him, and Blackie jumped right up in the back of the pickup. He said he'd take him out in a field. I saw his rifle. He had a gun rack."

"Well, see? You were right. You had to holler to get the job done."

"I know, but how come I feel so awful? I didn't know about his troubles. How was I supposed to know? I was just trying to do the right thing, and now the dog is dead, and I feel awful!"

Jack put his arms around her and petted her, caressing her neck, running his hand up and down her back. "You did the right thing," he said. "You were great. Don't feel bad. We don't even know if this guy's telling the truth."

"I know it!" She looked up at him and laughed. "I think he's nuts. I mean, I'm sorry if his son got gored by a bull, but I don't see what that has to do with—"

"Exactly."

"The sheriff said—"

"You did just right. Listen, this is really all my fault. I should have taken care of this. I should have had my own rifle and shot the dog myself."

"Don't be stupid. We don't want guns in the house."

"No, but if you're living in the country you ought to be prepared for things like this. It's irresponsible not to be. You shouldn't pawn this kind of trouble off on somebody else."

"But that's what he's paid for. You're talking rot."

"I don't know."

"Anyhow, it's done."

"We can be glad of that," Jack said. "I just wish you didn't feel so bad."

"I'll get over it. If only he hadn't smiled like that. Ooh, it was creepy."

"I'm sorry."

"Okay."

During their final days in the farmhouse, as Jack and Abby concentrated on cleaning and packing—carting canning jars and old clothes to Goodwill, clearing out cupboards, sweeping and scrubbing—they barely gave the dog a thought. But at the farewell parties thrown by their friends, Abby told, with gusto and skill, the story of her encounter with the constable. She lowered her voice to imitate him, demanding gruffly, "You Preus? You the party that called about the dog?" She held her audience, and when she delivered her favorite line—"I've got a boy was gored by a bull, a nervous wife, and forty fresh heifers in the barn"—they howled.

The last of these parties was held the night before the movers were to come and haul their things off to the warehouse. They drove home from this affair in silence, both of them exhausted and dizzy from drink. When they pulled up in front of the house, Abby sucked in her breath so sharply that Jack was alarmed. "What?" he said. "What is it?"

"Oh," Abby said, leaning forward, her hand on her heart. "Just a shadow." She breathed again. "I thought it was Blackie."

"You sound disappointed."

"I am."

Jack turned off the motor and cut the lights. "Blackie's dead."

"I know it. We killed him."

"It was the right thing."

"I know."

"What else could we do?"

Jack rested his arm on the back of the seat. Abby moved over and leaned her head on his shoulder. They sat there in the dark for some time, too tired to move, with no real eagerness to go inside. Inside, the house was bare. The walls were blank, and the windows, stripped of their curtains, looked raw. The furniture, pushed every which way, seemed anonymous now. It could have belonged to anyone. The bed was still up but unmade. They would break down the bed in the morning. Just now there was little reason to go inside. They sat there in the car, the white wall of the house rising up in front of them, darkness all around, as if they were parked at an outdoor movie and the show was over, everyone had gone. They sat there quietly, the two of them, resting, half their lives behind them, half their lives to go.

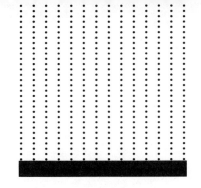

MY

FATHER'S

WAR

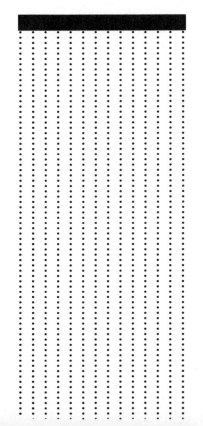

It's Christmas, and we're all snowed in, trapped here with our parents. The rain we ran into near Red River Falls quickly turned to sleet and then to fat, wet flakes that clogged the windshield wipers. We just made it. The radio says a foot with more to come. We're going to be stuck here for days.

I can predict what will happen. At first we'll enjoy being stranded, all our plans and schedules canceled. We'll feel free, as if we were kids again, and school had been called off. We'll be babbling, trading stories, nibbling divinity and fudge and sugar cookies until we're sick of sweets and jittery with coffee. By tomorrow night we'll be growing quiet. We'll play some Scrabble, maybe, or attempt to assemble a puzzle with a thousand impossible pieces. The conversation, as if muffled by the snow, will be no more than murmuring. By the second day we will be reduced to paging through the family photo albums we've already memorized and turning the leaves of the latest encyclopedia yearbook, unable to explain how just a year ago these meaningless events seemed so significant. We will enter silences as long as hallways, as large as empty rooms, and catch each other gazing through the windows at the snow. "What are

you thinking?" "What? Oh, nothing." By the third day
we'll be feeling claustrophobic. The tension between my
mother and my brother's wife and mine will start to
snap. This huge old house, where we did not grow up,
which holds no memories for us, no hope for the future,
will seem a dull hotel. We'll pile outside and dig the cars
free, shoving and laughing and stoning each other with
snowballs. And finally: pack up the presents and the
dirty clothes, kiss, hug, and drive away, hollering *good-
bye* and *have a safe trip* and *happy new year, happy new
year!*

In the meantime, here we are. It's Christmas, late,
and the women are in bed, exhausted from the travel
and the cooking and the awesome effort that courtesy
requires in my mother's house. My mother is an expert
at Christian nastiness. She disguises her animosity with
kindness. Her compliments are cruel. She has not only
worn out our wives, who have smiled bravely through
the evening, but fatigued herself as well. And so the
women sleep, while my father and my brothers and I
sit around the kitchen table, glad to be together.

"Tell us about the Christmas of the red bobsled," I
say to my father, and he smiles.

This is what we do best in my family: dream and
reminisce. The future, as we see it, is mostly a mirage.
We do not trust the present, either. It's too ephemeral,
too slippery. But the past, the past is both mysterious
and permanent. Happiness, we seem to think, as well
as all important pain, was something strange that happened to us long ago. I suppose we are pathetic, but we
think this halting talk, with which we try to find ourselves somewhere back in time, is fun. It's probably my
father's fault. He teaches history, and we have inherited
his interest, his backward attitude. And so, although
we've heard the story a dozen times before, I ask him
once again: "Come on. Tell us about the Christmas of
the red bobsled."

"Well," my father says, "that was during the Depression. Normally my dad would spend the winter building summer cabins at the lake—inside work, finishing and cabinets—but that sort of thing dried up when the Depression hit. So he went out West that year, and finally he found a job. They were building a dude ranch, and he was out there in Wyoming all through the fall and on into the winter. We missed him. Along about Christmas he finished up and caught the train back to Pike Lake. It was Christmas Eve day, I remember, and the train was late. We were watching for him all day long, and late that afternoon, here he came, trudging up the lane. There was a blizzard—that's why he was late—and he couldn't get a ride from town. Nobody was going anywhere. So finally he just walked the four miles home, and here he comes, hauling this red bobsled. He'd made it in his spare time. I guess they liked him on the ranch, because they gave him all these magazines, and the sled was piled high with *National Geographics*. Was that a gift! We were snowed in a lot that winter, I remember, and we'd sit beside the stove for hours, reading up on Africa and looking at the pictures."

"Of bare-breasted women, I'll bet," Dave says.

"Hot stuff!" Johnny laughs. "Magazines! But then you didn't have TV in those days, did you, Dad?"

"TV? We didn't have a radio." He pauses, as if listening. Snow sifts like sand against the windowpane. "I loved that bobsled, though. I had this path, and if I got a running start I could go from the playhouse all the way down through the orchard, past the house, right past the clothesline, and clear on down the lane. Every time it got a little faster. You could hardly steer that thing, but all you had to do was keep the runners in the track. I kept trying to see how close I could come to the clothesline post, and each time I came a little closer. Goodness. That was crazy. I could have killed myself. It sure was fun, though. I sort of hogged the sled, I guess. Everyone was mad at me, but that was about the best Christmas. Boy, that was fun."

I can see him, my little father, in a ragged mackinaw
and stocking cap, having fun, playing chicken with a
clothesline post. My father is easily pleased, like so many
of his generation. It has to do with the Depression, I
think. A plate of canned peaches and a piece of homemade bread is his idea of a special treat. It's the same
with Christmas presents. He thinks that socks and hand-
kerchiefs are something. "Just what I needed!" he says,
and he means it. As soon as he opens his presents he
puts them on to demonstrate his pleasure. He is wearing
now, and has been all night long, the red flannel shirt
that Dave and Martha gave him, a silly necktie that his
sister sent, and the dark blue stocking cap that Johnny
bought for him. He looks like a nut. A goofy old man,
sliding toward senility. I envy him. To him, aftershave
is frankincense. The dimmest memory excites him.

And so I say: "I remember that. You were so selfish
about that sled we finally had to gang up on you and
take it away. And then you got so mad you set the house
on fire, and your father fell off the ladder when he tried
to put it out and broke his back. But the house burned,
anyhow, and we had to live in the playhouse all winter
long. Remember? We almost froze to death."

"What!" my father laughs. I love to make him laugh.
He barely makes a sound—just a hiccup and a series of
small sighs. "What are you talking about? Broke his
back! You weren't even born yet. And that was a different winter entirely, the winter of the fire."

Dad is such a dope. Slow, deliberate, always trying
to untangle the facts. The perfect straight man. It's a
kind of game we play, Confusing Father. Dave winks
at me and passes the plate of cookies.

"The fire happened earlier," my father says, pushing
his bifocals back up his nose. Another ten years, I think,
and he'll be blind. Or deaf. Or dead. "Two years earlier,
I think. What happened was, we were all in bed except
my mother, who was blowing out the lamps, and before
coming up to bed she looked out the window and saw

this orange glow on the snow, the reflection of the fire, don't you see. So she yells for my father, and he comes barging into our bedroom, where the trapdoor to the attic was, and he's carrying the ladder and hollering, 'The hatchet! Get the hatchet!' So I ran downstairs and grabbed the hatchet that we used for splitting kindling, and I climbed partway up the ladder to hand it to my dad. I can see it now as plain as day: the attic all aglow and those orange and yellow flames around the chimney and my father chopping at the roof as fast as he could go and the sparks and his hair just flying. You remember that head of hair he had," he says to me. I nod.

"Yeah?" says Johnny. "So what happened? Did you get it out?"

"So my father hollers, 'Get some water!' and my brother Raymond ran and got the slop pail." My father laughs. "We didn't have any running water, you know. That was about the only water in the house. So that's what Raymond brought, and my father threw that on the flames. It did the trick. It was just a chimney fire, not so big but plenty scary."

"But did he really break his back?" Johnny says. "Grandpa?"

"Wouldn't you like to know," I tease. Dave is just four years younger than I am, but Johnny is nine years back of Dave, so he has missed out on some of the family legends.

"No, now, that was at the icehouse, wasn't it?" says Dave.

"Right. That was when Grandpa was working at the icehouse. They ran these cakes of ice down a track from the building to the boxcars," I explain to Johnny. "And one day one of those blocks of ice broke loose and came roaring down the track like a freight car. This other worker had his back turned and didn't see it coming, so Grandpa knocked him off the track, but he got caught instead, and broke his back."

"His leg!" Dad says. "He broke his leg, that's all. He

never broke his back ever. Where on earth did you get
that idea?"

"I don't know," I laugh. "You must have told me."

"I told you no such thing. He broke his leg, that's
all, and he was laid up all that winter."

"Reading *National Geographics*," Dave says.

"Probably," my father says. "Probably."

"I never heard that story," Johnny says. "I never knew
that Grandpa was a hero."

"Oh, sure. He did all kinds of things. Too bad you
never knew him. *Baby of the family,*" I sing, and he sticks
out his tongue.

"Should I make more coffee?" Dave asks.

"I don't know," my father says. "Any more and I'll
be up all night."

"So what?" I say. "Did you think you were going
somewhere tomorrow?" We watch the snow swirl
against the window.

"Siberia," Johnny says.

"Go ahead," I say to Dave. "Make another pot. I
want to hear about when Dad was a hero."

"What? When was I a hero?"

"In the war, of course. I want to hear about the war."
This is curiously true. As a boy I begged my father to
tell me how it was when he was in the war, but he
would never talk. Not much. He let me wear his uniform on Halloween once, and I was allowed to look
through a box of snapshots of his army buddies, but he
was stingy with his memories. "Who's that?" I'd ask,
pointing to a soldier sacked out underneath a palm tree.
"A friend," my dad would say. "He died." "How?" I
wanted to know. "What happened?" "Japs," he would
say, and that was all. "The Japs got him."

And then there was a long period when I couldn't
care less. Vietnam blew up when I was in high school,
and I went away to college, and my father's generation
became the enemy. People I'd known and respected for
years suddenly despised me. Discussions with neighbors

exploded into arguments, arguments broke down in angry insults. I was furious for days at a time. I studied maps of Canada, and I decided, if and when the time came, I was going north. My father—a quiet patriot who believed in God and the wisdom of presidents—allowed me my opinions, but he didn't want to hear them. To get along at all, we had to declare the whole area of foreign affairs off-limits. Home on vacations, I bit my tongue till I thought it was going to bleed. I tried to respect his silence, but, in a mad moment just before the '72 election, I tore the cover off a *Ramparts* magazine and mailed it to him. The cover was a color photograph of the slaughter at Mylai, and stuck in a corner of the gruesome scene was a Nixon campaign poster: RE-ELECT THE PRESIDENT. My father never mentioned it. He didn't have to. His generation had their way in that election. But my generation was right, by and large, and in the end we won, more or less. Still, it makes me squirm these days to think of our self-righteousness. Lately I've been thinking how different my father's war must have been from ours, and I've grown curious, not so much about the reasons it was fought, but about the feel of my father's own experience. And so I say: "Come on. Tell us about the war."

"Aw," he says, placing a slice of salami on a cracker, "that old stuff."

Johnny agrees, "I've heard all that before."

"You have?" Dave says. "He never told us anything." Dave is removing the carcass of the turkey from the fridge. He sets it on the table. He's got a potbelly already, my little brother, and he's going bald fast. In the sixties, I remember, he looked like a lion.

"I'm not surprised," I say. "I read somewhere not long ago how fathers never tell their sons about the war. While the kids are growing up it's still too close, and by the time they want to talk the sons aren't interested. And so they tell their grandchildren. You came along so late," I say to Johnny, "you're almost like a grandson.

So that makes sense. But Dave is right. He never told us anything."

"Oh, I did, too."

"No, you didn't. What? What did you tell us? I never heard a thing except you had a friend from Upper Michigan whose name was Kyle Aho. I remember that because I thought his name was just hysterical. And you told me how you slept in the jungle with a knife so you could cut your way out of your hammock in a hurry. And in the morning how you had to empty out your boots because of scorpions. And once, when I was little, you told me how a bullet hit the beach beside your elbow. Another foot, you said, and I never would have been born. That scared me. So I remember that. What else? Something about Manila, I can't remember what. And Johnny, of course. You told us how your brother died. But really, that's about it."

Dave says, "I remember once how mad you got when I took your dog tags from your dresser drawer. 'Those are not playthings,' you said. 'Those are not for you.' But that was funny, because I was looking for that box of army pictures when I found your dog tags. I thought: Wow, these are really neat. So I put them on and went on searching for that box of photographs, and what should I come across but these little rolled-up things, and I wondered, What the heck?" He laughs. "So I walk out in the living room with the dog tags round my neck and the box of photos in one hand and a rubber in the other, and I say: 'Hey, Dad, what's this?' "

All of us are laughing, my father included, but he's looking at the floor. He's still embarrassed!

"So Mom says, 'Come on, Harvey. Time to have a little talk. I'm not telling, that's for sure. This is up to you.' She was pretty much amused, but you were flustered, sort of mad, and you said: 'Put it back. Put it all away. Those are not for you.' Poor Pop," he laughs.

"Well, what did you want to know? About the war,

I mean," my father says. He cracks me up. War is easier than sex. And that's one thing I want to know—how a man so fastidious and shy managed to survive the war. I just can't see him as a soldier.

"Begin at the beginning," I tell him. "I'd like to hear it all."

He thinks I'm teasing. He says, "Really? I thought you were a pacifist. You and Dave."

"I am," I say, "sort of. That doesn't mean I'm not interested. There are things I want to know. I mean, I can't imagine how a wimp like you got through the war."

"A wimp? I'll have you know—"

"All right, all right. Just kidding. But here you are: you don't smoke, you don't drink or swear or chase the women. So how could any self-respecting soldier—I mean, did you have any friends? It seems like you would have been one of those guys who got picked on all the time."

"Hey, I had lots of friends! I got along okay."

"Oh, yeah. Kyle Aho. I forgot."

"For crying out loud. You don't know anything."

"Okay, okay. That's what I'm saying. I really would like to know. Because we missed all that, Dave and me. Vietnam was stupid. I wouldn't do it any different. But what I'm saying is, when we get together—friends and stuff—and we talk about the war, it's all about the draft and Canada and jail and things like that. And I don't understand you guys, you older guys. I'd like to, because you're all such hypocrites. That's what ticks me off, and that's the very thing I find so fascinating: the way you all insist the service was such a horrible experience, and World War II was awful, and 'I just hope my boys never have to go through what I went through.' So serious and superior, that little piece, it's almost automatic, like the pledge of allegiance or something. 'I just hope my boys . . .' But *then*, and this is what gets me, you'll talk for two hours about what a terrific time you had and all the pranks you played. Well, not you, maybe, but a lot of guys like you. Guys I've known."

"I know," Dave says, "I know exactly what you're saying. There's this guy at work, he's in his fifties, and he was just a kid in World War II, but he was in it. But he'll do that. He'll tell me how he wouldn't go through that again for anything, the worst period in his life, the pits, or so he says, and then he talks my ear off. He tells the same dumb story every time. You'd think it was the high point of his life or something. I don't get it."

"Well, you have these friends," my father says. "You're close. You don't forget that." Suddenly, I see something. My father has no friends. I can't remember one. Acquaintances, of course, people that he works with at the high school, but not one man you'd call a friend. Nobody to talk to.

"Okay," I say, "so how did it start? For you, I mean. I mean, did you enlist, or what? Was the war already under way?"

"No, no, I was drafted. This was 1941, the fall of '41."

"Before Pearl Harbor, then. Did you know the war was coming? Was it clear? What did people think?"

"Well, the war was on in Europe. We didn't know if America would get involved in that or not. But they were drafting, and my brother Raymond enlisted in the navy, and then that fall my name came up, and I was drafted. So I had to go down to St. Paul for my physical. Me and Eddie Eberhardt, a neighbor down the road, we took the bus down there together."

"And there wasn't any question in your mind?" Dave says.

"No, not really. You weren't too happy about it. You just went, that's all."

"This wasn't Nam," Johnny says with some disgust. "This wasn't hippie-dippie days."

"I understand that," Dave says. "I was wondering, that's all."

"You," I say to Johnny. "What do you know? You're so dumb you think Dave and I were hippies. We had long hair and we didn't go to Vietnam, so we were hippies. You're as stupid as the newspapers. You want to know something? Of all the guys I knew back then, there wasn't one, not one, who would have called himself a hippie, except as some kind of joke. It wasn't true. It was just the newspapers. They look at something they don't understand, and they have to have a name. So all of us are hippies. Dumb. And you're as dumb as they are."

"Well, jeez. Excuse me for breathing."

"I don't care. I'm trying to explain something. You guys, you younger guys, you think it's all so funny. The sixties, ooh! Flower children. All that shit."

"Sam," my father says.

"It wasn't funny. People got killed. People went to jail. Okay, so a lot of us acted like spoiled brats. At least we had a few ideas of our own. At least we had the guts to stand up to our parents. You guys, you're all so goddamn normal you make me want to puke. What do you want? Money. Now there's a brave idea. That really takes balls. Money."

"Sam," my father says. "I wish you wouldn't talk so tough."

"I'm sorry. But criminy, these younger guys make me mad. Bunch of momma's boys."

"Hippie," Johnny laughs at me. "Flower child."

"Okay," I say, "so I get a little out of joint. But I've got reasons. I was talking to a neighbor kid the other day. He's about your age, and you know what he told me? He just enlisted in the marines, and you know what he said? He could hardly wait to go kill Communists. He said it's what he's wanted to do all his life. I can't believe this! Why did we even bother? Chicago, Vietnam. What's the point? We got a bunch of warmongers coming right behind us. He wants to go kill Communists! The ignorance! Don't you guys read books?"

"Naw. We just play video games. Gimme another quarter, Dad."

"That's exactly how it looks to me."

"Sam," he says. "We're not like that. That's just one guy. People are worried about getting a job, for sure, but it's not as bad as you think. What have *you* been reading, *Newsweek* magazine?"

"All right," I say, "I guess I'm guilty. But I just hate the way our generation gets dismissed. To read the magazines, to watch TV, you'd think we'd all been killed at Kent State. Sorry. We're still here. Where do they think the nuclear freeze came from? These old galoots," I say, not looking at my father, "would love to believe we all marched off to jobs in insurance offices. They want to think we were just an aberration, just a little snow on the TV screen. They want to think the war never happened, that nobody said no and went to jail, that no one got his legs blown off for nothing."

"One thing I never understood," Johnny says, "is why you guys weren't drafted."

"Deferments," Dave says. "They didn't take you out of college. And later on, under Nixon, they had this lottery, and both of us came up with lucky numbers. So that was just dumb luck."

"And so were the deferments, when you think about it. If we'd been born black or poor, chances are, we'd have ended up in Vietnam. Because it was a class thing, too. Minorities and lower-class kids fought the war for the middle class and wealthy. Don't they always? I think they did the same thing in the Civil War. Didn't they, Dad."

"What?" He's been thinking.

"In the Civil War. Couldn't you pay someone to go in your place if you were drafted?"

"That's correct. In the North, they did that."

"So I'm not saying we had such lofty principles. Some people did, some guys really paid a price. I know one guy who went to jail, and he was wrecked for life. He's never been the same. I know a vet who was spit on by protesters when he walked off the plane in California. He joined the Veterans Against the War, and a month later he got spit on by the VFW. I think of guys like that, and I feel awful. I had an attitude. I was against the war. I marched, and I wrote some letters, and I voted. Big deal. I didn't do enough. Most of us didn't do enough."

"Speak for yourself," Dave says.

"I am!" I say. "Okay? So you got busted once. You want to hold that over me forever? Big hairy deal. You hardly stopped the thing single-handedly. Basically," I say to Johnny, "it was just a stupid war, and you got out of it any way you could. I mean, I should go halfway round the world to kill a bunch of dirt-poor peasants in pajamas? I've got no argument with them. Let them grow rice, for Christ's sake."

"Flunk your physical," Dave says. "That was one way out. I had friends who fired pistols off beside their ears so that they'd flunk the hearing test. Some took dope. My best friend took his mother. Held her hand the whole time. Hardly a profile in courage, but it worked. The doctors thought he was psycho."

Everybody laughs. My father shakes his head. He still can't understand this. "See," I say, trying to explain to Johnny, "it was just a crazy time. People were going nuts. You'd have to be nuts to enlist, right? But I knew some who did that, too. There was this guy in my dorm, Tom Fitts, and he was going goofy. He didn't want to be in school, but he didn't know what else to do. He'd quit going to classes. He just sat up all night, smoking dope, reading science fiction, listening to music. So one night, it's early winter, and he takes this bet. For ten bucks his roommate dares him to run to the supermarket and back in nothing but his briefs and cowboy boots.

It's snowing out, and half a mile to the supermarket, and most of that is right along the highway. But some other guys get in on it, and pretty soon the kitty's up to ninety bucks. So he did it. We're standing there cheering as he comes up to the dorm, and he goes around collecting his money from everybody, pink and blue and laughing like a lunatic. And the next day he goes and joins the navy."

"Very weird," Johnny says.

"But that's not the end of the story. We'd get letters from him, and the odd thing was, he seemed to be getting a kick out of boot camp. I don't know. I guess he liked being told what to do after drifting like he'd been. I suppose it all seemed nice and clear. But then he was sent to San Diego. He was walking around out there one night with a pretty good buzz on, and it was Christmas, the holidays. He was stumbling around down there by the base, and he came across this place where they were storing ammunition. Chain-link fence runs all around it, and on the fence they'd put up this gigantic sign: PEACE ON EARTH, GOODWILL TO MEN. He just went nuts. He tried to climb the fence, got all cut up, and he's hollering and bleeding all over the place when a couple MP's pick him up. Two days later he filed for conscientious objector."

"Oh, my," my father says.

"And you know what? They gave it to him. Three days before his hitch was up."

"It figures," Dave says.

"Yeah, but," Johnny says, "I don't understand. Why did it take that sign to tell him how he felt about the war? He enlisted, after all. He must have thought what he was doing."

"Sure, he did. What do you think he was doing up there in his dorm room night after night? Look," I say. "It's not so simple. Your parents tell you one thing, and your friends say something else. They teach you all this stuff at school, and then you go to church. You read and talk and think and think until you don't know what to think. It gets confusing. You just wait. You'll get your turn. What do you think they're cooking up for you right now, down there in El Salvador?"

"Aw, they'll never get away with that. Too many people remember Vietnam."

"You wait," Dave says. "They give a war for every generation. Just look at it. World War I. WWII. Korea. Vietnam."

"And lots of little side trips along the way," I say. "The Bay of Pigs. Dominican Republic. Got to keep the boys in shape, got to test the new equipment."

"Yesss," Dave hisses, placing his fists on the table. "Ve must protect zuh nation from zese inferior races! Zese chews. Zese awful chipsies! El Salvador, she is full of chipsies, Mein Führer! Ve must destroy zem."

"Bananas," I say. "We have a vital interest in bananas."

"Lebensraum!" Dave says.

"The Monroe Doctrine!"

"The Fatherland!" He's on his feet.

"ITT! Coca-Cola! IBM!"

"Remember Alsace-Lorraine!"

"Boeing! Chrysler! Honeywell!"

Dave has his arm in the air, saluting Hitler. Johnny hoots and giggles. He's more mature than we are, but we're more fun.

My father says, "Shhh! You boys! The gals are trying to sleep."

"Sorry," I say. "I forgot." We sit, and I say, "Gals? *Gals?* Where have you been? Pass me that turkey, will you, Herman?" I say to Dave, and he slides the heavy platter across the table.

"You boys," my father says. "You think you're pretty funny, but you don't know what it's like. My brother Johnny died because of Hitler."

"Okay," Dave says. "So tell us about it. Where were we? You'd just passed your physical, you and Eddie. So then what?"

"So then," my father says, looking at us warily, "so then they shipped us off to Georgia, to Camp Wheeler, for basic training."

"Boot camp," I say and try to envision my father with his head shaved, being bossed by drill instructors barking obscenities that must have sounded, to my father, like a foreign language. "How did you like that?"

"To tell the truth, I rather enjoyed it. The train ride was fun. That was the farthest I'd ever been from home. And then when we got there, I liked the exercise. They weren't too hard on us at first. Mainly what we did was march. What I didn't like was that Eddie and I got split up. They divided you according to height, and he was a short guy, so he had to go with the smaller fellows."

I say, "They sorted you out according to height?"

"That's right. They started with the smaller men, and then every inch or so they'd form a new platoon until they reached the tallest men, the heavyweights. They thought it looked better that way when we were on parade—more uniform—and you can see their point. You can't have your lines bobbing up and down. So whenever we marched, the tall platoon went first, then the medium fellows, and the little guys, they'd go last. I was in the middle somewhere."

"A platoon of midgets!" Dave laughs. "What strategy! What cunning! Send in your short guys to bite them in the leg. Sneak attack."

My father smiles. "It seems funny now, but we did look pretty sharp. We got good at that close-order drill. The bad thing was, you just got to know the guys in your platoon, and then when we left boot camp, they broke us up again."

"The military mind," I say. "They don't want you to form any human attachments. It's a machine. That's what Mumford says. You're all replaceable parts. Everybody's equal. Now there's democracy."

My father frowns. "Mumford?" he says. "Who's Mumford?"

"Just someone I read. I'm sorry. Go ahead. Then you went out West?"

"To San Francisco, yes."

"No, wait!" Johnny says. "Wait a minute. Tell them about the invasion!"

"What?"

"You know. The invasion of Georgia. Jeez, that's the best part."

"Well," my father smiles, "as I said, at first we had it easy. Just a lot of marching, calisthenics, and so on. But there was this one sergeant. He kept telling us, 'Look out. You think you're having fun, but we're going to get into this thing yet. You watch. Something's going to happen.' I've wondered about that since. He seemed to sense something, he seemed to know. And sure enough. Pearl Harbor. Boy." He shakes his head. "We hadn't even seen a rifle yet. That was on a Sunday, and that same afternoon they issued us our rifles and showed us how to fire. They put us out on guard duty that night. We had our posts and our brand-new rifles, and we sat there staring off into the dark. Just kids, and were we nervous. It was raining, I remember, and we were miserable, just running wet. Along toward morning I turned to the guy on guard with me, and I said, 'Well, I guess they're not coming.' "

Dave snorts and chortles. "Oh, my God," he gasps. "That's terrific!"

"I told you it was good," Johnny giggles.

" 'Well, I guess they're not coming,' " Dave says.

"Guarding the Gulf," I laugh. "Protecting Atlanta from the Japanese."

"Well, we didn't know!" my father says.

"I know! I know! I can see it!"

" 'I guess they're not coming,' " Dave says with rel-
ish, and I see the phrase will soon be famous. He trea-
sures family foolishness. He'll quote the dead with great
affection, tell you something funny that Grandma Thorsen said some forty years ago.

My father is absently biting his fist, gazing at the
tabletop. I say, "Dad? What is it?"

"That week," he says, "the week after Pearl Harbor,
I got a package from home. I opened it up, and my
father had sent me a hunting knife. It had a blade like
this." He measures eight inches between his index fingers. He stares and then looks up. "He was thinking of
hand-to-hand combat, I suppose. I suppose he was
trying to help." He smiles and shakes his head.

I can see the sheath, the open package, wrapping paper, and the blade as bright as a mirror in my father's
hand. I can see him testing the edge on his palm, prod-
ding the pad of his thumb with the point. "Good grief,"
I say. "What a gift."

"He meant well," my father says, "but that sure
scared me. That made it real. The day I got that knife
was the day the war began. For me."

"Do you still have it?" Dave says. "I'd like to have
that knife." He looks surprised by what he's said.

"I wish I did. I lost it in the Solomons. Interesting to
think who might have picked it up, where it went. It's
probably still out there in the jungle somewhere, . . .
rusty now. Goodness. That was . . . forty years ago.
This is history, boys!" He beams at us. "I am history!
You're looking right at it." He laughs his silent laugh.

"Don't forget the pillow, Dad," Johnny says.

"Yes, my mother sent me a handmade pillow in the
same package. It was like a baby pillow, like you boys
had when you were small. I took a lot of ribbing about
that pillow, but I was glad to have it. It sure beat sleeping
on your pack. And then when we were on the march,
I'd stuff it in my knapsack, slip it like a cushion between
my kit and my back. I had that pillow a long time, but

the jungle, you know, so humid. After a while it got sort of moldy, and I had to throw it out. You weren't supposed to carry a lot of extra stuff, but I had that knife, and the pillow, and a Bible."

I smile helplessly. I have always liked my father.

Dave says, "So then you went West?"

"And then we shipped out. Well, actually we spent the winter up in Pennsylvania. Indiantown Gap. That's not far from Three Mile Island, where they had that nuclear accident. I saw it on the maps when it was in the papers here a while back, and I thought, 'My land. That's where I was in the war. Indiantown Gap.' But we weren't there very long. They pushed us through training in a hurry after Pearl. They got awfully serious then."

"Is it true," Dave says, "that Roosevelt knew about Pearl Harbor beforehand and allowed it to happen?"

"Oh, I don't think," my father says. "He wouldn't have done that. Roosevelt was a great president."

My father teaches history! "There are no great presidents," I grumble.

"Nobody knows," Johnny says. "I did a research paper on that last year. It looks as if he maybe did. He wanted to help the Allies in Europe, but he couldn't get into that without a good excuse. So there's your motive. And there's evidence the military knew about the plans of the Japanese. The strategy was on the table, all mapped out. Take the islands, take Alaska, work your way down. In fact, the Japanese had made a practice run some years before. The military knew all about that."

"You're kidding."

"No, I'm not. You can look it up. But nobody knows for sure. If Roosevelt let it happen he covered his tracks pretty well."

"I don't believe he did that," my father says. "Roosevelt was a great man."

"There are no great men," I tell him. "Gandhi beat his wife."

"Gandhi?" my father says. "What's Gandhi got to do with this?"

I look to Dave for help. He rolls his eyes and smiles. He's more forgiving than I am. My father is a dupe. He believes what the TV tells him. He voted for Nixon. Three times. "Nothing," I say. "Forget it."

"So then you shipped out," Dave says.

"Yes, and I'd never been on a boat like that before. It was just enormous. There were hundreds of us, and as soon as we got out on the ocean most of the boys got seasick, and there weren't near enough toilets. Well, you can imagine. It was a mess. And quite a number of fellows were hanging over the rail. Oof! Was I sick. I thought I was going to die. I didn't care what happened to me. I just lay there in my bunk, and the second day Kyle Aho came by. We were friends by then, and he asked how I was doing. I guess I looked pretty bad, and he said, 'Have you eaten anything?' 'Eat?' I said. I said I couldn't even think about food. He said, 'You've got to eat something. That's the secret. I'll go get you something good.' His father was a fisherman on Lake Superior, see, so I guess he knew about these things. Anyhow, he went up to the what-do-you-call-it, the galley, and you weren't supposed to do this, but he must have made friends with one of the cooks. Because he told the cook, 'I've got a friend down there who's dying. He needs a fried egg sandwich.' And he did it. Kyle brought me that sandwich, and I ate it, and right away I felt fine. I was okay after that."

"Saved by a fried egg sandwich," Dave says.

"It was like a miracle. That Kyle. He was pretty smart."

"Oh!" I say. "That must be why you always tried to feed us egg sandwiches when we were kids and had the flu. I thought you were crazy. A fried egg sandwich! Yuk."

"I guess that's true. I never thought of that. It worked

so well for me that time I was seasick, but I suppose the flu is different."

"Is this when you drank all that Coca-Cola?" Johnny says. "He's always talking about those little green bottles of Coke."

"No, that was later. That was on my way home. They issued you these tickets, and you were only allowed so many Cokes and so many beers, but you could trade them. And that Roger Handy, he liked his beer, so he was always happy to swap with me. They were the small ones, you know, those little blue-green bottles, cold and wet. I'd take them out on the fantail and sit in the sun and drink this Coke that burned your throat and think about home and everything that I was going to do. That was good stuff."

"Yeah, but wait a second," I say. "Suddenly the war is over. Let's keep this chronological. You're on this troop ship. Then what? Where did you go?"

"That's just it. You never knew. You never knew what you were doing. Only the higher-ups knew that, the generals and so forth. You just had your orders: 'Dig in. Move out. You two go on guard.' Later on, when I was a runner, I'd get to know a little bit because I was in and out of headquarters, but even then it was mostly gossip. That's all you really had to go on. And going over, on the boat, nobody knew anything. A lot of the fellows thought we were headed for Europe. Some said Alaska, but it kept on getting hotter, and then they announced we were passing over the equator. The next thing we knew, they were telling us to prepare to disembark because we'd reached New Zealand."

"How long did it take?" I ask. "How long were you on board that ship?"

"Three weeks, I think. A long time. It was quite a large fleet. You'd look out, and there were cruisers and destroyers, aircraft carriers, everything. It was really something. Oh, and then, how could I forget this? One day we heard the guns go off. We thought they were practicing, but this went on for quite some time, and we were getting tense. We were in the war zone then, and they had ordered us to stay below, but finally I decided I'd rather get my head shot off than die down there and never know what hit me. So I went up on deck."

"Yes?" Dave says. "And?"

"Well, my goodness, it was a battle! We were smack in the middle of a battle! I could see land, and the ships' guns were pounding the shore, and the sky was full of planes. There were dogfights everywhere, mostly over the islands. Once in a while a plane would get hit and go down trailing smoke. Just like in the movies. Except that this was real."

He stops. I look at Dave, who shrugs. "Dad?" I say.

"I was thinking of this plane, this Japanese, a Zero. He came right at us. You could see the insignia. He was crippled, but he kept on coming. A suicide plane, I suppose. Finally they got him. My lands. I guess it was our guys who got him because they quit firing and the gunners down in front of me were jumping up and down and hollering and so on."

"Good grief."

"Well, yes. Pieces landed in the water just a few yards off the ship! And just about that time my lieutenant stuck his head out the hatchway and started swearing at me. He asked me what I thought I was doing, and I told him I was only watching. He said, 'Thorsen, you get your butt down here before I kick it off.' But he was curious, too. He asked me what was going on, and I said, 'Airplanes. It's an air war. I think we're winning.' 'Good,' he said. 'Now get back to your group.' I told the guys what I had seen, and, naturally, they all wanted to go have a look, but I said, 'Boy, you better not. The looey really got after me.' So we just sat there, and that was no fun, sitting down there in that hole. You didn't know what was going to happen. But then the guns quit firing, and we were told there'd been an air war, but we had won. And this was the Battle of the Coral Sea."

"Hey," I say, "I think I've heard of that."

"Of course you have," Johnny says. "That was a turning point, one of the major naval battles of the war."

"I was there," my father says. "I witnessed that." He thinks for a minute. "I didn't really contribute a lot," he says abruptly and laughs. "I guess you'd have to say that I was just a spectator. But I was there. And that's a fact."

"History," I say.

"Yes," he says. "Now wait a minute. That's not right. That plane, that Zero, maybe that was in the Philippines, when I went up on deck." He pushes back the stocking cap, disturbed. "Isn't that something? I can't remember."

"Well, for Pete's sake," I say. "What kind of historian are you? If you can't even remember—"

"I remember the plane. I remember that. I just can't place it, that's all. No, I think that was the Philippines. That's right. But there was a battle on the way down, too. I think it was—"

"Well, I'm totally lost now," Dave says. He gets up to pour himself some coffee. "I thought we were landing in New Zealand."

"I just can't quite—I can't remember everything in order," my father says. He seems both puzzled and amused by what his mind is doing.

"You're in New Zealand," I tell him.

"Okay. But not for long. Just two or three weeks, and then they shipped us to the Fijis. Suva. Nandi."

"Ohwa. Tagu. Siam," Johnny says, and the three of us laugh at the old Cub Scout joke.

My father says, "What?" He's somewhere else.

"Nothing," Johnny says. "Just a joke."

Dad looks at us with some distrust. "You want to hear this or not?"

"Yeah, yeah," Johnny says. "The Fijis. We're with you. Now what?"

"Nothing much. We were stationed there for quite a while, but we were more or less just waiting."

"Boring, huh? 'Hurry up and wait,' " I say. "Isn't that the phrase?"

"Yes, but actually I found the Fijis rather interesting. First of all the trip up from New Zealand was peculiar because they put us on the *President Coolidge*. This was an ocean liner they had turned into a troop ship, but they never finished the job. You could see where the bar had been. And they left the chandeliers. So here we were, going off to war, with these elegant, delicate chandeliers hanging over our heads. There were plenty of cracks about that. Later on, that boat went down with a lot of men on board, and many lives were lost. But for us the *Coolidge* was kind of fun. And then when we got to the Fijis, that was different. That's where I saw natives walk on coals."

"Really."

"They walked right through the fire. It was their religion. One night they had a festival, and I went over there with a couple of my pals. There was drumming, dancing, everything. A feast. Roast pig, I remember. At least I think that's what it was." He laughs. "They gave us some of that. And then several of the natives— the witch doctors or whatever—they got themselves worked up, and then they walked across these red-hot coals. Barefoot! Right through the fire!"

"I remember that," I tell him. "You had some pictures in that box of snapshots."

"Yes, I had to take some pictures, because I just could not believe my eyes! It was like something out of *National Geographic!*"

"Like Tibetans in the snow," I say. "Some sort of yoga."

"I don't know. I never saw anything like it. I wonder how they did that." He says this with such simple curiosity and awe that Dave laughs aloud and spills his coffee. "What's so funny?" my father says. "You don't believe me."

"No, no!" Dave says, wiping coffee off his chin. "I believe every word you're saying. It's just you. You've got a funny way of putting things." He giggles helplessly. " 'I wonder how they did that.' "

My father sighs and straightens the broad, gaudy tie he's got looped around his neck. "I think I better go to bed," he says. "It's getting awfully late."

"No. Dad," Dave says, "I'm sorry. Don't stop now. We haven't even seen any action yet."

"You were in combat, weren't you?" I say, trying to get him started again. "In the Philippines?"

"Yes," he says, still injured. "Yes, I was. I was coming to that. But if you guys think this was just a lot of funny business, I don't see why I should—"

"Dad," Dave says. "I'm sorry. I'm really interested in what you're saying. Really."

"Okay, then," my father says and settles the cap on his head. "Let's see, then. After the Fijis, they sent us to Guadalcanal."

"Guadalcanal?" Dave says. "That was really bad, wasn't it? Wasn't there an awful battle there?"

"Yes, there was. But that was earlier. We weren't in that one. That was the marines. We were their support. And this was usually the case with us, except for later, in the Philippines. The marines had already fought for Guadalcanal, and this was mostly mopping up. So there wasn't much resistance when we landed. Oh, the Japanese sent planes. They tried to bomb us as we hit the beach, but we got air support. The fighters intercepted them and drove them off, so that turned out okay. That wasn't so bad. The bad part started with New Georgia."

I say, "New Georgia. Now, where is that?"

"That's right there in the Solomons. That was the next large island up from Guadalcanal, and we went in there at night."

"At night."

"In rubber rafts. Oh, that was something. They loaded us up on Guadalcanal, and they put us on destroyer escorts. Exactly like destroyers except that they were made to transport men, and they packed us in just like sardines. But they used those destroyer escorts because they wanted to go fast. And then they sent us in, over the side, down the nets, and into these rubber rafts. That was foxy. Because they put us in where the Japs, the Japanese, weren't expecting us. They were thinking it was way too shallow there, but we went in at midnight when the tide was high, and those rubber rafts could float in a tablespoon of water. So we fooled them. We rode right in there on the tide. What was the name of that place, anyhow? Rice Anchorage. And there were many men landing like that, all over, in other places on the island. Well, they sent in the whole division, but our outfit landed there at Rice Anchorage."

"The whole division," Dave says. "But that's a thousand men or more. Isn't it?"

"Yes, it was. That would be several thousand."

"This was a major operation, then."

"You could say that, I suppose. Nothing compared to what they did in Europe, but it was a lot of men. Thousands of men."

"In rubber rafts."

"In rubber rafts, yes, and so we could only take our light equipment. We had mortars and machine guns, but that's all. The bigger boats were shelling an area farther down the beach, as if they were softening it up for us, as if we were landing over there. And that's where the enemy aimed all their guns. I still remember that, because, as we were going in, that entire area down the beach was all lit up with shell fire and fires breaking out, lighting up the jungle. But all the time, you see, we were over here.

"Nobody was talking. No lights at all, and it was black. And we were paddling and paddling and getting wet. You'd hear a shell go over now and then—over your head, over your shoulder, something from the ships—and it was whistling, like this: Wish!"

"Man," Dave says.

"It worked just perfectly. Everything was dark except where we could see these little blinking lights. And then the dark. And then those little lights would wink. And then the dark. And this was the signal. We followed those tiny lights right into shore. There was this Australian, and he had some natives with him, and they were signaling with flashlights to show us where to land. So we snuck right in there. And just a few hundred yards away, on down the beach, it was like thunder and lightning and forest fires. If we'd have landed there, we'd have been blown to bits. Literally blown to bits."

"Well," I say, "somebody was smart. You must have had one bright commander, anyway."

"Yes. That was pretty sharp. The funny part was, once we hit the beach, they told us to dig in, and it was coral. Coral rock. An inch or two of sand and you'd hit rock. So we got out our shovels and our trenching tools, and we did the best we could." He laughs. "We were pretty scared. Well, we were out there in the open! They could have shelled us anytime. But then they told us to move out, and I wasn't sorry to get off that beach. There was the jungle in front of us, and we walked right in, just waded in a few yards, and there we spent the night. I didn't sleep much, I can tell you that."

"No," I say, "I don't imagine."

"In the morning there was a little river ahead of us, and that's why we had stopped, and it flowed around like this," he says, drawing an invisible map on the table with his finger, "and poured into a bigger river that emptied in the ocean. And that was Rice Anchorage. We were sort of pinned down because of that river and I don't know what else, but we couldn't advance for several days. We were stuck, and it was coral rock. But at least we were off the beach.

"And then, all the time out there, why, all that night, we could hear PT boats scurrying around. And John Kennedy was out there."

"Is that right?" I say.

"Oh, yes. Bougainville. New Georgia. I can't think now. Was it Bougainville or New Georgia where he was? Well, it's all the same. It's right in The Slot, what they call The Slot. Islands on this side and islands over here. All kinds of islands in there. And that's where John Kennedy was."

"Not that night."

"I think it was. I believe he was there that night."

"Yeah?"

"I'm not sure, but I think it was. And then, afterward, every night we'd hear gunfights out there. PT boats roaring and taking off. Machine-gun fire. And we'd hear naval battles out there, regular naval battles. Big battles took place out there. They really stopped them in the Solomons. You see, the Japanese would try to reinforce their men on Guadalcanal, and they'd come down that Slot with soldiers and supplies. That was a tough battle for Guadalcanal, but after that we had a base, an air base. But the navy really stopped them. And that's when the tide of the war started to turn, and we were able to get to the Philippines, and so on. Fierce battles out there, big sea battles."

"And John Kennedy, huh? No kidding."

"He was there. And that's a fact. It's in the books."

"Why didn't you ever vote for him, then? I mean, there he was, protecting you, and you never even voted for him."

"But he was a Democrat. And Catholic and so on."

"Them Catholics," I say. Dave covers his head as if he were being attacked.

"Well, what about me?" my father says. "I was protecting him, too. He never voted for me that I know of."

"You never ran for anything," Dave says.

"Yes, I did. I did, too. I ran for the church board that one time. I won, too. Remember that? Where was John Kennedy then?"

Everybody laughs. "The only reason you won that job was because no one else wanted it," I remind him. "Besides, how could Kennedy vote for you, anyhow? He was Catholic."

"Exactly. That's exactly what I'm saying. Anyhow, that's where he was, and I think that's where he got shot up, where his boat was sunk, and he had to swim and save that fellow's life and so forth."

"But what about you?" I ask. "What happened to you? You're still stuck there in the jungle on that coral rock."

"Well, there we were, and that's where, every night, Washing Machine Charlie would come."

"Oh, that's where he was," Johnny smiles. "I was waiting for him. Old Washing Machine Charlie."

"Japanese. And every night he would come in his airplane, and he'd shut off his engine, and you'd hear the rush of the wind through the struts of his airplane. Whoo," my father whispers. "And then: Wham! Wham! Two big bombs would go off. Then the motor would start up, and he'd take off again.

"And everyone was warned: Don't fire at him. Don't fire your rifles at him. You'll give away your position. So we never did. Until finally, one night, some guy couldn't contain himself any longer, and he opened up. He shot every round in his rifle."

I say, "Kind of cracked a little bit, huh?"

My father laughs. He's looking at the wall as if he were watching a movie. "I think a machine gun started up, too! He was kind of low, and that's why they fired at him. And I believe they actually got him! He sputtered after that, and, I don't know, I think they got him. Because after that night we didn't have any trouble with him anymore."

"Man. So then where did you go?" I ask.

"And, you know, that was one of the worst things, for me, that I experienced in the war. Just that plane coming over. Hearing the rush of it. And then, where is he? Where are the bombs going to fall? I think most of the guys were that way. Just hugged the earth, you know. No place to go. Because you couldn't dig down."

"Oh, yeah. That coral rock."

"That's right. But finally we got rid of him, and then we advanced."

"But didn't you have antiaircraft guns or anything?" Dave says. "Couldn't you—"

"Oh, no. We came in on those rafts, remember. We didn't have anything like that. Nothing big enough. Oof! But then we moved inland."

"To rescue those marines," Johnny says.

"Yes. It wasn't a few days, and we had to go inland to relieve this group of marines."

He seems to be stuck or confused. "Wasn't there something about a slough, some swamp you had to go through?" Johnny says, trying to help.

"No, now, that was on the way back out of there. Oh, yes. You see, there was this marine outfit, and they had been sent in earlier, and their job was to make a roadblock. They were supposed to cut a supply line, this Japanese supply line, a trail that ran over the mountains down to the inlet. They were being supplied by their people over in Munda, and the marines were to go in and cut that supply line. And they had actually done that. But they were surrounded in the process, and they'd been hit. They were trapped in a terrible firefight, and our outfit was supposed to go up there, penetrate the enemy lines, break through the lines, and relieve them."

"The whole division?" Dave says.

"What? Oh, no. This was just our outfit, just our company. We had these native guides. They showed us the trail, and we got in there toward evening. And I remember this guy who was a cook in our company. Did I tell you about him?" he says to Johnny.

"I can't remember."

"He was from Akron. He was never on the line or anything like that. He was a cook, an older fellow, and he wasn't in very good condition. But he had to go along. Didn't do any cooking. Had to carry a rifle and pack, just like the rest of us. It was pretty tough going, and on the way up there he got completely worn out."

"Oh, that guy," Johnny says.

"And it was toward evening. He said: 'I can't go any farther.' And the company commander said: 'Well, you'll have to stay here, then.' So the company went on without him. He was the most forlorn-looking guy I've ever seen. Sitting there all by himself. And night was coming on. Sitting there with his rifle. His face was just like ash. And struggling for breath and so on.

"So we went on. But then the company commander called to me and said: 'I want you to go back and get that man's rifle. We might need it.' So I said, 'Okay,' and I went back. It was getting darker by now, and I retraced my steps. I was careful approaching him, because I was afraid he might think I was a Japanese. Then I called out to him. And he saw me." My father smiles as if he were greeting an old friend.

"I'd never talked to him very much, because, well, he was a different kind of guy. Older and so on. And back at camp he was always mouthing off. He wasn't doing that now. Boy, he was *quiet*.

"I came up to him and said: 'I have to take your gun. I hate to do it, but I have to do it. They told me I had to come and get it.' He said, 'Okay,' and he handed me the gun. I just hated to leave him there all by himself. Well, we sort of talked to each other. He said, 'Good luck to you.' And I said, 'Hope you make it back all right.' And then I left him."

"And there he sat," I say.

"Yes, and this was jungle, now, and I can't even describe it."

I try to picture it and end up seeing something like a painting by Rousseau: thick, mysterious, and threatening. "Whatever happened to him?" I ask.

"That's just it. I don't know. I never saw that man again. I don't know if he was killed, or if he got lost in there, or if he was transferred out, or what. But I still see him sitting there beside that trail.

"And then I left him, and I was all alone. It's night now, and I made my way back up that trail and caught up with the company. By this time we were in the area where those marines were supposed to be, and you could hear firing up ahead. We must have got into the phone lines, or I don't know if we had walkie-talkies yet or not, but they got in contact with the marine commander. We passed some dead Japanese. Then we got up there, and we stopped."

"Were those your first dead?" I say and hate myself for having read so much. I'm talking like some character in a fucking book, but this is my father! This is his life!

He says, "Yes. Those were the first, the first dead bodies I had seen. But we went in beyond that, and then the captain said: 'Dig in. Make yourselves as comfortable as you can. Try to get some sleep. And be sure your defensive positions are covered.' So they put out guards. And there was firing in the night. And then, before we'd settled in, one of the officers came around, and he told us: 'We're going to make a bayonet attack in the morning. So we'll wake you up, and you fix bayonets. We're going in. So get some sleep.' "

I say, "Sleep tight! Who can sleep after that?"

"But we did. We were so worn out. We did get *some* sleep."

"Good Lord."

"I know I did, because it was the firing of the guns that woke me up. They were firing machine guns and mortars and everything. Our boys were. Just mass stuff. Trying to soften up the Japanese, you see, before we went in there. So we got set.

"The company commander. Company commanders changed all the time! They were always getting killed or transferred or Lord knows what. But this one was a good one, I remember. Big guy. He was tough. He got up there, and he took out his .45. Big black .45. He waved it in the air, and he said: 'All right, men. Let's go!' He urged us on, you know.

"I think the First Platoon was supposed to go in first. So their scouts were asked to lead the way. They started in, like that, and then they stopped. Bogged down. They wouldn't go any farther. Scared stiff, I guess.

"Then our platoon was told to do this. So our scouts went ahead, and they kept going! Then one of the scouts turned, and he waved to our platoon leader to come up. But the platoon leader turned to the sergeant, and he said, 'You go up.' It was really the lieutenant's job, you see. But he told the sergeant to take his place. So that lieutenant was never really trusted after that.

"So then this sergeant, Sergeant Handy—he was from Chicago—he ran up and did the right thing. Little guy. Short guy. He was really a good guy, and he did the right thing. He dashed out there, and he'd run a few steps and then throw himself flat. Then he'd jump up and run and throw himself flat. He got up to where the scouts were, and then he came back. He said: 'The Japanese have left. They've gone in the night.' "

I lean back in my chair. Dave has both hands on his head, as if to keep the top from coming off.

"Boy, what a relief!" my father laughs.

"Whoa!" I say. "And there you stood, with your bayonets on."

"Man," my father says.

"But why had they left?" Dave says. "They had those guys surrounded!"

"I guess they'd had enough. They'd been fighting for a number of days. They'd lost a lot of men. And they knew that we were coming."

"That sergeant," Johnny says. "Sergeant Handy? Weren't you with him all the way through? Didn't you go out with him?"

"That's right. That's true. I did go out with him. And on the way back, on the boat, he read funny books all the way back to the States." He laughs. "Every time I'd look at him, here he'd be reading a funny book. And he was from Chicago. Roger Handy. Once, a few years back, when we were driving through Chicago, I stopped and called him up. It turned out he owned a beer joint. But he was happy to hear from me. That was fun to talk."

"But you didn't go see him?" Dave says.

"No, this was on the phone. Well, he was kind of out of the way, and it was a beer joint, and I had your mother in the car. You know."

"But you should have gone to see him!" Dave says. "What's the matter with you, anyhow?"

"Well, we had somewhere to get to. I suppose I should have. It sure was fun to talk."

"Let's go back up on that mountain," I say. "The Japanese had left. So did you stay there then?"

"For a while, yes. We had to help those fellows who'd been hit. They were glad to see us, I can tell you that."

"I'll bet."

"I can't forget their faces. The look in their eyes. They thought they were dead! They'd been fighting for days. And they were all torn up. Many of their friends were killed, they'd seen their buddies killed. And there were many wounded. So we helped those guys, helped fix up the wounded and took care of the bodies and whatnot. And then, I can't remember how, but not long after that, they picked us up and took us back to Guadalcanal."

"To regroup, or what?"

"To regroup, yes, to recover from what we'd been through. To get us ready for the next thing, which was Bougainville. But as soon as we got back, why, everybody started getting sick."

"Sick," I say. "What kind of sick?"

"I mean good and sick. It was the conditions we'd been through there on New Georgia. Terrible conditions. Just awful up in there. The water was bad. You had to use tablets, and some of the fellows forgot or thought they didn't need them, and they got malaria. Then it was raining. And the mud. It was tough going, and we didn't have enough to eat. Only about a third of a meal all the time. Then we were up there with dead bodies. And handling dead bodies. It's no wonder we got sick."

"What do you mean?" I ask.

"The bodies! We had to take care of the bodies at that roadblock. We put them in our shelter halves. Each man had a canvas shelter half inside his pack, and you put your half together with another guy when you made camp, and you were together, and that was your tent. Like a pup tent. Anyhow, we put the bodies in our shelter halves, and then we had to carry them down out of there. It was hot, so we had to go fast. So we took a shortcut through the jungle. And that's when we had to cross that swamp," he says, pointing at Johnny. "We were up to our waists in goop, and struggling with the bodies, and our feet were killing us. Oh, it was terrible conditions.

"And then, when we reached the beach, and we had rested some, then they sent us back along a certain trail. There'd been a battle. Marines again. They'd been going along a jungle trail, and they'd been hit. Most of them were killed. There should have been better scouting. But it's hard to scout in the jungle. You can't just go off in the jungle. So easy to get lost in there, and—

"We had to pick up the bodies. And the thing about the jungle is, the bodies decompose so fast. Hot. And wet. Steaming hot. And so. So I found the remains of one guy. And he was gone! Just bones. And the battle had happened just a few days before! I did what I could. I had to sort of gather up the bones. And I put them in my shelter half. And so. The tag was still there . . . the—"

"Dog tags," Dave says gently.

"Identification tags, yes, dog tags. So you knew. So I carried him back to the shore, down to the beach, and by this time they had a bulldozer there. The bulldozer dug a great big grave. A mass grave. They just lined up the bodies. Made sure one tag was on the man and one was put in the records."

"So that's why there's two," Dave murmurs.

"And then they just pushed them in and covered them up. I think those graves were dug up later on and maybe the bodies, the bones were sent back. I don't know. I don't know for sure."

"I never heard that," Johnny says in a choked voice. "What?"

"You never told me that."

"No. I haven't thought about that. Not for a long time."

This is my father. I've seen photographs of concentration camps and bodies stacked like firewood, but those were pictures. This is my father. And now I remember the nightmares my grandmother mentioned, and how, for months after he returned from the war, my father would wake up screaming in the night. He was twenty-three—ten years younger, then, than I am now.

"Those were the kind of conditions," he says, "and that's why we got sick. I never got malaria that I know of. I was faithful in taking the tablets they gave you, so I never got that, and we had shots for yellow fever before we left the States, but I got yellow jaundice."

"This is hepatitis?" I say.

"Hepatitis, yes, but we called it yellow jaundice.

When we got back to Guadalcanal I knew there was something wrong with me. I couldn't eat. I'd go up to the chow line, and I couldn't stand it. Couldn't stand the smell of food. But I was hungry! So I knew there was something wrong. I went to the doctor, and he said, 'You better go to the hospital.' They put me in the hospital—it was a tent hospital—and I got very sick that night. Fever. Sweating. Sort of delirious. The next morning the doctor came around and looked at me. He sat down beside my cot, and he talked to me a little bit. He said, 'You were awfully sick last night.' I said, 'What's wrong with me?' He said, 'Let me look at you.' He uncovered my legs, and he said, 'It's yellow jaundice.' I looked down at my legs, and they were yellow. And after that, of course, I got yellow all over. My face was very yellow. I got yellow as a Jap. It's from not having the right kind of food or bad food and stuff like that."

"Interesting," I say. "This was after New Georgia?"

"This was on Guadalcanal, but we picked it up on New Georgia. That's where we got it. And I was sick for three weeks.

"But that's when, one day, there was a stir outside the tent, and somebody was coming. Some people stepped inside, and I looked over there, and there was a woman! I hadn't seen a woman—a white woman, anyhow—in over a year. And here it was Eleanor."

"You're kidding!" I say. "Eleanor Roosevelt?"

"It was Eleanor Roosevelt. And I was very glad to see her. I suppose she stood a little farther than from you to me. She looked at us and greeted us, and she was talking. She made a little speech. How her husband was concerned about us. How she wanted to express her thanks. All that. Real nice speech. A very gracious lady." All of us are smiling.

"My ideas of her changed completely after that. I always had a soft spot in my heart for Eleanor. She did a very dangerous thing. Because it was dangerous in the skies, and she flew in there. The higher-ups in the military tried to persuade her not to go in there, and she said, 'I'm going!' And she flew in. Yes, she did. She did that. And visited the men in different places, went from tent to tent, one after another, and thanked us for what we were doing."

"What was the different idea?" I ask. "What was the different idea you'd had of her before?"

"Well, many people were making fun of her. They said she was trying to run the country. But she really did come overseas when her husband didn't want her to. She did a dangerous thing. And I always had a soft spot after that."

"I think you must be soft in the head," my mother says. We look up, startled. She stands in the kitchen doorway, clutching her quilted housecoat together at the throat. "What's the matter with you, Harvey? Look at the clock. It's after midnight! How are you ever going to get up?"

Nobody says anything, so I say, "Why should anyone get up? There's a blizzard out there. We might as well sleep in."

"Well," she says, "it's past his bedtime, anyhow. Good gracious, but it's cold in here! You know how you are, Harvey. You'll be stiff as a board tomorrow, sitting up in the cold like this."

"I've got a cap on," he says. "We were talking."

"Yes, and eating, too, I see. What have you done to that turkey, David? It's nothing but bones! I was planning on sandwiches tomorrow."

"Sorry, Mom," Dave says. He looks both surprised and guilty. "I guess I wasn't thinking. I was listening to Dad."

"You never did think of anybody but yourself." She sighs. "Well, put the food away when you're done." She goes to the sink and drinks a glass of water. Her skin is pale, almost translucent, and she looks emaciated as a saint. She seems to have stretched out over the years, grown taller, while my father has slowly slumped. I notice the crimped lines around her mouth, the sunken cheeks, and I think I must have loved her once, but I can't remember when. "What on earth have you been talking about?" she says.

"The war," I tell her. "We were asking Dad about the war."

"Oh, that," she says with disdain. "Well, come to bed soon, will you, Harvey? It's cold in there. And try to talk more softly. The girls are trying to sleep."

"Why don't you turn up the thermostat?" Johnny says.

"You haven't seen our heating bills."

"Put on another blanket, then."

"I don't have another blanket. We have some extra people in the house, you know. I only have so many blankets."

"Maybe you'd like us to go home," Dave says.

"You can't go home. There's a blizzard. I don't mean that. You're welcome here, you know that. It's just that I'm cold. Come to bed now, Harvey."

"In a minute," he says. "I'll be there in a minute." This is how he deals with her. Passive resistance. Delaying tactics. She snipes at him, and he turns turtle, withdraws to someplace deep that she can't reach. They never fight. The idea seems to be to maintain the peace at any price, and it's expensive.

"Well," my mother says. "Well, good night, then. Don't stay up all night. And clean up after yourselves. I don't want to see a lot of dirty dishes in the morning."

"Okay," Johnny says. "Sleep tight."

"Night, Mom," Dave says.

I say, "Night," and she retreats down the hallway, her slippers slapping the linoleum.

I've come to think there's almost nothing you can do about your parents except attempt to understand them, to minimize the damage. Even that much is difficult to manage. My wife had to teach me how to fight. I remember the first time I yelled at her. Twenty years of anger in that scream. She'd wanted it. She'd nursed that fury out of me with all the craft and patience of a witch doctor, but when I finally let her have it, she was terrified. She curled up in a corner of our bare apartment and whimpered for half an hour. I felt sick for having lost control. Yet, looking back, I see that night as the real beginning of our marriage. Here, in this house, no one hollers, no one cries. And after half a dozen years of scrapping with my wife, I'm still afraid of ending up like this. Because my folks were happy once. I've seen snapshots. I've heard stories.

Dave is clearing the food off the table, storing it in the fridge. Johnny stands and reaches for the ceiling. "I'm whipped," he says. "I might as well give up the ghost."

"Come on," I tell him, "you're the youngest. You're supposed to be used to this. Don't you guys stay up at school?"

"That's the problem. I was cramming for finals all last week. I'm beat."

I don't want the night to end. "Aw, sit down," I say. "We haven't even heard about the Philippines."

"You mean the Battle of Manila? All of that? I've already fought that one."

"Okay," I say, "party pooper." I get up and go to the window, cup my hands against the glass, and peer out into the night.

"Still coming down?" Johnny says.

"You should see it. Hey," I say, "let's go out there."

"Are you crazy?" Dave says. "It's freezing!"

"No, it's not. It's never so cold when it snows. Come on."

"I'll go," Johnny says, "but then I've got to get some sleep."

"Dad?" I say. "You want to go for a walk?"

"What?" He's still inside himself somewhere.

"We're going out to look at the storm. Want to come?"

"I guess not. You go ahead. I'll just clean up in here."

The hallway is always chilly. I shiver into my coat, pluck Dave's parka off the hook, and toss it at him. He groans and bends over his boots. "Hurry up," I tell him. "Johnny's already out there."

We stand on the porch and watch the snow descend. "Beautiful," Dave says. "Look how bright. It's the middle of the night!"

"I know. Isn't it weird? It's like an X ray. It's like another planet."

"Where did Johnny go?"

"I don't know. There he is. Look at him. He's ten years old." Johnny waves and lobs a snowball. "Come on," I say to Dave. "Let's walk around the block."

We wade off through the snow. It's knee-deep on the level, deeper in the drifts. A few strands of Christmas lights blink and glow along the street. Otherwise, the world is black and white and shades of gray. An abandoned car sits like a small white hill in the middle of the intersection. We stop to catch our breath. "Man, is it quiet," Dave says. "It's like after the bomb."

"Except that wouldn't be so pretty. Look at the load on the trees. Some of those branches will break before morning."

We set off again. "Those were some stories Dad was telling," Dave says. "I had no idea."

"Me either. I'd heard some of it, I guess, but I never knew it was as bad as that. He was really in it. I've never heard him talk like that. Too bad Mom had to spoil everything."

"Maybe we can get him going again tomorrow."

"I doubt it."

"Me, too," he says. "It's hard. I wish those two could get along."

"I wish they'd get divorced."

"Come on."

"I mean it. They don't do each other any good that I can see. The way she badgers him. It's embarrassing. Why doesn't he stand up to her?"

"I know," Dave says, "but he's hardly any better. He barely speaks to her. You notice how he goes away? Half the time he doesn't even answer her. That drives her nuts," he laughs. "They'd never get divorced. It's not the Christian thing to do."

"Yeah, right. The Christian thing to do is hate each other and pretend that everything is hunky-dory."

"They don't hate each other."

"No?"

"Well, maybe, but there's something else there, too. They have their friendly moments. You've seen how they remember things together. Sorting through photographs and stuff."

"That's piss-poor consolation for the bitterness."

"I suppose," Dave says. "But they've been through a lot. They're companions, anyhow. They've got that, their history."

"It's not enough."

"Really, Sam, it's not so bad. They still like to sleep together."

I say, "Bullshit. Cowshit, fuck, goddamn."

Dave looks at me and laughs. "What's the matter?"

"It's just so fucking fun to swear! Christ, I can barely talk in there for fear I'm going to blurt some filth and give the old man a heart attack. I'm afraid he'd die of disappointment."

"It's a strain," Dave smiles. "Especially for a smut-mouth like you. What can you do?"

"It's their house," I say. "But it pisses me off. It makes me feel like a fucking hypocrite. I used to brag about how honest I could be with my old man. 'I can tell him anything,' I used to say. Who changed? Did we? Hypocrisy. That's what I used to accuse his generation of."

"Quit beating yourself. You said it: It's his house."

"All right. So I'm excused. But, God, I'm getting old! I'm just like everybody else. That's what I hate about growing up. That's practically a definition, isn't it? Realizing you've got the same capacity for crap as everybody else. Just another asshole in the rain."

"Snow," Dave says. "In the snow. We're going to be up to our assholes, too, by morning. Look at this." He breaks trail through a drift, and I come up beside him.

"You really think they still like to sleep together?"

"I know it," Dave laughs. "They stayed with us a couple days last summer. We put them in the guest room, and you know what that's like. There's just that single bed. So I borrowed a mattress from the neighbors and laid it on the floor. We thought Mom could use the bed and Dad would be all right there on the mattress. It was comfortable enough. But you know what? When I brought them coffee in the morning, they were both down on the floor. They'd pulled the mattress off the bed and pushed the two of them together. There they were. Snug as a bug in a rug." He laughs. "Martha couldn't believe it."

"No fooling," I say. "That surprises me, too."

We turn into our street, and the snow stings our faces. Dave grunts and raises his arm like a shield. We lean into the wind, and then, for some relief, turn and walk backwards for a bit.

"Look at that," I tell him. "Look in the streetlight. You can really see it."

"It's like a million feathers."

"Confetti," I tell him. "It looks like confetti to me."

"No, it's not. It's coconut. Shredded coconut. Definitely coconut."

"You're disgusting. All you ever think about is food." I give him a shove, and he stumbles and falls in the snow.

"Cruel," he groans. He rolls over on his back and looks up at me. "You haven't changed. You're just as mean as when we were kids."

"I'm sorry," I say, laughing. "Was I as bad as that? Here." I offer him my hand. He sits up slowly, then grabs my wrist and yanks me into the snowbank beside him. "Betrayed," I say, "by the old Indian trick." I sit up and shake the powder out of my cap.

"Serves you right," Dave says. "No, you weren't so bad. You just did what older brothers are supposed to do. Ran away. Hid my toys. Washed my face with snow. Stuff like that. You were okay."

I sink back in the drift. The snow is cold but comfortable. "This is kind of cool," I say. "It's like a featherbed."

"Remember when we lived in Rock Rapids and we'd go sledding every night after school?"

"Sure," I tell him. "Jackson's Hill. That was a terrific hill. And that reminds me. Did I ever tell you about the Christmas of the red bobsled?" Dave laughs. "I remember everything," I say. "Skating on the river. Remember that? How we'd steal matches from the kitchen and build big bonfires right on the ice?" I sit up and look at him. "What in the hell are you doing?"

"What does it look like, idiot? I'm making an angel."

"Good God. I haven't done that in a hundred years."

"I know," he grunts, flapping his arms in the snow. "That's because . . . you don't have kids. You *are* getting old . . . if you can't . . . remember angels. You should have . . . some kids."

"We can't afford it. Are you and Martha?"

"Maybe. Can't decide. Come on," he says. "Don't just sit there. Make an angel."

"Dave," I say, sinking back, "we're too old for this." I smash the back of my head in the snow to make a good impression, then flap my arms and kick sideways, as if I were swimming on my back. Snowflakes flicker in my face. I close my eyes, and suddenly I feel a mem-

ory, fragile as a cobweb, floating toward me through
the dark. I stop and think, listening, and then I see my
father in a pool of light, kneeling on the kitchen floor.
He has a hammer and a screwdriver, and he's trying to
open something. It's tough and brown and hairy. It
scares me, because my father has just mentioned witch
doctors and headhunters, and I think the thing he's
working on might be a shrunken head. Remembering,
I understand the foreign language he was speaking. The
Fijis and New Guinea, Bougainville, the Philippines.
Inside my memory, though, I can't understand it, and
so I ask my mother, who's unpacking groceries. "It's a
coconut," she says. "They were on sale. They grow on
trees, like apples. Not around here, but where it's hot.
Across the ocean. Your father used to eat them when
he was in the war." She laughs and puts a hand on my
father's shoulder, leaning over him. "How's it coming,
honey?" "I don't know," he says. "I seem to have forgotten how. Wait a minute. Here we go." He hammers
on the screwdriver, and the bright shaft disappears inside
the shell. He grunts and pulls it out. "Get a glass," he
says, and I watch with fascination as he tilts the coconut
and fills the glass with juice. He takes a sip and smiles.
Then he hands the glass to me. "Go ahead," he says.
"Try it." I sniff the stuff and say, "What is it?" He says,
"Milk." "Milk is from cows," I tell him. "That's right,"
he smiles, "but this is different. This is the milk of the
coconut. Go ahead. You'll like it." I taste it and smile.
"It's good!" I say. "It's sweet!" "I told you. Let Mom
have some." She drinks a little, then hands it back to
me. "You can finish it," she says. I drain the glass and
lick my lips. My father pounds the coconut. It doesn't
want to break. He makes a lot of noise and finally cracks
it open. "There," he says and holds up half the shell.
It's white inside. "That's the meat," he says, pointing
at the white. I say, "Meat?" "That's what you call it.
That's the meat." He pries a piece free with a fork.
"Here," he tells me, "try some. Eat it." I put it in my

mouth. It's good and chewy. He hands my mother some and eats a piece himself. Kneeling there on the floor, he seems happy. "We used to eat these all the time," he says, "when I was in the war." "When was that?" I want to know. "Was I there, too?" My mother laughs. He says, "You weren't born yet. It was a long time ago, when I was in the army. A long way from here. On the islands in the ocean overseas." "Oh," I say. "Can I have some more?" "Sure," he says. "We've got plenty."

"Earth to Sam, Earth to Sam," Dave says. "Come in, please. Are you asleep, or what?"

"What?" He's standing over me. "I was just remembering," I murmur, "the milk of human kindness."

"My God," he says. "You're getting as bad as the old man. Come on. Get up. You'll freeze to death." He offers me his hand. "Be careful, now," he warns. "Don't wreck it."

He hauls me up. I step out of my angel and turn to admire the impressions we've made. "Look at that," Dave says. "It's art!"

"That's a laugh. They'll be buried by morning."

"You can't bury angels," Dave says. "Besides, it's not the product but the process that counts. The experience. Where have you been, anyhow? This is exactly where modern art is at. Performance. Here today, gone tomorrow, just like life. We could make a living doing this."

"Bullshit."

"That's what they said about Picasso. You're just a philistine. You only prove my point. This is worth money, boy. I'm giving mine a title." He leans down and writes *Finite Angel #1* and signs his name. "Come on," he says. "Aren't you going to sign yours? They're worth more if you sign them."

I write *Look Homeward Angel* in the snow and sign it *Thomas Wolfe*. "Clever," Dave laughs. "Way too literary, though. You'll never make it in New York. Let's go. I'm getting cold."

We shuffle up the hill to our parents' place. "Look at the cars," Dave says. "They must be twice their normal size." His Volkswagen is slewed sideways in a drift. The rear end sticks out in the street. He walks over and clears the snow off the windshield. "You think they're going to plow?"

"Not tonight. It's Christmas. Besides, they won't do anything until it quits. You're all right. We'll dig you out tomorrow."

"Toyota running all right?"

"Jim-dandy," I tell him. "Sixty thousand miles, now, without one serious repair. It's made me a believer."

"Ouch! What the hell?"

I say, "It's Johnny," and another snowball puffs the powder at our feet.

"That little asshole," Dave says, digging the snow out of his hood. Another snowball sails by. We duck behind the Volkswagen. I can hear Johnny laughing.

"Let's get him."

"The snow's too dry," Dave says. "I can't make it stick."

"You have to clear away the powder. Use the stuff that's underneath." I make myself two snowballs, stand up to throw, and get hit in the neck. "Christ," I say. "The little bastard's got an arm!" I fire both snowballs and miss by six feet.

"He was a Little League star, remember? We taught him everything he knows," Dave laughs.

I crawl around the car to get a look and see that Johnny's built a fort. He's dug a hole and heaped up snow in front of it and piled a supply of snowballs, neat as cannonballs, where he can reach them easily. He spots me, throws, and ducks out of sight. "Look," I say to Dave, "he's dug in over there. We'll never get him this way. Get yourself an armful, and we'll charge."

"Right," Dave says, looking up. "You go round that way. I'll come in from here."

"Ready?"

Dave says, "Go!" and we race across the street, throwing on the run and hollering, "Yee-haw! Geronimo!"

Johnny can't escape the hole he's dug himself. Dave leaps the bank and grabs him before he can flounder out of the fort. "Get him!" Dave shouts. "Wash his ugly face!" Dave holds him by the shoulders while I scoop up a handful of powder and scrub Johnny's face.

"Okay, okay!" Johnny shouts, spitting snow. "I surrender!"

We all fall back, giggling and gasping for air. "Oh, man," Johnny laughs. "I really got you guys. You never knew what hit you."

"Don't gloat," Dave says, "or you'll get another faceful."

I haul myself out of the snowbank. "Let's go in," I say. "I'm pooped."

Johnny says, "You old geeks got no endurance. Bunch of wimps."

I give him a stiff-arm in the back. He slips but keeps his feet and runs up to the porch. Light still glows in the living room, and the Christmas tree blinks. My father stands in the picture window, looking out at us. I wave and follow Johnny to the porch. The three of us stand there, stomping the snow off our boots and watching the storm. Then Dave says, " 'Well, I guess they're not coming,' " and we laugh and go inside.

My father meets us in the entry with a broom. "Here," he says. "Here, now." And one after another, as if we were sides of meat being basted, he turns us slowly round and brushes off the snow. "That looked like fun," he says. "Is it cold?"

"Not so bad," Dave says, "once you get used to it. My hands are frozen, though."

"Come on in the kitchen," my father says. "We'll turn on the oven."

Once we're in the kitchen, I see the old man has changed into his bathrobe. He's still got the stocking cap. His feet are insulated by heavy wool socks and a pair of ugly slippers with inch-thick soles that look like sponges. His calves are covered by the white waffle pattern of his long underwear. He asks me, "Is it drifting?"

"Is it ever. We're really socked in. That's quite an outfit," I tell him. "We should have given you a nightcap."

"I don't need one. I've got one. What's wrong with this one?"

"Nothing," I laugh. "There's nothing wrong with it, but we could buy you something a little more stylish."

"Once you get to be my age, you could care less about fashion. I want to keep warm, that's all." He turns on the stove and opens up the oven. "Here," he says, dragging over two chairs. "Have a seat. This ought to thaw you out."

Dave and I sit down, rubbing our hands and faces. "Is there any coffee left?" Dave says.

"I thought you might want some," my father says, "so I brewed another pot. Though how you guys can sleep with this stuff on your stomachs is beyond me." He hands us each a steaming mug. The hot ceramic warms my fingers. "Go ahead," he says. "Put your feet right up there on the door."

"I remember when we used to do this," I tell him, "when we were kids. In the mornings in the winter you'd be making pancakes or whatever, and we'd sit in our pajamas with our feet propped up like this."

"I got that from my father," he says. "That's how I remember him. We spent a lot of time in the kitchen in the old days. Well, it was the only really warm room in the house. And that's how I remember him—sitting in a flannel shirt, reading something, with his feet inside the oven. That was a wood stove, of course. These electric ones are different. It's a different quality of heat. It seems to me that these give off a cold kind of heat, comparatively speaking."

Johnny comes in with his sleeping bag in hand. He says, "Good night, you guys."

"Where you going?" I ask him. "To sleep in a snowbank?"

"I'm on the couch. Dave and Martha were assigned to my old room. You know how it is. Us young ones always get shoved out in the cold."

"Poor thing."

"Aren't you going to warm up first?" Dave says.

"Naw. This is goose down. I'll be toasty in a minute."

"All right, then. See you in the morning."

"Night," he says. "Don't get me up too early."

"Ha," Dave says. "Mom will take care of that."

"We won't," my father says. "Sleep tight."

My face and fingers tingle as they warm. The coffee helps. Dave shivers and moves his feet closer to the heating coils.

Then my father says, "I found this in the attic. I thought you might be interested." Almost shyly, half amused, he hands me a sheet of yellow paper that looks like a diploma. A form filled in with names and dates and signatures.

Dave says, "Dad. You shouldn't be going up there. It's like a meat locker up there."

"I know it. But you boys got me thinking."

"What is it?" Dave asks me.

"It's his discharge papers. Look at that. See, here it says the date he left the States, and when he got to Bougainville, the Philippines, and here's when he got back. 16 June 1945. And here it says the shots for yellow fever. What's this, Dad?" I point. "This here. It says decorations."

"Oh," he says, leaning over my shoulder, "that's nothing. Those are just your service ribbons that you got to wear. You had a different one for each campaign that you were in. It's just a bar, a small colored bar, and then I think there was a little star in the middle if you'd actually seen action. That's all it was. And then, here, see, you had your service stripes—hashmarks, they were called—and they went on your sleeve and showed how long you'd been in."

"I see. But then what's this? What's this about a Bronze Star?"

"Does it say that? Let me see that."

"Right here. Look." I hand the paper back.

"I never noticed that," he says, astonished. "It says so, though, doesn't it?" He laughs. "He must have put me in for that after all. I thought he was only talking. Huh. I never got it, though. They never gave it to me."

"What?" Dave says. "Who put you in for what?"

"Oh, this Lieutenant Carver. He told me he was going to see I got a Bronze Star, but he never did. At least I never got the medal. But now I look at this I have to think he really did do that. It's here on paper, anyhow." He laughs, as if he were speaking of a Boy Scout merit badge. "Isn't that funny? I never noticed that. After all these years."

"You ought to write for it," I tell him. "They'd have to give it to you. You really ought to have it."

"Oh, I don't care about it now." He thinks a minute, smiles. "Maybe I should, though. Maybe I should do that."

"Of course you should," Dave says. "If you don't want it, I would. It would be a souvenir, a family heirloom, sort of."

"What did you do?" I say. "How did you earn it?"

"I don't know," my father scoffs. "A Bronze Star isn't anything. It's not for bravery or anything like that. It's for, well, 'meritorious service' is what they call it. Those were the words. 'Meritorious service.' That's all it is. Now, the Silver Star, that meant something. But not the Bronze."

"But you must have done something," I say. "Everybody didn't get them, did they?"

"Oh, well," my father says, "I remember this Lieutenant Carver. He was what you call a ninety-day wonder."

"A what?"

"A ninety-day wonder. He wasn't a real officer back in the States. He went to school overseas. In the Fijis, I believe. They were short of officers, you see, so you could put in for this course. And he did that. He was just a sergeant in another company before, but he went to school, and they made him a lieutenant, and then he came into our company. Along with his pal, Lieutenant Overbeck. We had a couple of these guys, these ninety-day wonders."

"Terrific term," Dave laughs.

"Yes, well, this Lieutenant Carver, he was a ninety-day wonder, but he was all right, and he kind of liked me. We shared a foxhole once. I think this was the Philippines. We were together for a couple nights, and we were talking. He didn't act like a lieutenant then. It was more like we were buddies. He was married, and he had a couple kids, and we talked about our families. All of that. And he told me then that he was going to see I got a Bronze Star."

"How come, though?" I ask. "Just because he liked you?"

"He'd seen some things, I guess. I never knew for sure. Maybe it was in Manila. I thought it might be that. It wasn't really anything. Except that it was fighting in the street, and we came to this house. It was a real nice house. Or at least it had been, before the war. There was a courtyard, and we were in that courtyard. There was a gate, a large gate, and I saw where this wire was down. Telephone wire. They'd had it strung up on that gatepost, but now it was down on the ground. And I could see where vehicles were passing back and forth. Trucks. And tanks. Why, they'd chew that wire up. As a runner, see, I knew about communications. I figured we needed it, so I ran out in the street and picked up the wire and crawled up that gatepost. I shinnied up there near the top and fixed it, fastened that wire back in place. Now, I don't know if he saw that or not, but

I thought that might be it. Because I slid back down. And I ran over to the building. And I turned around and looked. And a shell landed right there and blew it all sky-high."

"Oof," Dave says.

"I think they saw me from that City Hall. There was a tower, and the Japanese had lookouts, they had spotters up in there. They must have seen me. Because I remember: I ran over to that building, and I turned around and looked, and the whole thing blew."

"My God."

"It might have been a worthless wire! But I couldn't say. I couldn't see any breaks in it. So I thought I ought to do that. And I turned around and looked, and the whole thing went."

"So you think that's why you got the medal," I say.

"I thought it might be. Except I never got it. Oh, who knows? Maybe he saw something else. But he told me several times he was going to do that."

Dave is reading the discharge paper. He says, "I'd forgotten you made corporal. How was that? How did you become a corporal?"

"I became a *corporal*," my father smiles, as if rank were a joke, as if Dave had said "general," "I became a *corporal* because Frank Plummer got in trouble with the first sergeant. They had an awful argument, and I was there. The first sergeant demoted him right on the spot. And when he'd gotten rid of Frank, he turned to me, and he said, 'Thorsen, you're going to be mail orderly. You're going to take over Plummer's position.' And I told him right back, I said, 'I don't want it.' He said, 'Well, you're going to take it.' I said, 'I don't want it.' He said, 'You're going to take it.' I said, 'Frank is a good friend of mine. What will he think if I take it over?' He said, 'That doesn't matter. You're going to take it.' And he started to threaten me. 'You're going to take it, or I'll put you on the front lines. Permanently.' Words to that effect. I'll tell you what it was. It was just as if he'd said he'd see me killed. And he meant it, too. He was a terrible guy. Not only that, but morally, too. You know what I mean."

I say, "But you had to work with him all the time, then."

"Yes, I did. And he was no good. He was a bad man. And then the postmaster back at regimental headquarters, he was mad when the first sergeant fired Frank, because Frank had been good at the job, and now he had to train in someone else. I couldn't blame him, but he didn't give me a very warm welcome. So that was hard. He was plenty mad there for a while, but we got along pretty well afterward. I had to take it."

"Sounds tough," I say.

"It was. It was hard at first. And exactly the thing that I predicted happened. Frank was really angry with me. He thought I'd been cozying up to the first sergeant. I said, 'Frank, I didn't want it. I told him and told him, but he wouldn't listen.' Well, we settled it, finally, sort of patched it up. But it was never the same. I lost a good friend there. Frank and I had been good friends, but that spoiled it."

"Well, where was this?" I ask. "Where did all this happen?"

"This was, let me see, this was Bougainville."

"But I don't understand this mail situation. I mean, I know you were a runner, and now you're a mail orderly. What's going on? Were you a member of a communications platoon or something?"

"I don't know why it was, but they picked on me for a number of these jobs." He laughs. "I don't think they knew what to do with me."

"A man of your talents," Dave smiles.

"Well, I could read! I think it was because I had some education. Many of the fellows in our outfit hadn't finished high school. We had a lot of boys from Kentucky and from Tennessee, mountain boys, and they were

good guys, but many of them couldn't even read. There
was nothing wrong with them. It's just that they were
ignorant. They hadn't been to school. So I guess that's
why I kept getting chosen for these jobs."

"Yeah," Dave says, "I notice here it says two
years of college. What was that? I didn't think you'd
been yet."

"Oh, that was Bible school. I'd been to Bible College
down in Minneapolis."

"Oh, yeah, yeah," Dave grins. All of us laugh. "Bible
College," Dave says.

"Well, it was more than most guys had, so I suppose
when they looked at the records . . . and I could type.
I could type a little bit, so they had me in company
headquarters a lot of the time. I'd type up the roster,
things like that."

"Oh," I say, "so you were being shifted around all
the time, then."

"Yes, and that was hard. Because I didn't really belong
anywhere. I'd be in company headquarters, and then
we'd go into combat, and they'd put me up on the line
with a rifle squad. Or they'd use me as a runner running
messages between platoons or back to headquarters. So
that was hard. You couldn't settle in and make friends
the way you wanted to."

"You warm enough?" I ask Dave.

"Fine," he says. I turn off the oven, and we move to
the table.

"So you were the company mailman," I say. "How
did that work? Did you have some sort of office, or
what?"

"It was really a good job," my father grins. "That's
why Frank was so upset. Because you were kind of free.
In the morning I'd take off for regimental headquarters
and pick up the mail. I'd walk down there or catch a
ride, but many mornings I would walk. And I enjoyed
that. Then I'd pick up my mailbag and trip on back. I'd

hold a mail call for the company, and all the guys would come and get their mail. You know how that is. Everybody likes the mailman."

"Sure," I say, "I'm always expecting my ship to come in."

"So that really was a good job. Except that later on it got complicated. Because of all the different things that were happening to the men. You had to have a list, and it got confusing toward the last, because a lot of men were killed. You'd have to send the letters back, and I just hated doing that. And in the Philippines the men were scattered around in different hospitals. So many hurt. I tried to find them, and I got to some of them, but I couldn't get to all of them. It was a mess. And their Christmas packages came late. And the packages were all sticky from what-do-you-call-it. That cake."

"Fruitcake?"

"Fruitcake. To this day I can't stand to look at that stuff."

"I never did like it much," Dave says.

"Well, I did. I used to like it a lot. But not after I had to handle all those packages. I really did try to get around to the hospitals, because we'd been cut up pretty bad, and those fellows needed some good news. So I'd bring their mail and try to talk to them a little bit and see if I could cheer them up. I thought I could do that much. I found Kyle Aho, I remember." My father looks at us, and I see from his face that he's about to tell us something. "He was in the hospital. And he had been shot in the penis. So I was awfully glad I could bring him some mail. They sent him home after that, of course."

"My God," I say.

"Yes," my father says. He looks away. "No, that mail orderly business, that was good duty, but toward the end it wasn't much fun anymore."

"No."

"So many guys got killed. You didn't know where

you were." He sighs. "I just pitied the poor guy who had to take over after me. I don't know how he knew where to begin."

My father's voice has grown so soft I have to strain to hear his last words. "You did that quite a while, then," I say.

"Oh, yes. Two years. It was two years or more."

"Did you ever think of becoming a mailman when you got out?"

"No, I'd had enough. I had other plans by then. I liked the freedom and the fact you weren't in action all the time. But then there was the lonely aspect. And there were times when it was very scary, too, because you'd be out there all alone. You had to find your way and make your own decisions, and there was no one there to cover you.

"For instance. I remember this one time, and this was Bougainville, and I thought I was lucky. I thought I'd got out of some dangerous duty. Because the enemy was out there. The Japanese were on the island, and we knew they were coming. They ordered our company out beyond the lines, across the river, to set up an outpost and send out patrols. But I didn't have to go because they had me working back at regimental headquarters. Well, it was just a few days, and then the word came down: You have to bring the mail up to the company."

"Oh, boy," Dave says.

"You can say that again. So I took the mail—just the letters, no bulky stuff—and I also carried a carton of C rations on my back. I went out by myself. I went along the trail. Crossed the river. I don't know how many times. Over twenty times, as I remember. It was shallow, though, thank goodness."

"The river's winding back and forth, or what?"

"The river winds around in there, and I was going out alone, because I heard some noise up ahead. And I had my gun with me, too. I thought, Boy, what's coming? So I got off to the side. I hid. Well, here came some

of the men from our company, and they were carrying
a stretcher. Here one of my best friends had been bit by
a scorpion. And he was in agony. Just writhing in agony.
Just terrible. They were taking him back to the hospital.
He got all right after that, but he was really in pain.
That's why, there on Bougainville, you had to shake
your boots out every morning. Scorpions. Centipedes.
You were in for it if you got bit.

"But then I got up to the company and made my
delivery, and the guys were really glad to see me. They
were glad to get some mail. Then I took off, and I made
it back all right. That was beautiful out there. I remember the trail going up along a cliff and the river down
below so beautiful I just sat there for a little bit. And
the birds! Birds you can't imagine. Trees and flowers I
had never dreamed. I'm telling you, the jungle is like
nothing else on earth. I forgot about the war there for
a while, listening, and looking round at everything. It
was like when you're a little kid, and an afternoon goes
by and you don't know if it was just a minute or a year.
I watched these ants, I remember, a whole crew of ants,
and they were building something, carrying these tiny
twigs and leaves and things. And then I'd look way off.
The hills all green and blue. The river down below. I
don't know how long I sat there, but I made sure I made
it back by sunset."

"For sure," I say. "That would be too creepy out
there in the dark all by yourself."

"Not only that, but you have to be careful what you
do, because it's not just the enemy. You can be fired on
by your own men. You know. You can be killed by
your friends."

"I can see that," Dave says. "I can see how that might
happen."

"But I don't understand this, Dad," I say. "What's
going on here?"

"Where?"

"Here on Bougainville. What are you doing here?"

"Well, the situation was, we were sent to Bougainville to guard an airstrip. We had to set up a perimeter around an airfield that was being built. So they could bomb the other islands out there. Bougainville became a real base for future operations to the west. So we had to keep the Japanese from coming in on that."

"This wasn't an airstrip that you captured, then?"

"No, we built it. The Seabees came and built it. Just amazing what they could do in no time. Bulldoze, clear the jungle, pile up the trees. Like a miracle the things that they could do.

"And then the Japanese. They knew we had landed, and they came across the island. They were coming, and we knew they were coming, and we had to build fortifications. We even dug trenches there along the hillside and all along the front. It was practically like World War I the way we were dug in.

"But we were fortunate, our company, because we had a little river ran in front of us, and then a sort of lake—swampy, with malaria and mosquitoes—off there to the right, between us and the other companies. Then we had a road right behind us that the Seabees built so we could bring supplies to all the companies strewn out along the line."

"You had some time, then," I say.

"Yes, we had some time. And this was strange. This was different, because we were on the defensive now. Before we'd been on the move. We were always attacking, you might say. But now we just kind of waited for them. Sent out patrols to see where they were, make contact, see how far they'd come. And we sat there for nearly two years."

"Two years!"

"It was nearly two years, altogether, anyway, that we were there on Bougainville. A long time before they came and some time after, too."

"Good grief," Dave says, "but that's a long time. That's longer than I've been married."

"It was time enough to think, I'll tell you that. And it was there on Bougainville, sitting there beside that swamp, I thought that I might want to go to college."

Dave laughs. "Oh, yeah? And why was that?"

"I don't know why it was, because I'd never thought of it before. I couldn't imagine I could really do it, because we never had the money for anything like that, but somehow I latched onto that idea. I think it was because I couldn't understand the war. Not really. Because by this time I had friends who were getting killed, and I wanted to know why. I wanted to know what was going on. As a whole. All I had were pieces. So many parts I couldn't understand. All kinds of things. Like there was one night, earlier, we made a landing. This was only practice, but no one seemed to know what we were doing. We had no idea where we were. The rumor was New Guinea, and there was talk of headhunters and cannibals, but they never even told us. I think it was New Guinea, and I've looked it up on maps, but even to this day I don't know if I was ever on New Guinea! It was that kind of thing that really bothered me."

"I can see where it would," I say.

"And then I had this feeling. I knew this was history we were doing, that this would be remembered and written up in books. Not any special thing you were doing as an individual person but the whole thing as a whole. I knew it was important. I had seen Eleanor Roosevelt, and once I even saw MacArthur. But what was going on exactly? And how did I fit into this? That's what I wanted to know. And so I got the idea I would go to college, and I'd study history, and maybe some day I could teach it. I didn't know how. There wasn't any money. But I had that idea, and then, afterwards, the GI Bill came along, and so I got to go to Augsburg."

"I see," Dave says. "But then what happened? Did the Japanese attack?"

"Wait a sec," I say. "This is important. Did you ever figure it out? Do you feel you understand it now?"

"Not really. Not the way I wanted to. But some. Better than I did. I looked it up on maps, and saw where I had been, and read about the strategy, and saw where all of this fit in. But I have to say I had a kind of hunger that reading and my classes never really satisfied. A hungering to understand about my friends and why they died. Places where we were and the reasons we were there. I don't know. When you go through something, it's never quite the same. But I think I did the right thing in going to the war, and I'm glad I went to college and found out what I could. Even if— Even if it left the things that mattered most relatively unexplained."

"You mean?"

"I mean about your friends and the situations you were in. The real feel of things. And why."

"You had been to Bible school," I tell him. "You were a Christian."

"Yes."

"So how in the world did you square the war with your religion? How could you go off to kill and still believe the things you did? I mean, if I may ask."

"Yes," my father says. "Well, that's a question, and I didn't like to think of it, but I felt I had to do it. I thought about that more than once while we were there on Bougainville and waiting. I had my Bible, and I prayed, and I thought about it quite a lot."

"And?" I say. "What about it? Doesn't the Bible say to turn the other cheek and love your enemies? I'm not attacking you."

"No," he says. "I know you're not. The only thing I can say is what I thought of then and what I still believe. I can't see how you turn your cheek to Hitler and the Japanese. I don't know. Maybe Jesus could. I didn't have the faith for that, I guess you'd say, and, anyhow, once you see your buddies killed, your friends, you know,

you don't think along those lines. Besides, the Bible
says to love your enemies. It doesn't say you're not
going to have any."

"I never thought of that," I say, startled by what
strikes me as a fresh interpretation of a tired text. "That's
a real idea."

"It's a thought."

"But you can't call killing love."

"No," he says, "you can't. But I believe there's such
a thing as evil, and it has to be fought."

"So do I! But it's inside us, too. That's what makes
me sick about this country. We always want to think
the wickedness is somewhere else. Like Reagan calls the
Soviet Union an Evil Empire. That lunatic. We're supposed to be the good guys? It's this will to innocence
that's wicked. You want to quote scripture, how about
the one that says not to sweat the speck in your brother's
eye when you've got a goddamn log in your own eye?"

"It doesn't say goddamn," my father says.

"Okay. But that's the verse that best applies to us, as
far as I can see. We ought to print that mother on our
coins instead of what we've got. I mean, if there's *one*
thing we learned from Vietnam it ought to be that the
Kingdom of Heaven isn't all we've got within us.
There's a whole pile of bloody shit right alongside."

"Sam," my father flinches.

"Hey, cool it," Dave says. "Vietnam hadn't even happened yet. Who are you arguing with?"

"I don't know," I say, suddenly exhausted. I lean
forward, put my head in both hands.

"Listen," my father says. "I don't like your language,
but I think I see what you're saying, and the truth is, I
know it better than you do. But it's not all inside you,
either. Some of it is actually out there. The fact remains.
Hitler was out there. And he was a demon."

"Human," I say wearily. "One of us."

"That man was possessed. He had the devil in him."

"Yes. But what about Dresden? What about Hiroshima?"

"We had to do it."

"Did we?"

"We couldn't help it."

"The devil made us do it."

He gives me a long look. "I can't answer all of that," he says. "All I can say is I prayed about it. I tried my best to think it out. Do you know Dietrich Bonhoeffer?"

"Yes," I say. "Not personally."

"What?"

"Sorry. Joke."

"It's not a joke. He was a German and a great theologian. And he decided to assassinate Adolf Hitler. But he was caught and killed. But then you say you know about him."

"Yes, I've read about him."

"All I'm saying is, if a man like that could decide on such a thing, then I have to take some comfort. Because he was a deep thinker and a great man, and I was just a guy, but I had to decide, too. And it so happened that I came to more or less the same conclusion. I don't know. It was all I could think of."

"That's all I was asking."

"Yes," he says. "Well, you have the New Testament, but then there's Joshua and Jericho and so forth. You have to think of that. And even Jesus, when you think about it, overturned the tables in the temple and drove the money changers out. He did it with a whip, and that was violent."

"But that was different. That was bankers. That was loan sharks."

"I can't argue with you, Sam. I haven't read as much as you have. I can't win an argument. I'm only saying what I thought."

"I'm listening."

"And there were many wars in those days, back in

Bible times, and there were many battles, and even Jesus
did some things."

"I know," I say. "The Bible is a bloody book."

He holds me with a long look. "What would you
have done?" he says, his voice rising. "It's not so easy
to think! And if you haven't got the Bible, then how
do you decide? You think your own mind? You think
you're so smart that you can figure all this out?"

"No," I say. "I'm sorry. I know it's hard."

"It was not an easy thing. Not any of it. And I'm
sorry that it happened. We didn't ask for war, but there
it was. I felt I had to do it. I guess we disagree on that.
But I thought then, and I still think, that this was what
you call a just war. And that's all I can say. I'm sorry.
They killed my brother, and they tried to kill me."

I say, "I'm sorry. I know it. I didn't mean to be smart.
It was a different kind of war. I think you were probably
right."

No one speaks. The windows rattle, and I can hear
snow sift and slide along the walls of the house. Then
Dave coughs and says, "I'd like to know what happened.
There on Bougainville. You sat there waiting, but did
they ever actually attack?"

"Yes," my father says, then lapses back into silence.
I think he's getting tired. In fact, we're all worn out,
but we seem to have decided, the three of us, without
discussing it, to see this thing through, to get my father
off the islands and bring him safely home. "I remember
when they came," he says, "because I was on the line.
I was there. I saw this. I was up on the line, and a patrol
had been sent out. We knew the Japanese were close.
We kept track of them. And here we heard this racket,
a real ruckus, and firing. And this sergeant ran out in
the clearing and waved to his men to come on, hurry
up! He crouched there in the clearing. He waited until
the last man got past. And then he sprayed the bushes
back in there to cover them. Then he came on, and he
got all his men across that clearing."

"You saw all this!" Dave says.

"I was right there."

"And this is daylight?"

"Right in plain sight of everyone. He got decorated for it later on. Because that sergeant did the right thing, and he showed he cared about his men. It was really a courageous thing to do. Out there in the open. I think he got a Silver Star for that."

"I can see why."

"He got his men across the line, but then we knew the Japanese were there. But the thing about it was, they really didn't hit us. They hit the company to the left and the company to the right. Because we had that little river right in front of us. They didn't like that. And over here we had that lake. So we were kind of lucky. We had some casualties because we had patrols that were hit, and several men were killed that way. And then we took artillery."

"Well, did the Japanese follow that patrol right in?" I ask.

"We had a line where we'd cleared away the brush and jungle, and that patrol I was telling you about, they came across that clearing. But the Japanese were there, right behind them, and they were massed in the jungle right across that clearing."

"Man. So this is when they came?" Dave says. "In broad daylight?"

"Oh, yes. They came by day. They came at dark. Whenever."

"How long did this go on?"

"For a number of days. It was a terrible racket. We had 90 millimeter guns right behind us, firing at the hills, trying to hit the incoming lines of Japanese. They'd fire over our heads. And then the Japanese were firing in, too. Racket all night long. Well, we had built these bunkers. Our company hadn't been hit yet, and one night I was in the dugout. I was the only one in there. We had men down below, on the line, and I was in company headquarters, back a ways. And a shell came and hit the corner of the dugout. All kinds of dirt came down. I thought the whole thing was coming in on me. But it held. We built them pretty strong. I got out of there, and I was just covered with dust and dirt. Pretty scared, too. But it was good that I was in there!"

"Man oh man," Dave says.

"And shells would land right down in company headquarters. That's how my Jewish friend was killed. Piece of shrapnel hit him right in the chest, and he was gone. He was in a bunker, and we heard a yell down there. I was near the front lines, but I could hear it. I was right there with the captain, and the captain told the first sergeant, 'Go down and see what happened.' So the first sergeant went down there. And he came out. And then he said it. He said, 'Shapiro bought it.' And I felt so bad.

"I didn't even go look. I didn't even want to see it. Because we were friends. Abe Shapiro. He was from . . . it might have been Chicago. Was that it? Someplace. I got to know him pretty well. He was kind of shunned by the rest of them. They knew he was Jewish. A lot of hatred of the Jews, you know, in those days."

I say, "But that's crazy!"

"I know. I tried to tell the other fellows. I told them he's not so different from you or me, but they weren't about to listen. And he was a real nice guy, Shapiro. We were interested in some of the same things, and he was a big reader, and we used to talk together. He was kind of feminine, in a way, and maybe that was part of it. Had a high voice and things like that. But there was nothing wrong with him. He was a good guy, but he was kind of all alone. Everybody shunned him. I didn't feel that way about him, so he used to hang around with me a lot. I talked to him quite a bit. But I felt so bad when he got hit!"

"This doesn't make sense."

"What?"

"I don't understand what's going on!" I say. "There's prejudice and hatred of the Jews by these Americans at the very time Americans are fighting Germans who are burning up the Jews in concentration camps!"

"Yes."

"But that's completely nuts! This is crazy!"

"That's the way it is, though. That's the way it's been. The Jews have always had that what-do-you-call-it, stigma?"

"Stigma? Yeah? Stigma?"

"They have that stigma held against them. That's how it was."

"Nuts."

"I know it. But that was Abe Shapiro. Och." He takes off his cap, as if he were at a funeral. I can see the memory still hurts, and I've begun to worry now about the things we're dredging up.

"So this was Bougainville," I say, trying to distract him. "But you say your company was never hit."

"No." He runs a hand through his wispy hair and pushes his bifocals back up his nose. "No, we never felt the brunt of it. We lost some boys to mortar shells, artillery, but they never came right at our company. That river, like I said, they didn't want any part of that. So we were spared, you might say. Because just to the left and right, those companies had very heavy casualties. The Japs tried to punch through in both those places. It went on for days, and they lost a lot of men."

"I'm surprised you weren't called on, then," Dave says, "you guys, your company, to reinforce those men. You'd think they would've used you to back them up."

"No, we couldn't do that. That would have left a weak spot, see, where we were. We all just had to hold our places, our positions, and we did. We finally threw them back. But that was something, and those other guys, especially the company on our left, Charlie Company, they really got clobbered. They were fighting night and day, and the casualties were very high, but they did it. They held the line.

"And I'll tell you how they did it. Everybody fought, but, finally, in the end, it was just one guy who did it. That's what it came down to. This one guy. Because the Japs were getting desperate, and they made a final push. It was a banzai attack. And they say this kid went crazy. He sort of went berserk. I didn't witness this, but this is what I heard.

"They said they thought what did it was, the Japs got his buddy who was in the foxhole with him. Right next to him. And it was bloody. There was blood all over him. And the kid got out of his foxhole! He climbed up out of that hole, covered with blood, his buddy's blood, and he got right out there in the open, on a little hill, and he had a BAR. That's a Browning Automatic Rifle. It's like a light machine gun, but it's not. But he grabbed that BAR, and he got out there, and he was absolutely and completely in the open. And he burned it up! He burned up the BAR. Firing and firing. They said he was like a madman. They said he had a couple of rifles, too, and he just fired everything till there was nothing left to shoot at. He just leveled them. Just flattened everything in sight. So the Japanese retreated, but even after they were gone he went on firing, firing into the bushes, shooting at the jungle, even after there was nothing left to shoot at. And that was that. Right there. That was the Battle of Bougainville. For all intents and purposes. Because they never did come back. The Japanese withdrew, and pretty soon our patrols couldn't even find them, and they had left the island."

"My land," Dave says.

"And he was just a kid! He got a Silver Star for that, and they made him a second lieutenant and put him in charge of a platoon. Promoted him right up out of the ranks. A battlefield commission. What was his name, anyhow? It was kind of peculiar, I remember. Funny name. Buford, something like that."

"Did you know him?" I ask.

"No, but I saw him a few times. I'd see him around. The first time I ever saw him, after that attack, I could hardly believe it. I ran a message over to Charlie Company one day, and he was there at headquarters, and someone told me, 'That's the guy.' And I could not believe it. He barely had any fuzz. He wasn't any older than, why, he was the same age as Johnny! Nineteen years old. And there he was in headquarters, and he was playing with a puppy. I thought, This is him? Because my goodness. But that was him. Beulah, that was his name. Leonard Beulah. I wonder where he got that darn dog."

Dave laughs, and my father looks up, surprised, and then continues. "But this Beulah turned out to be an excellent lieutenant. You wouldn't think he would, a kid like that, but he developed quite a reputation. We'd hear about him every now and then, over in our outfit, something he had done. And later on, in the Philippines, I think he even took over a company. That's what I heard.

"And I'll tell you something else. Years later, during the Korean War, I read a story in the papers about a major who had led a group of men behind the lines on a very dangerous mission and freed a whole bunch of prisoners. And the major's name was Beulah. It was the same name. Major Beulah. I'll bet you anything it was him. He was that kind of a guy."

"But this was a major," I say.

"Sure, but this was quite a few years later, and a guy like that, he would have risen through the ranks in a hurry."

"Oh, yeah. I suppose it could have been."

"I'll bet it was. Because he had that knack. He was good with his men, or so they said. You'd think it might be awful to be with somebody like that, but they said he was careful with his men. It was only with himself that he was crazy. Leonard Beulah. Michigan. I think he was from somewhere up in Michigan. And he was a genuine hero.

"That's why, earlier," my father laughs, "and I know you were joking, but when you said I was a hero I said I never was. Because I wasn't. I was just a normal guy. But this guy, this Beulah, he really was. He was fearless. And with somebody like that, I don't think that you could even call it courage. Because it wasn't. It was like he didn't even know there was anything he was being brave about. It was like he was a little crazy. I was never anything like that. I was afraid all the time."

"I should hope so," I say.

"Yes. Well, that was something. That was very scary all the time. But we did it. We held it, and the Japanese left the island, and that was Bougainville." He stares at the Formica tabletop as if he were reading the past in a crystal ball. Then he says, "Excuse me. I have to go to the bathroom. I guess I had too much coffee."

Dave laughs, and I say, "I do, too. What have we drunk, three pots?"

Dave says, "Too much. I know what you mean. I'll use the one upstairs."

My father pads off down the hall. Dave shakes his head, gets up, and pauses in the doorway. He grins at me and says, "I still think we should have called this The Pissin' Club."

"Get out of here," I laugh, and he heads down the hall. I hear him stumble and swear in the dark on the stairs.

We called it The Army Club. The membership varied from day to day, but there were usually five or six of us—boys about nine, ten, eleven years old—and we'd roam the gravel pits and pastures around Rock Rapids. We were practicing for when the Russians came. We had flags and wooden swords, hunting knives and BB guns. All of us were infantry except the Wesley boys. Their father had been in the navy, so they insisted they were sailors. When the Russians came, the Wesley brothers were going to mount their father's shotguns on a raft and patrol the Rock River. They could transport troops—the rest of us—wherever we were needed most. That was the theory, but our boat-building techniques would not support it. Every raft we built sank out of sight as soon as a sailor stepped aboard. So the Wesley boys decided they would be marines instead. We built bunkers in the gravel pits and planned to blow up the Rock River bridge. We dug a set of foxholes in the brow of Jackson's Hill and stashed supplies of peanut butter, crackers, first aid kits, and extra packs of BBs. Our parents might be unprepared, but we'd take care of them. We had more imagination than the planners at the Pentagon, and we lived in constant readiness. I slept with my BB gun beneath my bed, my jackknife on the nightstand.

We called it The Army Club, but at least once a day, out on patrol after school, somebody would say, "Okay, halt, you guys. I've got to take a leak." And then, the operation synchronized, we'd line up on the riverbank, unzip, and somebody would say, "I *still* think we should have called this The Pissin' Club." And so we'd stand, giggling and pissing proudly into the river below.

Only one member of The Army Club actually grew up to join the army, and that was our leader, Jerry Wesley. Wetpants, we called him, whenever we were mad. Years later, when I was out of college and working in St. Paul, I heard that he was living there in town. In a melancholy mood one Sunday afternoon I found him in the phone book. I had to say my name three times. I asked what he was doing now, and he said, "Playing army. Just like in the old days." He laughed and explained that he was in the national guard and had just returned from a week of running around in the woods at Camp Ripley. Thirty years old, I thought, and he's still getting ready for the Russians. In his other life, he sold insurance. I could hear his wife and children going at it in the background. He had a hard time concentrating on the conversation, but I asked about the kids we'd grown up with, and he told me what he knew. Everyone had left Rock Rapids. Most had gone to college. No one else had gone into the service, but as far as he knew, he said, everyone turned out all right. He meant, he said, that nobody had tried to save the world. I didn't bother telling him about the protests I'd been in or that Dave had gone to Washington and spent a week in jail. He sounded dumb as a brick, and I had no desire to wreck our friendly memories, and so we reminisced about The Army Club and laughed. A baby howled in the background, and he said, "Listen, I'm glad you phoned, but I really have to go." I didn't call again.

My father enters the kitchen, blowing his nose on a Kleenex. Has he been crying? Not Mr. Calm. Not Mr. Imperturbable. It must be the start of a winter cold. He sits, and I put a hand on his shoulder as I pass to take my turn in the bathroom. Standing over the toilet bowl, I weave a little, as if I were drunk, although I haven't had a drop all day. Not in this house. This house is dry. Some brandy would make the blizzard nice and cozy, but we'll have to survive the storm on coffee. And maybe that's enough, I think, because I seem to be slightly giddy as it is, feverish, light-headed. It's just fatigue, I think. My father's monologues have worn me out. Listening to his memories, trying to interpret them, I'm beginning to suspect the fight went out of him forty years ago. I think he must have used up all the juice you need for arguments back there in the war. At least that might explain the edgy peace that rules this house. I flush the toilet, flip the switch, and return to the kitchen to find my father in stitches.

"Look at this," he laughs. "Look what the cat dragged in."

Dave is holding up my father's old dress uniform. He

lifts the hanger high, as if he were hoisting a heavy stringer of fish, and he grins as if he expects to have his picture taken. "Where the heck did you get that?" I ask.

"In the attic. I was looking for that box of snapshots, but I couldn't stand it any longer. Man. It's like Alaska up there!"

"Put it on," I tell him. "Did you try it on?"

"Are you kidding? This thing was made for a midget. Here, you try it."

My father and I are the same size. I can wear most of his clothes, but I can't begin to get into the jacket. "You sure this thing isn't Japanese?" I say and hand it to my father.

"You boys are out of shape, that's all," he taunts us. But it doesn't fit him, either. He exchanges his bathrobe for the jacket, and he slips it on all right, but there's something wrong with the shoulders, and his belly swells the waist so that the coat won't button. He sucks in his stomach and manages to twist the button through the hole. "There," he says, "you see? Nothing to it." He grunts and blows, and all of us laugh. He looks ludicrous. "Well, it used to fit," he says. "I cut quite a figure once. You ask your mother."

"Sure," Dave says.

"I did. I really did," my father puffs, struggling out of the jacket. He stands there in his underwear, like a child in pajamas. He is old, old. Unbelievable. He slips on his robe and ties the belt. "I looked pretty sharp, boy. I don't know what happened."

"You put on twenty pounds and lost your posture," I laugh. "That's what happened. You turned into a hunchback."

Dave drapes the jacket back on the hanger, hooks the hanger through the handle of the fridge, and drops an olive-drab cap on the table. "My land," my father drawls. He strokes the flat, wool cap, then picks it up. He opens it like a wallet and peers inside.

"Come on," I tell him. "Put it on."

He settles it, front and back, and pats it into place. "What do you think? Pretty snazzy, huh?"

"At least it fits," I say. "You didn't get a fat head, anyway."

"You wore it like this, you see. And then if you wanted to make a big impression, you'd cock it at a little angle, like so." He snaps a half-salute and laughs. "Oh, my goodness," he sighs. "There's history for you."

"You look like the VFW," Dave says. "You look like one of those Legion guys."

"I do?"

"Say, how come you never joined those groups?" I ask. "You qualified, didn't you?"

"Of course I qualified. I just never saw the point. Half those guys were never really in it. And those who like to brag about it, well, I never saw too much to brag about. I was trying to forget it! Besides, it's just a lot of drinking."

"Oh," I say, "okay. Are those the service ribbons you were telling us about?"

He slides back in his chair and slips his hand inside the jacket to plump the pocket and lapel, like a tailor testing material. "These are the ribbons," he says. "And you see there's a different one for each campaign. This was for Guadalcanal, I think. I forget these others. This was New Georgia, with the little star, here. And this one," he says, touching a red, white, and blue bar as if he were pressing a button, "this one was the Philippines." He rubs the bar lightly, then abruptly gets up and goes to the window. I glance at Dave. He shrugs and rolls his eyes.

I say, "Dad?"

"It's still coming down!" he says. He turns and checks the clock. "We better get to bed. It's almost two." I can see where his breath has fogged the window, but even as I watch the vapor clears, and the glass goes black.

Dave says, "What's the matter, Dad?"

A blast of air hits the window at his back, and my father flinches. He turns and runs his fingertips along the edges of the pane. "I should have put putty," he says. "I should have weather-stripped." He turns to face us. "I can't talk about the Philippines."

"Come on," I say. "You told it to Johnny."

"No, I didn't. Just Manila. Even that was hard."

Dave says, "You could tell us this one time. Couldn't you?"

I say, "What's so bad about it?"

"Well, that's where all my— That's where— I don't like to think about it."

"You don't have to," I tell him. "We can quit."

"All right," he sighs and sits. "If you really want to hear it."

"I really want to hear it," Dave says. "Just one minute." He gets up and refills his mug. "Sam?"

"Okay," I say, "but this is it. I already feel like I'm on drugs."

My father sits and thinks. Dave slides my mug across the table, takes his chair, and hunches forward, his hands wrapped around his heavy coffee mug. He works in a shop that restores old furniture, and he never gets his hands completely clean. The fingernails, the cuticles, the knuckles bear traces of varnish and stain. Steam rises off our coffee and evaporates.

My father says, "The Philippines. The Philippines were MacArthur's idea. The Philippines were Mac-Arthur's revenge. Because he was defeated there, you might remember, and that's when he was driven out, and he said that famous saying. What was that?"

" 'I shall return,' " I tell him.

"That's it. 'I shall return.' And he did."

"And you were there," Dave says. "You were part of that."

"I was there, and nobody went in ahead of us this time. This was in Luzon, the northern province, and we landed at Lingayen Gulf. We had to fight our way down to Manila. It was, oh, a hundred miles, and we had to walk. We had to march on Manila."

"This was where that kamikaze almost hit your ship," I remind him. "Where you went up on deck and watched the dogfights? Where you saw the Zero? You were telling us."

He looks at me blankly.

"The plane!" I say, as if he were hard of hearing. "The suicide plane!"

He jumps a little. "Yes!" he says. "I think that's where it was. I think it was. They bombed us on the beach. But, you know—" He looks at a corner of the ceiling so long that I turn and examine it myself. "Isn't that funny?" he says. "I can't quite see it. I'm really hazy on that landing. We lost a lot of men there, too. I just can't think."

"It was a long time ago," Dave says at last.

"But I should remember! They were calling for medics. We came ashore, but I can't—" He looks at us apologetically. "I can't remember."

"That's okay," I tell him. "You saw so much I'm not surprised it gets confused."

"It was landing craft, wasn't it? Yes. They ran us in, and dropped the ramp, and we rushed out in the surf. You had to hold your rifle up to keep it dry. And that was bad, because you had your hands above your head like this. You had your hands up! And they were shooting at you!"

"I see it," I say, "yes."

"I can't . . . we made it to the beach, and we went in, but then . . . we lost a lot of men. It's really hazy. It keeps fading on me. Somehow, finally, we got them on the run, and they withdrew. Then we headed for Manila, and there were skirmishes and battles all the way."

"And you were in those," Dave says.

"Clark Field, and that's a fact. An air base, and we took it back, and that's where I was almost hit. Going across that field where the grass had burned off. The tracer bullets had started a fire. The Japanese were over in the hills, and they could see us coming, and they were firing. I hadn't been under much fire before. Rifle fire. There's a cracking noise. Bullets crack when they come over. Going through the air like that, they crack. And it's hot. It was a hot day, and this burned-over field was smoldering, but I was so tired I threw myself down. To get a breather. And something hit the ground beside me. I looked down, and there was a bullet that hit the ground right by my side. Six inches. They tried to kill me! They shot right at me!"

"I thought this was the beach," I mumble. "You used to tell me this was—"

"What? No, this was in a field, a burning field. Everything was charred and smoldering. Boy, that was close. I had so many things like that. Close calls. Washing Machine Charlie. Mortar shells. That time that I was in the bunker, and that time I tried to fix the wire. I could have died a hundred times. I don't know why I wasn't killed, except that it was really just the grace of God that I came through at all."

"You had to have us," Dave says.

"What?"

"I say, you had to have us. We were waiting to be born. You had to make it through the war so we could get born. We were waiting for you."

"Oh, okay," my father says, smiling uncertainly. "So then I jumped up out of the ashes and made a run for it. Bullets cracking all around me. What was I doing there? I don't know, unless I must have had to bring a message to one of the lieutenants. That's what it was. I kind of circled around, and for a while I was ahead of all our men. I was even ahead of our scouts. But I circled back and came in to company headquarters. I came back to where the captain was, and the first sergeant, and another man was there. I was walking around, and the bullets were cracking all over, but I didn't even notice

them because of what I'd just been through. I was in a
daze, I guess. This man I'd never seen before was huddled in a slit trench with the captain. He said, 'Soldier,
why don't you get down? Don't you know those are
bullets up there?' So I got down. But it was the battalion
commander, and he'd come up to see how we were
doing. I don't think, right then, I knew what I was
doing. But the company was doing all right.

"But then, that night, there was a banzai attack. That
very night. You could hear them screaming. Turn your
blood to cottage cheese. They are a crazy people. I was
back of the front lines a bit, and we'd been told to dig
in. So I was in my foxhole, and the guys were right in
front of me. I was back a few yards, a rod or so, and
company headquarters in back of me. Well, the guys
were firing like mad, but I couldn't fire, because the
guys were right in front of me. So I had to hold my
fire. All I could do was huddle down inside my foxhole.
Shell fire, mortar fire coming in. I'd pop my head out
once in a while and look out. Then the firing suddenly
ceased. And I popped my head out. And there was a
guy there, and he tried to make a fool of me. He said,
'What are you doing? You been down in that hole all
this time?' And there was a lieutenant there, and everybody looked at me. I said, 'What do you want me to
do? Fire my rifle and hit you guys?' But this guy was a
guy who had a lot of senseless what-do-you-call-it.
Brava-do?"

"Bravado," I tell him.

"Bravado. Yes. Well, he was killed," my father says,
with a shocking hint of satisfaction. "Not that time but
later on. I was coming off that hill, knowing I was going
home. I came off that hill and down the trail, and he
was in a mortar company, and they were down the hill
behind us. He was sitting on an ammunition box outside
his foxhole. Fully exposed. And shells were landing all
around. Whenever a shell would land close by, he'd kind
of flinch. But again he was just showing off. How brave

he was and everything. Well, I went past him, and I yelled out to him good-bye. I said, 'I'm going *home.*' I got back to the area where I was supposed to be, and a little later Roger Handy came. And he told me this guy had been killed. He was hit by a shell. And so. He was from Ohio. Can't remember his name. But that's how he was. He was always doing things to get the attention of the officers. But he was just a private, and he never got to be anything else. I guess the officers could read him, too. And he was killed."

"But what happened in this banzai attack?" Dave wants to know.

"We threw them back. They were coming across that field, but they didn't get anyplace. We had more firepower, far more firepower, and they had to fall back. So we took Clark Field and kept on going." He stretches and then adjusts his glasses with both hands.

"So you were some time," I say, "getting to Manila?"

"Yes, we had to walk, and it was quite a ways. We'd stop whenever a firefight broke out. You'd hear the fighting. We'd wait till that was over, and then we'd proceed. And there was a place . . . let's see now, how was that?"

He's lost again. I say, "How was what?" to bring him back.

"I'm trying to think. I'd been sick. I had an ingrown toenail, and it was giving me a lot of trouble. I was limping along, and I got a fever from it. We came to a place where our barracks bags had been brought up. And the captain knew about me. He knew I was having trouble. He said, 'You stay here with so-and-so.' I can't remember this other guy's name, but he was a redhead. The captain said, 'You guys guard the barracks bags, and we'll go on. The truck will come along tomorrow and pick up the bags, and you can rest and get a ride and then catch up with us.' And so we did that. We were all alone, and we went into a house, a bamboo house on stilts, and we thought, Well, maybe we can stay here tonight and sleep inside this house. We were laying out our bags, but then I got to thinking, Boy, there might be a lot of lice and stuff in here. So then we thought, Well, let's go out and sleep on top of the barracks bags.

"But that was scary, too, because we were just two guys, and we never knew what was happening. And every once in a while there in the Philippines we'd meet some Filipinos who had guns and various weapons. Later on I found out they were Communist. But they were trying to help us. They were guerrillas, I guess you'd say. Ragtag outfit. They'd use anything they could get their hands on—old relics and machetes, anything. They were all around in there, and we weren't too sure of them. And there were Japanese all over. So we didn't sleep too well that night. We kept waking up. Any little noise. We were on top of all those bags. It made a nice bed, a big, soft bed, and I remember looking at the stars and the different constellations. And we sang some songs up there. We made up songs and sang some hymns we knew. But soft, because we were afraid. In the morning we got on the truck, and I went and found the medics, and they fixed me up."

"I guess you didn't get a Purple Heart for that," Dave says, smiling. "I guess they didn't give a medal for an ingrown toenail."

"No," my father laughs. "That sounds dumb, but it was awful painful." He winces, and he says, "I still remember that. I could hardly walk. But then I got all right, and we proceeded on down." He's weary now and pauses, the memories fading in and out. "Had to stop now and then for somebody to clear the way." Dave's eyelids flutter. He's got both elbows on the table, his chin in his hands. "We got into a firefight at a place called Abando. I think we lost a couple men. As I remember."

I say, "Dave, wake up."

He says, "What?" and his eyes open wide. "What happened?"

"Watched a church burn to the ground. Some other things. Then we proceeded on down, and we came to Manila."

I say, "Manila. This is the capital. This is where you almost got blown up? Where you tried to fix that wire?"

"This is Manila, and there's the university, and that's our base. There was fighting around the university, and then we stayed there for a while. And then the word came down: Take City Hall.

"I can't remember everything that happened. We had an acting captain because we lost our captain there. He was a good man. Strong. He went out on patrol, and he asked his radio man and one other fellow to go along. He was going to go out and find out how to get to City Hall. He was going to scout it out himself. He wasn't sending someone else. He was doing it himself. So he went out there. And he got killed."

I say, "No."

"Yes, he was. And his radio man was hurt, and the other guy got killed. They hit a mine."

"Ach."

"So then this Lieutenant Carver took over. I liked him. He was a good guy, but I don't think he had enough training to command a company."

"Oh, this is the guy you were telling us about," Dave says. "Isn't this the guy who was going to get you the Bronze Star?"

"That's the guy. Lieutenant Carver. He was just a ninety-day wonder, and he made some serious mistakes. But we didn't know what we were doing! We'd been in the jungle all this time! We knew what we were doing there. We had experience in the jungle. But here we were in town! How were we to know? We're in the city now. Fighting in the streets and house to house. This was just like Europe, but here we're in the South Pacific!

We had no idea how to go about it. And we'd lost our captain. He was a smart guy, but he was dead. Well, this Lieutenant Carver was promoted to command the company. Never got his captain's bars, but he was told to take over."

"I don't like this," Dave says.

"We had to take that City Hall. But we couldn't seem to do it. We got some men inside the building, in the lobby, but they'd make a little progress, and then they'd be shoved out. Couldn't make any headway. Japs inside, and they'd shoot them up. Awful."

"Well, for crying out loud," Dave says. "Why didn't they give you—"

"Shut up," I tell him. "Just shut up and listen."

"I had to bring a roll of wire. I had to bring a telephone so the guys inside could talk to headquarters. They had to have a wire in there.

"So I ran over there, and I got inside the building. And here were all kinds of small arms ammunition exploding in the outer room. And it was a fire in there, blazing fire. And I didn't know where the guys were! I looked around. I found an entrance and got in. And here were all the guys down below. Up overhead, this balcony. So I looked at them, and they were all staring up at this balcony.

"I'll never forget as long as I live. The guys turned around and looked at me. And it was in their eyes. Their eyes had such a look I can't forget. Then they all turned and gazed back at that balcony. They had their guns out. But there were Japanese up in that balcony. And they'd pop up and shoot down on the men below. Our guys. Our guys were getting killed. But by the time they got their guns on him, he'd be down below again, below the railing up there, down below that concrete wall.

"I've often thought since: Why didn't they use a grenade? Why didn't they throw a grenade up there? But they must have been afraid the grenade might hit the

walls and come back down on them. That's what I have
to think.

"So here I am, and I'm trying to set up that telephone.
I was trying to set *that* thing up. Then the sergeant who
was in command in there, a good friend of mine, Roger
Handy, Roger said: 'We can't stay here! We have to get
out of here!' He said, 'Thorsen, take the phone out.' So.
I picked up the telephone. I picked up the wire, and I
pulled all that behind me. And as I was going out, I
tripped and fell headlong. And at that very second a
Japanese took a shot at me. The sergeant told me afterwards. Roger said, 'You would have been killed. It was
a good thing you fell, because I saw the bullet land right
between your legs as you were sprawling out.' If I'd
been standing I would have been shot. So it was a good
thing. I was pretty shaky after that, but I got up and
got the wire and the telephone outside."

I say, "Dad!"

"And then when I got out, there was a fellow over
by the window. He said, 'Come over here and help me!'
He said, 'Guys are coming out of a room up here.'
They'd been in there, trying to make some headway,
and now they were coming out. And he said, 'There's
a personnel mine right below this window, and if they
jump on it, they'll be dead, and so will I.' He said, 'I've
been trying to catch these guys as they come out and
pull them away from the wall where the mine is.' He
said, 'Help me!' So I went over there, and one after
another the guys came out, and as they jumped, we'd
pull them! So they'd be sure not to hit that personnel
mine. I don't know how many guys came out."

"Well, did they know about the mine before they
jumped?" I ask.

"We'd yell at them. 'There's a personnel mine right
below here! So jump! Make a good jump, and we'll pull
you to the side!' So one after another they came out. I
don't know how many guys came out. But all that were
coming out came out. The rest of them were dead. Or

about to die, I guess. And then we took off for the other building where the rest of the company was." He pauses, breathing hard. "But that's really bright in my mind! Even tonight."

"Yes," I say softly.

"After all these years."

"That was bad," I say. "Was that the worst? That must have been about the worst."

He says, "Oh."

"But how did you finally take that City Hall?" Dave says.

"The next day," my father says, "they called in another company. I was there in headquarters when the battalion commander called. I was answering the phone when someone called, and he wanted to know what was going on, and he started asking questions. I said, 'I don't know.' And I said, 'I don't know! I don't know!' He said, 'Who is this, anyhow?' I said, 'Corporal Thorsen.' And he said, 'Well, put somebody on there who knows what's going on!' I didn't know. The common soldier doesn't know anything. So I yelled at the first sergeant, and then Lieutenant Carver got on the phone, and I heard him hollering. You see, he'd never been a captain. He'd commanded a platoon, but never a whole company. He didn't have the experience. He didn't know *what* to do. Well, the battalion commander wanted to know what was going on and why weren't we taking City Hall. So the next day he sent up another company to help.

"And what they did was, they somehow or other got up on the roof, and they worked their way down, room by room, floor by floor, to the bottom of the building. You've seen it in the movies. How they kick in the door and blast inside, and that's what they did.

"I wasn't in on that. I was back at headquarters with the first sergeant, but this Lieutenant Carver went along. This is what I heard: that he insisted on being the one with the flamethrower. And that was high risk. Because he was exposed. They'd kick in the door, and he'd stick that flamethrower in there, and he'd be in the doorway then, and, whoosh!, he'd blow that fire in there and try to burn them out."

"Good God."

"Yes, and afterwards he was strutting around and bragging all about it. He really did do something there, he could have been killed all the time, but I think he was a little off his rocker. Because the reason he insisted on doing that, to be the one, I think he felt he had to redeem himself. Because it was because of him a lot of men were killed the day before.

"You see, the thing about it was, this Lieutenant Carver kept sending in Lieutenant Overbeck, who had the third platoon. He sent him into that lobby. He sent him back time and again. And this poor lieutenant would come out, and every time he'd lose more men. But Carver wouldn't change his idea. Or he couldn't think. I don't know. But he kept sending them back in. And every time they'd lose more men. I heard them talking. Overbeck said, 'Steve! We've got to think of something else. We're getting killed. I'm not taking my guys in there again.' But Carver wouldn't listen, or else he couldn't think, because the two of them were arguing, and finally Carver said to Overbeck: 'And that's an order.' And Overbeck looked him in the eyes and called him something I won't say. And then he turned away and went and did it. And the last time Overbeck went in with what was left of his platoon, the guys came out again, and this time they were carrying Lieutenant Overbeck, and he'd been shot in the head. And he was dead."

"Oh," I say, "no."

"Yes, he was. He was shot in the head, and he was killed, and what you have to understand about this is, Overbeck and Carver had been friends. They'd been together all the way. And I think Lieutenant Carver thought he'd killed his own friend. I think he felt as if he'd pulled the trigger. And that's why he insisted on the flamethrower when they went back the next day. I think he had to take the risk, redeem himself somehow. He sort of did and he was bragging all about it, but it didn't really work."

"It didn't work," I say.

"It didn't work, because I think this was Lieutenant Carver's trouble afterwards. Afterwards, after Manila and after the reservoir, I went to see him. Because I really did like him, and it wasn't his fault. He just didn't have the training! He didn't know what he was doing, and all those guys got killed. I don't know what happened to him in the end, but I think he really suffered. I think he had a problem. A serious problem. Because when I was going home, I went to see him in Manila, and I found him in a hospital. In bed. But he didn't have any wounds that I could see. I think it was internal. In his head. I think he felt responsible for everything. And he was in the hospital. We said hi, and then we talked. And then I had to say good-bye, and, as I was leaving, he said, 'I'm still going to get you that Bronze Star.' But he was talking kind of crazy, and there was something wrong with him. So I never thought he'd do it, but I guess he really did."

Dave takes a deep breath and blows it out.

I say, "So this was Manila."

"And that was Manila. And that was too bad about Lieutenant Overbeck and all those guys. That was terrible. But that was Manila.

"And I'll tell you something strange. I saw it! Years later. Just a couple years ago, I saw it."

I say, "What? Saw what?"

"Manila! Your mother and I went over to Grace Lutheran over in Ryerson because they were having a program one night. We went over there, and we were with some people we know from Ryerson, and they'd invited us. It was in the basement of the church. There were some missionaries. They were from the Philippines.

They gave a nice talk about their work and everything. And then they showed a movie. It was all about the Philippines, and there were pictures of Manila, and suddenly I saw it. There it was! I saw that City Hall! I thought, My land. That's it! That's where I was almost killed! And it was just the same. I saw the tower and the entrance, and I even thought I saw that window where those guys came out, and I thought we'd all get killed. I made them stop the movie. I made them run it back so I could take another look. I told them stop it, stop the movie, and I said how I was there in World War II, and I had to have another look. And they were good. They did it for me. Boy."

I say, "That must have been a funny feeling."

"It was, you know. It was the strangest feeling. There it was."

Dave makes a sound like a cat, and I look over at him. His face is twisted, and I think he's going to cry, but he controls it. He swallows and places both hands on the table. He says, "Don't you think we ought to go to bed?"

I say, "What? Not now!"

And my father says, "No. I want to say this now. I've told you everything but this. I told you the beginning. Now I want to say the end. The beginning was the day I got that hunting knife. I told you that. Now I need to tell the end of it. And this is how it went." He looks up at the ceiling. Dave still has his hands pressed hard against the tabletop, as if he might get up and leave at any moment.

I tell him, "David." He sits back in his chair and fidgets with his beard.

"This is how it went. After the Battle of Manila we were there in town for some time, and I knew that I was going home. The rotation system had come in, and my hitch was almost up. And we'd been told: 'You're going home. Pretty soon. Your name is up next. You and Sergeant Handy.' " He laughs. "Old Roger Handy.

We were together, and we knew our time was almost up. But we couldn't get out of it. We had to go on this last campaign. And try to take back the reservoir. For the city of Manila.

"The Japanese were up there in the brow of that hill, and they saw us coming across that field. They started shooting at us. I can still hear those bullets crack. We just had to keep going across that field till we got to the bottom of the hill, and then they couldn't see us so well."

I say, "Everybody's running?"

"Yes, and I think some guys were hit. I heard them yelling out for medics. But not in our company. We all made it. But then we had to start up that hill. It was tough going. It was steep. It was hot. But we struggled up that hill, and finally we came toward the top, and it was evening. We were told to dig in, so we dug in. I had as my companion a little Chinese man. And he started talking to me in the dark. He said, 'You know, I knew Lieutenant Overbeck wasn't going to make it.' And then he had some reason for it. He saw a black cat. Somebody walked under a ladder. All these crazy things! I got mad at him. I don't know if I finally told him to shut up, or what. But he was talking so . . . all these weird things! So I had to put up with that. Then during the night there were scary things happening, because there were Japanese all around the mountain down below. We'd gone through their lines. And they tried to climb up there and get us."

"They knew you were there," I say. "They knew you were coming!"

"Yes, but finally the dawn came, and we got ready to advance. But some big shells started coming. Mortar shells. The Japanese could see us! They were on top of that hill, and now they were zeroing in. They walked the shells closer and closer. They were landing way in back of us at first. But gradually they worked them up the hill."

"I don't like these mortars," Dave says. "You think

about combat, you think about war, you think about someone shooting at you. That's one thing. Someone you can see. But this is like an accident! I mean, you can't even see who's killing you! Just blam, and there's a piece of metal, and you're dead. It's like an accident!"

"It's not an accident," my father says. "They're aiming at you. But I see what you're saying. It's true. Because you can't see them. If you're close, you hear a kind of poof. Then it's quiet. You're waiting, and you're waiting. And then it's just explosions."

"Ach!" Dave says.

"But then! Our company commander yelled at me, he said: 'Thorsen! Pack up! You're going home!' And my land. 'Bring your rifle, and get out of here.' They kept your rifle. So I had to run out of there without my gun."

"But you're on the move!" I tell him. "You're going up that hill!"

"Yes, but we're still in our holes. It's early in the morning, and we're just getting ready, starting out."

"Yeah, but why did they decide like that? Right in the middle of everything? Did they phone it in, or what?"

"I don't know! I don't know! I suppose. We had radios by then, and they must have called the orders in that I was going home."

"Okay."

"So then I knew that I was going home. And I could hardly believe it. So I got my things in order. But I'd been with these guys a long time. Three years, with some of them. I wanted to say good-bye to them. But the shells were coming closer. But I had to say good-bye. So I ran over to the different foxholes. I said, 'Frank!' I said, 'I'm going home!' And I shook hands with Maynard. I told him so long, too. And Alan. I got to him, I know. And Mike. And Daryl. All those guys. Anderson, Delano. I said, 'Good luck to you, good luck. I'm going home. Good-bye! Good-bye, you guys.' And the shells were coming closer and closer. And then, pretty soon, guys all around me: '*Thorsen! Get out of here! Get out of here!*'

"So I took off then. But I was feeling bad. In a way I felt bad, and in another way I was just exuberant. I dashed out of there and got away from the shells. They were landing all around. And a little while later some shells hit right there, and several guys were killed.

"And my best friend. Alan Hanson. He just kind of went to pieces. Roger Handy came, afterwards. He got out of there a little later, but he didn't get the word until after that attack. He had to go through that, and then he came down after me. And he told me all about it. My best friend, this Alan Hanson, was right near a fox-hole that got hit. Roger told me who'd been killed. And Roger said, 'Hanson kind of went to pieces.'

"We were good friends. We were in the same platoon. And he was very young. Only nineteen. But he was from Minnesota, too. Pine City. He was a Swede, and he and I hit it off right away. We had quite a bit of things in common. We were both Lutherans. And then he thought he might want to be a teacher, too, and we would talk about after the war. He had only been there about a year, but we were friends, and I was older, and I guess you could say he looked up to me.

"And then the next day we got word. He'd been killed. He'd gone back to the company." My father's voice wavers, but it doesn't break, and he continues. "He'd pulled himself together, and he went back to the company. They advanced up that hill. And some mortar shells hit, and he was blown to pieces."

My father is breathing and breathing. I say, "No."

Dave says, "Don't tell me."

"But that's what happened," my father says. "That's how it went. And this is what I hate to think. Because they went on up that hill. And this is it. This is what I can't forgive! Because the mortars came again. Because the Japs. And they killed them! And they killed them!"

I hear my father breathing, and then he adds, quietly: "They killed all my friends."

I can't look at him, and so I look at Dave. His hands are spread on the table, and his eyes are liquid bright. Tears start leaking down his cheeks and trickle into his beard. And then my brother blurs because my own eyes are brimming, and I feel I'm just beginning now to understand my father. My father has no friends. My father never cries, not even now, and isn't that why Dave and I are forced to do it for him?

I clear my eyes with my fingertips and see my father sitting stiff and trembling, as if at attention, transported, distant, gone.

I say, "Dad? Pop. Dad." I say, "Dad? Are you all right?"

He says, "What? What's the matter with you guys?"

"You were telling us," Dave says. "You were telling us about your friends." He dries his eyes on a dishtowel.

My father looks at us with some surprise, a little fear, bewilderment. "Well, yes," he says. "They were killed. Going up that hill. The mortars came and got them. Not all of them. But most of them. They called it a hundred percent. That's how they listed our outfit: a hundred percent casualties. But several guys came out of it. Some were badly wounded, but they made it, and a few weren't hurt at all. So I don't know why they had to call it that. But that's what they said. A hundred percent. Some guys were wounded more than once. I guess that's why they called it that. It wasn't really all of them, but most of them.

"But that's what's always been so hard. Because I wasn't up there, see? I got out of it. I got off that hill just before the worst of it. So why was that? You feel, you know, you almost feel as if you have to live for all these other guys. Except, of course, there's no way you can do that. Except you think of it. Years afterwards. Even now. It's like you've got these ghosts. You think of them."

"Yes," I tell him, "I can see that."

He looks at the tabletop and smiles faintly. "But then, and this is how it went. I got off that hill, and I was back where they told me to go, back in a safe area, and pretty soon here comes Roger Handy. He told me what he knew, and then a little later we heard the rest of it and got reports. But this was odd, because the two of us were friends, and we had gone through everything, but after we heard what happened on that hill, we sort of stopped talking. We didn't want to talk about it. But we were going home. We had to wait a couple weeks, and it still wasn't real. But then they put us on a train, a narrow-gauge railroad with little cars, and we traveled quite a while."

"You're still there?" Dave says. "You're still in the Philippines?"

"Yes, but then we got down to the coast. We stayed in a camp. I don't know how long it was. But finally we were loaded on a ship.

"We had a rough passage all the way. High seas, rough seas. The front of the ship would rise up like this, and we were down in the hold at night, and the bow would go up like that. And then: Whoom!" He smacks his hand on the tabletop. "Just like that. Whoom! And it was like that all the way back."

"That was a long trip, too!"

"Three weeks. And Roger read funny books all the way back to the States. He wouldn't talk to me. He wasn't talking to anybody. I guess he talked to me once or twice. But every time I looked at him, here he'd be reading a funny book." My father grins. "He was really engrossed in those funny books. Didn't talk to anyone. But I could understand that. So I just sat out there and drank those Cokes and looked around at the ocean. It was rough. But the skies were clear. I thought about what I was going to do. Or thought about nothing at all. It was over. That Roger Handy," he laughs.

"I guess he'd had enough," I say.

"Aw, he got a raw deal, too. I think that was part of it. He should have been made first sergeant. He worked his way up, and he was shooting for first sergeant, but they never gave it to him. And that was too bad, because he was a smart guy. He really earned it. He was kind of small, and maybe his authority wasn't established the way it should have been. But you can't go by size! He was good."

"That's too bad," I say. "And he opened a liquor store? After the war? This was the guy in Chicago?"

"That's right," my father laughs. "A beer joint. He ended up running a beer joint. My goodness." He shakes his head and smiles.

"But then. When we landed in San Francisco: I'm actually getting back there! We went to Angel Island. That's near Alcatraz. We had to stay there two weeks. They had to see if we had any bad disease. Yellow fever, VD. You know. Guys were fixed up if they had jungle rot and things like that. They wanted to see if we had any more malaria. But then one day we were told we were going to get on a train."

"You're going home," Dave says.

"But I had to travel all the way across the United States. Practically. All the way to St. Paul. Get off the train. Go to Fort Snelling. And be discharged from there."

I pull the discharge paper across the table and read the date aloud. "16 June 1945."

"Yes, it's early summer now. But then the day I got discharged it was late in the afternoon. So another fellow and I—he was from North Dakota, and we'd gotten acquainted on the train—we decided we'd get a hotel room together, stay overnight, and take the train up north the next morning. So we did that. And I decided I was going to call home."

"Oh, no," I say. "This was when you—"

"Yes," he says, "this is how I heard. I called home. And Nancy answered the phone. My sister. Her voice.

And we talked, then. And I said, 'Well, how are the boys? How's Raymond? And Johnny?' And she said, 'Haven't you *heard*?' I said, 'Haven't I heard *what*?' And she said. She told me then that Johnny had been killed. And oh."

"Damn it," Dave says.

"It was supposed to be a happy occasion, and here we were crying. I'd been gone for four years, and I'd been sick, and I could have died a hundred times, but I had made it through the war, and here I was. I'd come home to this. Then my mother got on the phone, and we talked, and she told me how it happened."

"It was in a jeep," Dave says.

"He was a driver, and this was in Europe, and it was just a few days more, and then the war was finished over there. But he couldn't make it. His jeep hit a mine, and it turned over on him, and it crushed him. There was a colonel with him, too. He was driving that officer somewhere, and both of them were killed.

"Well, that wrecked everything. Johnny was the youngest. He was everybody's favorite. Mine, too. But he was dead. And after everything we all went through. After all this time.

"I still remember that. Talking on the telephone and hearing those voices and then getting hit with that news. And afterwards how I was slumped against the wall. It just took the wind right out of me. This guy from North Dakota came back into the room, and he was good to me, but there really wasn't anything that he could do."

"Damn it," Dave says.

"But Raymond was all right and everything," I say.

"Raymond made it. Raymond was fine. But Johnny was gone. And there it was again! Why wasn't it me? Why did it have to be him? You see? Because he was so young, and everybody liked him. Why wasn't it me?"

"But that's a crazy way to think," I tell him.

"I know it, but I couldn't help it. I was thinking all the way home on the train the next day. It really messed

me up. I had thought I was okay. I thought I'd forgotten
the stuff I'd been through, but I got very bad on the
train. It all started coming back, everything I'd seen,
and I got it all confused with Johnny. I had a window
seat. I remember that. This old lady gave it to me. The
uniform, you know. She said, 'You sit over here so you
can look at everything.' And so I did, but I couldn't
really see it. Because I kept on thinking, and I had these
flashes. We were getting up there in the woods, up there
in the lakes and evergreens, and I kept looking at it, but
I couldn't really see it. It just reminded me of Johnny
and every other thing. I was feeling sick and sort of
dizzy, and I wondered if I didn't have malaria. We got
close to home, and the train went through Ojibway,
and I could remember the time Johnny and I had hiked
the railroad tracks from Ojibway all the way home to
Pike Lake. And we went by Wolf Lake, where we always fished for bass. That stand of birches where we
camped. I loved those places, but I couldn't see them!
Because I had these flashes, and they were like explosions. I remember at the end I had my forehead pressed
against the window, hard against the glass, but I couldn't
see a thing. So finally I simply sat back. I didn't look at
anything. We came into the station. We pulled into Pike
Lake, and I got off."

I say, "They came to meet you."

"Oh, sure. Everyone was there. My dad. And
Mother. Nancy, Raymond. We hugged and kissed and
all that stuff, but everyone was crying. We drove up to
the farm, and it was late afternoon, and we just stood
there in the yard and talked. We kept looking at each
other, and I had to walk around the place and check on
everything: the house and barn and the playhouse and
the garden and the view through the woods to the lake.
Everything looked good. I was glad to be back."

"No kidding," Dave says.

"But it was funny. I wouldn't let them go inside. I
had to look at everything. So they stood there with me

in the yard, and it was quite a long time, but we stood there and talked and sort of touched each other, and it was getting to be evening. It was getting sunset, and I could see it shining on the lake. But then someone would mention Johnny, and somebody would start to cry. It was supposed to be a happy occasion. That spoiled it. Johnny wrecked it. But I was home, anyhow.

"But now it's getting dark, and finally my dad came over, and he put his arm around me, and he said, 'Welcome home.' Words to that effect. 'I'm sorry things turned out like this. You know how glad we are to have you home. Why don't you come on inside now?' So we did. We went inside, and my father lit the lamps, and my mother brought some food, and we had supper. It was coldcuts. Homemade bread. Canned peaches. It was good."

"I'll bet," I say. "So that was it, then? That was the end of it."

"That was about the end of it, yes. Raymond got a job right away, but not me. I remember I had to go down to the courthouse and sign some papers, and Oscar Peterson was there. Old Oscar. He was really glad to see me. He couldn't be nice enough. He had been on my draft board. He offered me a job right there. He said, 'Harvey, come to work for me. I'd sure like you to work for me.' And he offered me a job putting in some new kind of window. I couldn't see it, though. I wasn't ready for that."

"Well, what did you do, then?" Dave says. "Just unwind?"

"That was it. I was still kind of jumpy, and I had to settle down. So I asked my dad if I could paint the house. And that was crazy, because it was a shingle house. You don't paint a shingle house. But I had that feeling, and it was like a passion. I had to do something with the house. My father understood that. He said yes, okay, and he paid for all the paint. So that was my project. I didn't do anything else for the longest time. I'd go for walks. I painted the house. I did that. And then, my father had built a swing for the porch. One of those love-seat swings?"

"I remember!" I tell him. "I remember that swing!"

"Well, he had built that swing. And I'd sit out there every evening. Push and swing. Swing and swing. Not thinking anything. Just rocking. And they'd come out and sit with me. I can't remember talking. Just sit there in the dark and swing. It was peaceful. Somebody would sit with me. And I remember lilacs. When I first got back, the lilacs were in bloom, and I could smell that purple smell as I sat there in the dark.

"Yes. Well. I got better after that, but it took the longest time. I had some trouble what you call adjusting. It was hard. I couldn't get a good night's sleep. I'd wake up in a sweat and hollering, and it was like I couldn't get my breath. I kept waking everybody up. I have to feel sorry for my family. I sort of had the heebie-jeebies."

"I remember," I tell him. "Grandma told me."

"Yes. But then one night my dad and I drove over to the church at Powder Ridge—little country church— to see a program they were having there. It was talking and a lot of singing. They had a blind accordion player, and I went up to help him with his instrument and things, and there was a young woman there, and she was helping, too. And this was your mother. After-wards, at lunch, we got to talking, and I said—"

"Wait," Dave says. "Don't tell me. Let me say it. You said, 'How come a pretty thing like you is still running around loose? How come you aren't married?' Right?"

"That's right," my father laughs. "Those are the words."

"You rogue," I say. "You old devil."

"Well, that's what I said. And so we got together, we got married, and the GI Bill came along, and we moved to Minneapolis, where I could go to Augsburg. Your mother helped me out a lot. She really did. With my nightmares and the sweats and everything. She'd get up with me and rub my back and different things. She really pulled me out of that. And so it was. So we were married. And we've tried to love each other. I don't know. Things went kind of haywire for us a while back, but it's not like we haven't tried. Things were good between us for a long, long time. I don't know how you boys are finding it, but it seems to me that I have found the most important thing in marriage is a spirit of forgiveness. I wish that you could try and possibly remember that."

"Yes," I say, "I think I might remember that."

He looks at each of us, then crosses his arms. "So that was that. I got my degree and my first teaching job up there in Hackensack, and then we had you boys. You maybe won't believe this, but you boys were like a blessing. Really. Once we had you boys, it really sort of healed me up about the war. And then, when Johnny came along—and he was a surprise!" He laughs. "When Johnny came along, I asked your mother if we could call him Johnny, and she said that would be all right, and so we did. So that's about my story." He shrugs and smiles. "That's about it. That's all there is."

I nod and smile back at him. Dave yawns and shudders. My father says, "My land! Look at that. It's after three! You sure got me going, didn't you? We better get some sleep." He rises and groans. He puts his hands on the small of his back and rocks back on his toes. Then he carries our cups to the sink.

Dave says, "Okay. Good night, then. Thanks for telling us all this."

"Oh, you bet. Maybe you'd wipe off the table? Don't forget the lights. Merry Christmas, boys. It's good to have you home."

"Thanks," I tell him. "Same to you."

Dave and I sit still. I feel bleary-eyed, exhausted. Dave gets up slowly, brings the dishrag from the sink, and slowly wipes the table. He does it thoughtfully, as if he were polishing a piece of oak. He sweeps a heap of crumbs into his hand and stands there staring at it. "I never dreamed," he says. "I can't imagine." He looks at me.

I say, "Me, either. I never knew all that. Jesus. I know one thing."

"What's that?"

"I know why he doesn't drive a Toyota."

Dave grins, then sobers. He says, "They tried to kill him! Our old man!"

"Amazing," I say. "Absolutely crazy."

Dave drops the crumbs in the wastebasket, rinses out the dishrag, and drapes it over the faucet.

"You know," I say to my brother's back, "he knows things that you and I will never know."

"That's the truth." He turns and looks at me. "What are you saying?"

"He's been tested. In a way we never will be. He knows things about himself that we can only guess. It's a kind of calm. There's nothing left to prove. He's been through the fire."

"Barefoot," Dave smiles. " 'I wonder how he did that.' " He laughs. Then he says, "Hey! What are you doing, recommending war?"

"Not on your life. I'm just saying what he knows."

"Yeah, but I don't like your drift. Listen. This doesn't change a thing. This stuff Dad told us doesn't change a thing. Vietnam was wrong. Worse than wrong. And guys with his experience should have known it. Where were they back then? Waving flags."

His face is flushed. I say, "Who's arguing?" We laugh. I say, "It isn't over yet, is it? Vietnam isn't over yet."

Dave eyes my father's uniform. "Neither is World War II."

"No, and if you'd been through it, you'd think about things differently, wouldn't you?"

Dave yawns and leans against the sink. "I'm sorry,"

he says. "I'm too pooped. I'm calling this discussion off. Okay? Postponed on account of exhaustion. See you in the morning. Merry Christmas."

"And to all a good night. I'm glad we did this, Dave."

"Me, too," he says. "Night." He turns in the doorway and addresses the uniform hanging on the fridge. "And good night to you, Sir." He makes a mock salute, turns about-face, and leaves me smiling.

I sit for a minute, resting my head in my hands, then get up and switch off the kitchen lights. I use the downstairs bathroom and go into the living room to turn off the Christmas tree. My father is there, standing at the picture window. "Hey," I say.

He starts and turns. "Oh, hi there."

"I thought you were going to bed."

"I am. I just thought I'd check the storm."

"Still coming down?"

"It's over. See? Clouds broke up. You can see stars."

I step up beside him. What clouds remain are smoky, thin, and moving fast. There's even a piece of moon. "What do you know."

"It's going to turn cold. Clear and cold tomorrow. There's quite a wind yet. Roads will all be drifted in."

"You plan to sleep in that cap?" I ask.

"What? Oh, no," he laughs. "I just forgot." He stuffs it in the pocket of his bathrobe.

"I hope you'll be able to sleep," I say. "I hope we didn't stir up too many memories."

"Oh, I'm all right."

"There's one more thing I'd like to know."

"What's that?"

"Did you ever fire your rifle?"

He looks at me. "Are you kidding? I fired my rifle plenty of times." He gazes out the window, and then he adds, in a tone that mingles pride with shame, "I never killed anybody, though. Not that I know of."

I put my hand on his shoulder. "I really like you," I tell him.

"I'm your father. I'm afraid you're stuck with me."

"It's not stuck. It doesn't feel like that. It feels like I'm lucky to know you."

"Well, thank you. I'm glad to know you, too." He gives me a pat. "Night, Sam. Sleep tight."

"Right. Don't let the bedbugs bite."

"I won't," he says. "You either."

I stand at the window a while, watching the snow swirl and drift in long, thin streamers across the yard and down the street, filling in valleys and hollows, building on the cars, shrouding the bushes and trees. It makes a mysterious landscape. The scale of things keeps changing. Houses advance and retreat. The yard might be the Sahara. And suddenly it's summer, and the house across the street belongs to my grandparents. I see my father, a young man in uniform, standing with his family in the yard. Shades of green and lavender. Everything is hazy at the edges, but I see lilacs. I hear voices. The people seem a little awkward with each other. They're talking, but I can't make out the words. It's just a murmur. Shadows grow. And then the older man, the one with gray hair and suspenders, puts his arm around my father, and they turn and go inside. The windows bloom with light. And then a gust of powder hits the picture window and shatters my mirage, and I'm looking through the window at the shifting dunes of snow. The beaches of the moon, I think, and turn away.

The Christmas tree still glows. I stand staring blankly at the open packages spread beneath the tree. And then my brother Johnny moves inside his mummy bag and speaks. I go over to the sofa and smile down at him and watch his mouth move soundlessly, like the mouth of an old man in the middle of an afternoon snooze. His right arm has escaped from the sleeping bag, and his hand, resting on the carpet, like something separate, suddenly makes a fist. "Don't!" my brother says. "I won't," I say, "I won't." I run my fingers through his hair, and he gradually relaxes, breathing, sleeping, breathing.

The living room is littered. Paper everywhere. My mother will be on the rampage in the morning. I pick up wrapping paper, ribbons, discarded decorations, stuff it all in boxes. Cleaning up, I hum and sing a little, softly, beneath my breath. O little town of Bethlehem. I kneel beside the blinking tree, reach way back among the fragrant boughs, and pull the plug.

I think I see a ghost at the top of the stairs, but it's only my brother, just emerging from the bathroom. "Hello!" Dave says softly. "I thought you were in bed."

"I'm on my way," I whisper and put my hand on his side and go around him down the hall.

"Hey, Sam," Dave whispers.

"What?" We stand there gazing at each other in the thin, dim light. We are made of moonlight, starlight, clouds, and snow. My brother lifts a hand, two fingers forked. It is either a V for victory or the sign of peace. I see my brother's teeth. He is laughing in the dark. He says, "Peace, brother."

"You can say that again," I whisper. "Peace."

And then, like Odysseus before us, like Napoleon and Eichmann, like Eisenhower, Gandhi, and our father, like a million other men the wide world over, each alone and all together now, we enter darkened bedrooms where our wives are breathing softly in their sleep.